Sage Vector
and The Book of Space

First Edition 2024

ISBN 978-1-965942-00-0 (paperback)

CONTENTS

Dedicated to my son Sage, and my wife Lenette.

"Men at some time are masters of their fates.
The fault, dear Brutus, is not in our stars,
But in ourselves, that we are underlings."
- William Shakespeare (*Julius Caesar*, Act 1, Scene 2)

INTRODUCTION
Knowledge Is Power

I want to thank you for being interested in reading this book. We live in a time when picking up a book to read is becoming a rare thing. It is too easy and convenient to turn to a screen to do our imagining for us. One of the reasons why I chose to write this book was to encourage people to return to reading, or for many of our younger people, to choose reading over scrolling or streaming.

I love movies and YouTube videos as much as the next person, but there's one major drawback to watching them — the pictures are made by someone else, not us. When you read a book, you imagine what the story looks like. You interpret what the words mean. If you're a good reader, the pictures you create in your mind are richer and more rewarding than anything you could watch on a screen. Reading is exercise for your mind and practice for your imagination. Without it, you're left living in a world others make for you, instead of building one of your own.

What if you're not a good reader? Well, there's a good, simple reason why some people don't like to read — lack of a good dictionary. Yep, it's as simple as that. When you read words on a page, once in awhile you run into a word or phrase you don't know the meaning of. When that happens you've run into a small confusion. Reading is supposed to make you brighter, not duller, but when you hit too many confusions you definitely feel less smart. After awhile you'll toss a book aside and say it was too boring, or possibly you drop out of a class, or you even stop going to school. There are too many people in the world that gave up on reading only because they didn't use a good dictionary to clear up their confusions.

As far back as I can remember I always wanted to know about the world, but there wasn't a single book in my home when I was a little kid. I might not have become a reader at all, or even the person I am today, if it hadn't been for two influential TV shows in the early 1980's: *G.I Joe: A Real American Hero* and *Reading Rainbow*.

G.I. Joe: A Real American Hero was a cartoon series about special soldiers that fought against an evil organization called Cobra. At the end of every episode they featured a public safety lesson geared towards children. At the end of these safety segments they would say, "Now we know! And knowing is half the battle." I heard that line so many times, it really sank in. I understood that possessing knowledge put you in a strong position to succeed — it was half the battle! So I knew learning knowledge was something I had to pursue.

Then there was *Reading Rainbow*, a PBS show created to encourage kids to read books. It worked on me 1,000% because I was excited every time I heard the theme song tell me "Take a look, it's in a book..." or "I can go anywhere," and "I can be anything." Messages like that empowered me. I remember walking into the library as a kid and carrying out a stack of books, then bringing them back and getting another stack. I felt like a superhero.

Reading books has been my single greatest, most successful action in my life. It gave me an advantage in school. It also enabled me to learn things I would never be taught there. It allowed me to surpass the knowledge anyone in my immediate surroundings possessed, and it opened the whole world up to me. It gave me a powerful imagination. It made me more creative. It opened every door I could find or dream up.

Sage Vector and The Book of Space was written to emphasize the importance of reading, and hopefully encourage more people to read. The book is about a lot of things, but one of the big ones is why knowledge truly is power. I hope you enjoy reading the book as much as I enjoyed writing it. Remember to use a good dictionary when you come across a word you don't understand. There's also a small Glossary at the back of the book with some of the words you might not know. Make sure to use it often. Sometimes we think we know something, but we don't really, *truly* know it. Not until we take the time to make it become part of our life, part of our world. I hope you take the time to make this book part of *your* world. I think you'll have fun imagining it, like I have.

- David Carus

PROLOGUE
Earth's Future

It's been centuries since any war has taken place on Earth. 800 years into the future mankind knows nothing but peace. The nations of the world live and work together to share and grow resources, celebrating each other's diversity and individual contribution to the planet. Poverty, hunger, and disease only exist in history books, and no one is without a home to live in or a family to belong to.

The people of Earth organize themselves into groups called guilds. Each guild takes responsibility for a different part of the society. People are placed in guilds according to their passions, and human society works to everyone's benefit. Guilds are part of branches that are managed by government guilds throughout the planet. Governments are overseen by a global council led by one person — the philosopher king, who has ultimate authority over all aspects of life on Earth.

Ethan Tanaka, the eighteenth philosopher king, currently rules over the longest period of prosperity in the Earth's history. While the citizens of the world rest easy in their peaceful lives, the king remains vigilant. He understands too well that perfection is impossible, because nothing stays the same forever.

BUST A MOVE

The world outside was dark, except for the light of distant stars and the moon that softly lit the Salinas Valley. The mountains stood tall and stretched wide across the land, holding it all together like two giant protective arms. The air was cold and touchable, and floated gracefully across the empty streets like creatures at the bottom of the sea. Salinas was a city in slumber, but not everyone was asleep.

A small, black bird with a worm in its mouth landed just outside the window where Zimmer was. He first detected its motion a couple of houses away, and was now accessing one of the city's security camera feeds to monitor what the bird was doing. The soft blue light from Zimmer's eyes moved slowly back and forth as the bird ate. He scanned the latest news stories as they came through while he watched the bird, two cats, one dog, seven squirrels and hundreds of ants.

The sun was starting to break through the window blinds when Zimmer's eyes suddenly changed, and like the sun, they shot out a bright beam. Projected on the wall were historical images of men with microphones, and a song from over 800 years ago blasted from the small speakers around Zimmer's midsection. Over the footage of the men, displayed in an Impact font, was the current time: 6:00am. The robot observed how the bass of the music vibrated across his metal body while he waited for his human friend to wake up.

Sage Vector turned over in bed with a slight look of confusion, then gradually formed a grin, which then became a full on smile. His eyes tried to catch up to his ears, and he squinted at the projection on his bedroom wall. He was happy to see two artists from the twentieth century performing one of his favorite kinds of music — hip hop. He jumped out of bed and his feet made a big thump as they hit the wooden floor boards. Without a care in the world, Sage punched the air and started moving and rapping the words to the song for about a minute or so, until the light from the projection suddenly vanished, the music stopped, and Zimmer's eyes turned blue again.

"IT'S TIME FOR THE NEXT TARGET."

Sage shook his head, took a deep breath, and reached for the towel hanging behind his door and said, "All right Zim. See you in a bit."

Before his hand turned the doorknob he could smell the sweet aroma of freshly made tortillas drifting down the hallway from the kitchen. His stomach made a little growl as he made his way to the bathroom. Luckily the bathroom was empty, and he quickly locked the door behind him, turned on the hot water, and bobbed his head to the music still playing in his mind.

As the water washed over his body, Sage thought about the words of the song, repeating them to himself. He broke down the rhythm and word structure, and by the time he was finished with his shower he almost had a whole new verse constructed. He was trying to carry it in his memory until he could write it down when he heard a loud pounding.

"Hurry it up! I've got to get to school early today!"

"Calm down Sara, I'm almost done!"

"I needed you done five minutes ago. Wrap it up!"

Sage could see his sister's toes through the bottom crack of the door, tensely gripping the wood. She was ready to pounce like a cheetah. He could feel her impatience penetrating through the barrier between them, and when he finally unlocked the lock, she was inside the bathroom before he could place his first step outside of it.

Sara opened the window and a cool breeze traveled inside as she used her towel to fan the place of any little brother odor. Sage was at the end of the hallway when he heard the bathroom door slam loudly and echo towards him — one final communication from his big sister.

The smells from the kitchen were heavenly and drifted all around. Sage walked to the drink counter and waved his hand over it. A steel cup appeared and the faucet interface lit up.

"Water. Full cup."

"You should have some orange juice."

Sage looked down at his water filled cup, and then up at his mother and smiled.

"The body is like 99% water so you can't go wrong with the stuff, right?"

"Actually the body is more like 60% water."

"You know what I mean mom."

"Yeah, I know what you mean, but you need to get your numbers straight when you're trying to win an argument. I know you don't like it, but you should spend a little more time studying instead of..."

Sage turned his body slightly to the right and pretended to look out the kitchen window at some far away thing in the distance.

"You don't have your interface today, do you?"

"Thanks for reminding me mom, but I would've remembered and come back for it. It's not a big deal."

"Yes, it is a big deal. How are you ever going to be ready for the world if you can't study it and communicate with it?"

"I do study it, just not always through the interface. Zimmer has most of the info anyway. And doesn't real life count for anything anymore?"

"You know it does, but sometimes you have to get up close to ideas. Zimmer is convenient, but your interface puts the world's knowledge right in front of your eyes. And, why not take full advantage of learning from everyone that came before you? It'll save you time in the long run."

"I know mom, I know. I'll use it more often, I swear."

Sage could feel something hard poking his back. He turned around and saw Zimmer's outstretched hand holding his interface glasses."

"YOUR INTERFACE."

"Thanks man."

He grabbed the black, metal glasses and placed them over his light, brown eyes. He looked up to show his mom.

"See? All ready for the world."

Mrs. Vector smiled at her son, and she gave him a different kind of metal — an aluminum foil wrapped breakfast burrito.

"I'm sure you're anxious to get your day started."

"You always know what I'm thinking mom, that's scary."

"If you don't get moving I'll show you something even scarier."

"His personal hygiene?" interrupted Sara, looking impeccable and ready for a walk down a fashion runway.

"Very funny sis," replied Sage. He was half way to the front door when he turned around and said, "Hey, do you know what percentage of the human body is made up of water?"

"Yeah, like 60%."

His face tried to hide his surprise and he sighed.

"Whatever, everybody knows that."

His mom was grinning as he walked away. He was almost to the front door when he heard a slight creak of furniture, and then the voice of his father came sharply from behind him.

"Sage, did you think I forgot?"

Damon Vector rose from one of the chairs in the living room, looking over his son as if trying to find some small invisible thing that might attempt to harm him. He wasn't a big man physically, but his presence filled the room as if he were a giant. Sage was pretty sure his dad's thoughts could kill small living things. He had never seen a bee or fly get near him.

"Morning dad. No, I remembered."

"You told me you were going to come to work with me to talk to the guild leaders one day this week after school — and today's Friday."

"I know dad but I'm working on this big project that's part of my final assessment, and I'm almost done with it. Plus, the big game is tonight. Is next week ok?"

"You know it is son, but each week you tell me the same thing. I don't get it. You're going to be a builder, right? It'll do you some good to be seen at the guild. It's been too long since you've been around. Today we're constructing a huge perimeter wall around the home we've been working on. It should be a fun build."

"It sounds cool, but I really have to finish this project, and the guys need me tonight. Next week for sure, ok dad?" He backed away towards the door before his father could reply.

Just when he thought he was free, and he was about to see a sunny, bright Salinas sky, he was suddenly stopped by the towering figure of Bear Murrieta blocking the sun and his entire exit. Bear wore his usual dirty denim pants, thick, tan hooded coat, and heavy gloves. One of his huge hands projected outward towards Sage, and he waited for a fist bump.

"What's up kid!?"

Sage's knuckles gently bumped into Bear's clenched fist.

"Hey man, nothing much, just heading out for school and everything."

Bear put one of his enormous arms around Sage like a lasso and steered him back into the house.

"Listen, it's too early. I know you got a couple minutes. Hear me out for a second, okay?"

"Sure Bear, what's up?"

Bear Murrieta looked over at Damon Vector standing in the back of the room like a Roman statue and nodded slightly. Mr. Vector gave an even slighter nod back. Both men were certain their communication with each other went unnoticed by the young man between them. Sage gave a look towards Zimmer as if to say, "Do they really think I don't know what they're trying to do?"

"Old Jose is ready to retire any minute now. We know you're almost ready to wrap up this school thing soon. The timing couldn't be more perfect. He doesn't have any kids, and he already gave his replacement vote to your dad. All you have to say is yes and you're in. It took me and your dad a few years to get established in the guild and work our way up from apprentice, but because you've got so much experience helping your dad and me over the years, those old farts will let you jump right into full member status and pay. You'll be set for life right out of school. But we gotta let those dudes know you're serious and that you want it."

Sage was thinking about his art project waiting for him in his locker while Bear's words became background music. It wasn't until the silence penetrated his thoughts that Sage realized it was time for his reply.

He turned away from Bear and faced his father.

"I really appreciate the opportunity. I just need a little more time. Being a builder is an awesome job, and I know I could do it, but there's something inside of me that needs to be 100% sure. I'm at about a 90% right now. I just need a few more days."

Damon looked at his son with a mixture of compassion, disappointment and confusion.

"Your test results have Builder at the top for a reason. It's a perfect match. The system knows what it's doing. Everything is pointing in this direction. I don't understand why you're second guessing it, but it's your life. I've done what I can to help get you ready for it. But just know, that it *is* coming. This is not like putting off cleaning your room, or turning in an assignment late at school. What you do next will shape the rest of your days. I understand not wanting to pick the wrong thing, but understand that in life, you have to make choices. If not this, then what?"

Sage looked at the floor, then let his gaze wander to the wall, and he wondered what was happening on the other side of it.

"I know dad. If I could tell you, I would."

His dad looked to Bear Murrieta for some help with the puzzle that he called his son, but Bear just shrugged.

"Okay Sage, go do what you gotta do."

"Thanks dad."

Sage made his way around the mountainous frame of his dad's closest friend, and best worker. He reached for the door knob, and turned and pulled it. The brightness of the outside world hit his face and made him grin. Before stepping through the doorway he turned around one last time. The two men looked at Sage with great interest. He looked back at them for a couple of seconds then said, "Don't worry. I've got this."

Sage looked out at his glorious neighborhood in East Salinas coming alive. A few autos were floating down Steinbeck Avenue, and a man jogged past with an oxygen helmet. The vibrant colors of the murals on the sides of buildings seemed to glow, and the flower and vegetable gardens wrapped around homes complimented them well.

"Zimmer — chariot mode!"

The robot's eyes turned orange as he began to break apart and transform. His head adjusted, his arms flipped backwards, and his entire bottom section formed into a platform that hovered a foot above the ground. Sage hopped on and they were soon moving down Steinbeck Avenue towards the tech shops, food vendors and game rooms.

Salinas had a thriving game community consisting of dozens of rooms dedicated to everything from the latest VR, AR and AI games, to traditional physical games like chess and checkers. Game rooms were accessible day and night. People used them as social clubs, and they dropped in before or after, and sometimes during, work or school. There were a few people who could be found in one most of the time, either by employment or from complete dedication to a game or a club. Diego fell into that category. He was always the first to arrive and the last to leave Central Coast Coders.

Diego was typing and swiping away at his latest puzzle game projected in front of him when Sage pulled up to Coders. The resident game maker couldn't help but notice Sage hopping off of Zimmer. The droid transformed back to his normal self and followed his human friend into the game room where Diego excitedly waved them over.

"I think I finally did it!" he said.

"Did what?" asked Sage.

"I have completed my masterpiece. A puzzle game to end all puzzle games. One game to rule them all. Tetris can kiss my... well let's just say my game is truly epic."

"Awesome! Let's see it."

Diego punched a couple of times and swiped, then projected his screen onto a nearby wall. Dozens of colorful circles and bright ovals filled the empty space, floating there in a dream-like landscape. The beautiful shapes looked like they were slowly dancing with each other across a cloud-filled sky.

"I call it *Circ*."

"How do you play it?"

"It's ridiculously easy. All you do is grab a shape and try to squeeze it inside another one. When you do that you score. As the game progresses the shapes shift, and they get harder to manipulate, and if you're not quick enough some of them will shrink too small or grow too big, and then you lose. Wanna try it?"

"Hell yeah!"

"Okay, cool. Just sent you the beta version. Check your interface."

"Got it." Sage opened the file and Zimmer projected it in front of him. "Whoa, I love these visuals."

"Totally. See how many points you can get. So far I can only score up to 2000."

Sage moved his fingers and swiped, manipulating the round shapes in front of him faster and faster. His attention was completely focused on the game as a few other gamers began to gather around him. Diego watched Sage and the others' reactions intensely.

"He's already at 1,000," someone said.

A happy grin formed across Sage's face. "I think I've got this one figured out," he said.

Diego was totally confused when he saw Sage hit the 5,000 point mark after only a few minutes of play.

"What the hell is going on? How'd you get that many so fast!?"

Sage continued to swipe and move his hands. The whole room was watching him now.

"It's not too tricky once you get the hang of it. It's all about spotting the patterns and predicting quick enough."

"You can find the patterns that easy? I mean, everything's constantly moving in the game." Diego was even more confused.

"Yeah. I wish I could explain it better, but there are definitely things that repeat in the shapes, even with all of the shifting happening. Cool, I'm at 10,000."

Sage paused the game with his right index finger. "I'll have to play it some more later. Great job Diego. I think I actually do like this one better than Tetris."

The game maker was still in a daze but he slowly came out of it. Sage walked over to the member lockers and he put his face near one of them. It scanned him over with a small green laser beam. The locker door opened. Sage reached inside and he pulled out a small bust of a man's head.

"Who's that?" asked Diego.

"William Shakespeare."

"Oh yeah. Now I see it. That's pretty cool. You made it?"

"It's part of my sculpting course. I have to turn this in today. It's my final assignment. All goes well, I'll complete the course today."

"That's awesome man. I didn't know you were taking sculpting."

"Good, I'm not trying to advertise it either. If my dad finds out I'm studying art instead of construction, he'll probably kill me."

"Why? Being an artist is awesome. My brother makes the dopest designs for some of the big game companies. He makes big bucks too."

"You haven't met my dad. He's a builder, and his dad wanted him to be a builder, and now he wants me to be one too. I pick anything else, it's like I'm taking a chainsaw to the family tree. You know what I mean?"

"I feel you. So what's the plan? Build during the day, and at night turn into an artist caped crusader fighting villains with your markers and pens?"

"Honestly, I don't know. I have no plan. All I know is, I'm still trying to figure out what I want to do."

"Damn, you must be nearly done with school. What do the tests tell you?"

"They keep telling me to be a builder."

"Oh, damn that sucks... I mean, maybe it's not a bad job, right? How many other career options pop up for you?"

"Actually, a ton. But so far, nothing makes me nearly as excited as being an artist. Right now, that's like 57 on the list."

"57 is a lot of options. I only got 5, and game maker was always number one for me. I'm pretty lucky. Been here at Coders for ten years now, and I love every minute of it. The system is perfect as far as I'm concerned. Those engineers know what the hell they're doing with our data, 1000%. Maybe builder is what you should be man."

"I'm just not sold. Well, I better run, I've gotta get this project to my professor. See you at the game tonight?"

"Field ball at Trojan Stadium on a Friday night? You know it! I can't wait to watch you beat those Vikings bad."

Sage laughed then said, "Cool, see you there."

He walked outside and just before he was about to tell Zimmer to transform again, he saw his sister Sara with her entire entourage of friends packed tightly in a green convertible auto. It cruised by slowly, and his sister turned her head towards him, smiled, and waved. Sage was confused, but he raised his right hand up slowly and waved back. His sister's face grimaced in disgust at him, and shouted, "Not you, loser!" as she drove past him.

Sage turned around. He understood immediately who his sister had waved at. Joaquin Malcolm stood behind him smiling, dressed in a white dress shirt, dark brown tie and slacks, his messenger bag slung across his left shoulder.

"Of course it was you. As if my sister would ever wave to me in front of her friends."

"Don't take it too hard. You know deep down she loves you."

"Yeah, so deep down you need a submarine to find it."

"You ready for the game tonight?"

"Always. It'll be fun facing those guys again."

"The place will be packed. We have a real shot at breaking some records."

"I'll let you worry about the trophies and history books. I'm just happy to play."

"You're too humble. Sometimes you have to embrace the moment."

"Where'd you learn that line?"

"Nowhere. I just came up with it. Why, you like it?"

"Yeah, it's not bad. You should try it out on your supporters."

"What? You're not one of them?"

"You never have to worry about my vote. You've had it since we were kids, and you'll have it when we're old and gray."

"I knew there was a reason I hung out with you," laughed Joaquin. "So, you made any progress on your guild choice? You know you can extend your time in school if you need it."

"Are you kidding me? I can't wait to be done. No offense, but reading and studying ain't for me. I need to do something with my hands, move around, get some fresh air."

"Sounds like the Builder Guild might be a great fit. You know, you can always join me in the Government Guild, right? You get to do a lot of walking and talking, plus you get to use your hands to shake other people's hands."

"You're funny. I just can't shake the feeling I get when I make something beautiful — just something to look at. Building homes or walls is too practical. It's important, don't get me wrong. I just see what the artists in the Artist Guild are able to do, all of their detail, and it inspires me. I'd love to paint, sculpt or make something that lasts long after I'm gone."

"Sounds like you know exactly what you want to do."

"I guess you're right. The hard part is convincing everyone else."

"As long as you're convinced, everyone else will be too."

"Thanks man."

"No problem. If your dad kills you, I'll say something nice at your funeral."

Sage laughed, "I wouldn't expect anything less. Hey, you want to see something I made?"

"Definitely."

The heavy clay sculpture inside Sage's backpack took him most of the week to get just right. He carefully removed the white, cotton towel protecting it and showed Joaquin. His best friend looked it over and grinned.

"Shakespeare, huh?"

"Yeah!"

"I thought so. To be or not to be? That *is* the question."

"Ain't that the truth?"

"Hey, we better get going. School isn't going to finish itself."

"Cool, see you there."

Joaquin slapped Sage on the back lightly, enough to not make him drop his art project into a million pieces on the sidewalk, then rode off in his shiny, gray auto blasting a recorded lecture instead of music. Sage shook his head and smiled as he put the heavy bust of Shakespeare back in his backpack. Then he turned to Zimmer who had also watched Joaquin drive away.

"What was he listening to?"

Zimmer's eyes flashed. "DR. MARTIN LUTHER KING JR."

"Oh, cool. I thought it sounded familiar."

Sage looked out at the street bustling with activity and motion, excited to be a part of it. Zimmer was already in chariot mode when Sage figured out what music he wanted to hear while he rode off.

"Zim, play *King of Rock* by RUN-DMC, full volume."

***

The Alisal campus was massive and made up the heart of East Salinas. Old world stone buildings covered in ivy combined with more modern styles of art to create an atmosphere meant to elevate young people to intellectual heights. Department buildings representing all of the major branches of learning spread out from the center of campus like branches of a tree. But instead of a tree standing in the center of it all, something bigger took that powerful position in the heart of Alisal University — the Trojan Horse.

It was more than a statue or a mascot to the people of East Salinas, it was like a religious symbol, or a way of life. Beyond being the community's spirit animal, the Trojan Horse was also a usable campus building. It was a place of learning, a memorial, and even a playground. It stood 50 feet tall and 80 feet long. It was constructed with every material imaginable to meet all of its intended purposes. One could walk inside the horse and make their way to the horse's head and take in a panoramic view of the entire city of Salinas. Lectures were often given inside the monument, while the lower parts were used as a popular playground for young children who enjoyed climbing and sliding down the horse's legs. And all around the horse were hundreds of years worth of names etched into its body to remind everyone that they were part of something bigger than themselves.

Sage liked to watch the kids running around the feet of the horse, slide out from its hooves, and fall laughing onto the grass. But today, as he approached the statue, he couldn't help but notice many of the children's mothers looking at something on their interface glasses. Usually these same mothers talked non-stop while their children played, but today they were all silent as they stared in front of themselves.

"Zim, anything I should know about?"

Zimmer's eyes flashed red.

"BREAKING NEWS. ALBERTO EINSTEIN BEATS A.I. MEGA SUPER CHESS COMPUTER."

"Wow, that's big news man. I forgot that match was today."

Sage looked at the mothers who wore huge smiles and were cheering, calling their kids over to watch the final moves in the match that was being replayed over and over again. One mother told her son, "Anything is possible mijo, watch what Alberto does. Man is greater than any machine, because he is the maker of machines. Not even an A.I. mega super computer can match what human beings can do. Mind over matter mi amor."

Alisal always had an air of excitement to it, but Alberto Einstein's victory added a whole new layer. Sage could feel the energy all around him. Einstein dedicated his entire life to chess, beating every human champion by the age of 12. The whole world followed his unbelievable determination to be the first human to beat A.I. in two hundred years. Everyone thought it was impossible because technology was far too advanced, but he kept telling people that human ingenuity was far superior to machine level thinking. Alberto Einstein's huge smile filled every viewscreen around. It was a remarkable day to be a human being.

The outdoor chess tables were more crowded than ever. Game pieces were tossed in the air in celebration, and more than a few tears of joy fell from the cheeks of the regulars. Sage was a pretty decent chess player himself, and he was tempted to play a game before heading to class, but he knew that wasn't the best idea. As he stared at the jubilant chaos in front of him, he noticed some familiar black hair rising above an old hardcover copy of *Romeo and Juliet*.

Sage walked eagerly over and could hear the words of Shakespeare coming out from behind the book. When he was close enough to have his shadow appear on the green grass near her, Robin Vasquez's big brown eyes looked up at Sage. Her smile was infectious, and her face communicated curiosity and wonder. She was suddenly struck by an opportunity in front of her and smiled wider.

"O Romeo, Romeo! Wherefore art thou Romeo? Deny thy father and refuse thy name; Or, if thou wilt not, be but sworn my love, And I'll no longer be a Capulet."

Robin waited.

Sage, enraptured and definitely confused, replied, "You really know your stuff."

Robin's head sank a little, and she took a slow, deep breath.

"Sage, don't you remember the next words?"

"No, why would I?"

"Don't you remember — in English? Mr. Marlowe had us read this part of the play. I read Juliet and you read Romeo."

"It's kinda coming back to me. You know I'm not that into reading books so much. But it's really awesome that you are. Every time I see you, you're with a different one."

Robin looked at Sage with great sympathy, like a small bird that fell out of its nest into the grass and has a broken wing. She couldn't help but try to nurse the poor boy back to health.

"Here, take the book. Read the next line." She pointed at the proper spot on the page.

Nervously, Sage read aloud, "Shall I hear more, or shall I speak at this?"

"I think you've spoke plenty Vector. It's my turn now!" said a deep, loud voice from behind him. Sage turned and looked at the sudden appearance of Francisco Castillo who reached for the book in his hand.

"Hey Francisco. I have to get going anyway."

Robin looked disappointed, "Are you sure Sage? You'd be great at this part. Why not stay for a few more lines?"

"No, it's okay. You're in good hands with Francisco here. He knows this stuff better than me. I can't wait to see your next performance though. You'll be amazing."

The aspiring actress and playwright beamed at the compliment, and her eyes were left hungry for more. Sage gave a big smile and let all the other things he wished to say stay hidden behind it.

Francisco cut through the silence.

"Thanks for holding things down. I've got it from here. Good luck with the game tonight."

Robin came alive, putting both hands on Sage's shoulders. "Sage! Tonight's game is huge! You must be so excited!"

"Yeah, it'll be fun," he said modestly.

"I'll be there, but I'll have to leave a little early to get ready for our performance. It starts after the game if you want to drop by."

"I'd love to see it. Is it *Romeo and Juliet*?"

"Yep. It'll be a beautiful night for it too. The amphitheater under the stars will be pretty memorable."

"Oh, before I leave, I want to show you what I made." A more genuine excitement grew inside him as he reached into his backpack. He unwrapped Shakespeare and pointed his gaze directly at Robin.

"What do you think?"

"Sage, you made this? It's incredible!"

"Yeah, it's for one of my classes, but I was thinking after I turn it in for a grade that maybe you would want to have it?"

"I would love it! Yes! Thank you!"

"Great! You'll be seeing him again soon."

"I'll put him right on my book shelf next to his books."

"How many do you have?"

"Books of his? Only the big ones — *Hamlet, Macbeth, Merchant of Venice,* and *Romeo and Juliet* here." She pointed at the copy still in Francisco's hand.

"I'll be on the lookout for some of the others for you."

"You don't have to do that. All of his works are online."

"Yeah I know, but physical copies are pretty cool."

"Yeah, they definitely are."

"Sage, is it okay if I take a look at that bust?" interrupted Francisco, handing *Romeo and Juliet* over to Robin.

"Sure, here you go." Sage carefully carried his sculpture over to him. Francisco lifted Shakespeare's head high so that it faced his own. He stared at him intensely, almost like he was sizing him up, trying to decide whether he should fight him or not.

Francisco spoke to the bust dramatically, "Do you bite your thumb at us, sir?"

Robin sensed her acting friend was crossing a line that wouldn't end well.

"Francisco, stop playing around."

"Is the law of our side if I say 'ay'?" he replied.

"No," said Robin annoyedly.

Francisco held Shakespeare out a little further away and altered his voice as if to pretend to be the famous bard answering back.

"No, sir. I do not bite my thumb at you, sir, but I bite my thumb, sir," he said. On those last few words, he jammed his thumb into Shakespeare's mouth. He was starting to laugh loudly at his perceived cleverness when he suddenly realized the additional pressure from his thumb made the clay sculpture unbalanced in his other hand. Shakespeare started to tip backwards and Francisco's arms were too late to catch him.

English literature's most famous playwright, and Sage Vector's most important school assignment, lay broken and lifeless in the green grass of the Alisal campus. His head was split practically down the middle, from his forehead down to his chin and neckline. Both halves were looking in opposite directions, with their rough, rocky insides exposed for the world to see. Sage reached down and touched one of the jagged, hard pieces of clay and remembered how wet and smooth it had once felt in his hands. Shakespeare was once again a distant memory.

Professors Row

Professor Garcia was like most of the faculty at Alisal University. He was more a resource or mentor than an actual teacher or professor. Since the world's knowledge was instantaneously at the fingertips of every student, and because A.I. could help them cut through the maze of information with ease, it was left to educators like Professor Garcia to see that students could actually do something with what they learned. It was his job to see the actual application of learning demonstrated in the real world. His primary task was reviewing assessment projects, and next on his schedule was examining a clay bust of William Shakespeare by Sage Vector.

The art classroom of Professor Van Garcia was a working studio as well as a personal office. There were a great many omnibus titles and coffee table editions of art books from every era of human creativity neatly alphabetized all around the giant room. The cleaning lady wondered whether Professor Garcia or his students ever used any of the massive books that surrounded them each day, and for a time she stopped dusting them to find out if her suspicion was right. She let the dust pile for an entire academic year. She had to wear a protective mask and gloves when she finally removed the thick dust from every single volume in the studio's collection of books. From that day forward she treated Professor Garcia with more directness and less formality, but he was none the wiser, having previously ignored the woman as much as he had ignored his books.

Garcia sat at his oversized desk with a pile of student sketches stacked high to his left, and a slender, red fine-tip marker pen gripped tightly in his right hand. He was annoyed each time he selected a new sketch to look over, yet strangely pleased each time he left it with his unforgettable, violent red pen strokes. The short man's legs swayed pendulously just above the floor, and he squinted through his big, round, purple glasses at the time flashing on his Picasso themed watch. His student should have been here five minutes ago. Professor Garcia relished in the fact that he could use this information as additional arsenal in his constructive criticism to help the young man, if and when he finally arrived. He continued grading, leaving a sea of red ink in his wake until he heard the rushed footsteps just outside his studio door.

"Professor Garcia. Sir, I apologize for my lateness. I was trying to make my work acceptable due to some unexpected circumstances."

The art professor did not look in Sage's direction when he replied, "Mr. Vector, art is filled with unexpected circumstances, but that is no excuse for lateness."

"You're right professor, but here it is. I hope you find it satisfies the requirements of the assignment." Sage carefully placed his work in the center of the oversized desk in front of him.

"What in the world..."

"It's a bust of Shakespeare."

"A bust...of Shakespeare?"

"Um, yes, sir."

Professor Garcia took his right index finger and placed it on Shakespeare's forehead and traced the crack in his center all the way down the front of his face to his neck. A tiny bit of glue was left on the edge of the professor's finger. He pressed it against his right thumb to feel the stickiness of it. He raised his finger to his nose and sniffed it as if he were trying to decipher the contents of a wine he was about to drink.

"Well, what do you think Professor Garcia?"

"What do I think?" he replied. A look of confusion had permanently settled across his face. Sage wasn't sure whether he wanted to hear his answer, or if he should just run before he exploded.

"Young man, it's terribly brilliant."

"I know, it's terrible. I worked on it all week just to have it break this morning."

"You broke it this morning?"

"Yes."

"Remarkable."

"Just my luck."

"Luck has nothing to do with this at all. It is truly great work."

Now Sage was the one confused. "I'm sorry... what? You mean, you like it?"

"No, I love it."

"You do?"

"Of course. The theme is genius. A bust that is bust! And your choice of Shakespeare is really thought provoking. It's quite a statement, very revolutionary. I completely agree that the English language is antiquated and belongs in history books. What better statement for this assignment than a real declaration of the visual over language? You have really captured the sentiment and mood of our current times. What led you to have such a breakthrough idea and concept?"

Sage didn't understand half the things his teacher said, but he understood very well that he just dodged a bullet because his professor was praising him. He wanted to say something smart and insightful in response, but he was at a complete loss for words.

After a few seconds of waiting, the professor broke into a huge smile.

"Wow, you really are good. One day I'll be taking your class in this room Mr. Vector. What better response to my question on your critique of language than to remain quiet and refuse to utter a word? I love it! It goes without saying, you have completed your requirement and passed this course. Very well done."

Sage picked up his bust of Shakespeare and slowly walked out of the room. He wanted to say thank you but thought it might jeopardize his grade. He carefully placed his art assignment into his backpack, then walked down the corridor to exit the building. It was time for him to check in with his next professor.

He wasn't more than twenty feet from his Government professor's office when Sage caught sight of Joaquin heading towards him. The young, future government leader was surrounded by his student staff, and was busy giving them orders when he suddenly spotted Sage. He gestured with his raised right hand to give him a second. Joaquin gave one last instruction to his followers, and they scattered in all directions as he walked confidently towards his best friend.

"Where you headed?"

"Professor Adams. Gotta check in with him."

"Cool, I was just about to do the same. Where are you coming from?"

"Art. I just had the strangest encounter with Garcia."

"Oh yeah?"

"Yeah, I showed up late with my assignment. It broke in half, and I'd just spent the last half an hour gluing it back together. I thought for sure I was going to hear hell for it, but then he tells me he loves it, and that I'm making some really genius statement on the English language being antiquated or something."

"What'd you say to that?"

"Nothing."

"Nothing?"

"I didn't say a word, and he thought I was an even bigger genius!"

"Oh man, that's hilarious. Sounds like you lucked out."

"Not really, come to think of it."

"Why's that?"

"Just when I thought I was going to be an artist, I'm starting to think it's all a bunch of subjective mumbo jumbo. I mean, is something great because someone says it is, or is it great because a lot of someones say so? And who's to know who's right? How will I ever know if what I'm making is any good?"

"That's a pretty deep philosophical question. It's like that old analogy, if a tree falls in the woods and no one is there to hear it, does it make a sound? At the end of the day, if you're there to hear it, or there to make art or anything else, I think your opinion matters doesn't it? You just gotta believe in yourself and think what you're making is good, because if you think it's good, that's what matters the most. Everyone and everything else is gravy."

"I like that. How'd you get so damn smart Joaquin?"

"Books, my friend. Lots of reading and studying of books."

"There you go again. Thanks for reminding me for about the thousandth time. Books are all right but I just struggle when I stare at the words. Audiobooks are better but even they lose my interest after awhile."

"They definitely require focus, but I think you just get too distracted."

Sage was watching Robin walk with a couple of her girlfriends far off in the distance. Joaquin waved his hand in front of Sage to break his gaze and got his attention back.

"Why don't you stop beating around the bush and just ask her out?"

"What? No way man, I couldn't handle the rejection if she said no."

"Dude, you've been in love with her practically your whole life. Isn't the torture you're putting yourself through worse?"

"I'm going to tell her, eventually."

"I've heard that one before."

"School's almost over. I'll tell her then. That way, if she rejects me I won't have to see her every day to remind me. I'll tell her soon, when the time is right."

"Well, I hope your strategy works."

"I have confidence in myself."

"Uh, huh. Say, why don't we both go in and see Adams at the same time? It might make it easier for him, killing two birds with one stone and all that. Plus, he'll be less likely to come down hard on one of us if the other is there. Sound like a plan?"

"Sure, why not? My day can't get any weirder."

The two friends walked together into the office of Professor Adams who was standing by a window looking out at the Gabilan mountains. He was dressed in an impeccable navy blue suit, shiny, black dress shoes and his hair was combed straight and parted. His appearance was half city mayor and half Jay Gatsby.

"Hello boys, to what do I owe the pleasure of this fine visit?"

Joaquin spoke first, "Professor Adams, we were both on our way to check in with you about our course progress. We thought you might be able to see us both at the same time."

"Is that right, Mr. Vector?"

"Yes, sir. We don't mind if the other knows what you have to say. We usually tell each other anyhow."

"I don't see any fault in your logic. All right, go ahead and take a seat boys, although I doubt you'll be here long."

"Thank you Professor Adams," they both replied, nearly at the same time.

"Academically, you're both doing fine. Mr. Malcolm, you've got just about the highest grade one can have with me, and I don't have to tell you the future you've got picked out will also be positively affected by the performance I've seen from you this year. You're on your way to a fine career serving the public in our illustrious government. I'll be passing you officially later this afternoon."

"That's great. Thank you sir."

Professor Adams nodded.

"As for you, Mr. Vector, I'm afraid you're a bit of a mystery sandwich I can't seem to figure out. Your assignments are also fine, but each time I go over your work I'm never sure whether you're being properly diplomatic or overly clever. Your approach and level of consideration is always enjoyable for me to take a gander at, but it often reminds me of a crossword puzzle or Sudoku game. I sit down, and the time just goes."

"Um, thank you?"

"Well, I'm not entirely sure I mean it as a compliment Mr. Vector. There are times I think your solutions are really something special, and other times I'm practically convinced you're pulling one over on me. Which one is it Vector?"

"Sir? I just write what I think is right."

"You just write what you think is right..."

"That's right."

Joaquin gave a side glance to his friend who met his look with a carefree shrug.

"Mr. Vector, your test results suggest you are best suited for the Builders Guild, is that where you're headed?"

"I'm not sure. I'm still considering my options."

"Interesting. Although Builder is at the top of the list, you rank high enough in practically every field to consider most guilds as options. Is that right?"

"Yes sir.""That sort of undermines the whole point of the placement system doesn't it?"

"Yes sir."

"Are you leaning towards one guild over the others?"

Sage looked at Joaquin who nodded in encouragement.

"Well, Professor Adams, I'm leaning very heavily towards the Artist Guild."

"You want to be an artist?"

"Yes sir."

"Fascinating. Are you any good?"

Sage opened his backpack and handed Professor Adams his latest work. The government professor looked it over thoroughly. He seemed to be searching for something he couldn't quite find.

He turned Shakespeare's head around so that it it was looking directly at Sage. "It's broken. It's cracked down the middle."

"Well, it's a busted bust. It's supposed to be a statement on the antiquity of the English language, and how visual art is superior to the written word."

Professor Adams was taken aback, then grinned.

"You don't talk like that. Who fed you those lines? It was Garcia, wasn't it?"

Sage was cornered, and replied embarrassingly, "Yes sir."

"I knew it. The man talks like he lives in a surrealist painting. Salvador Dali couldn't have a practical conversation with the guy. Listen, this ain't half bad. It's a shame it broke and had to be glued back together. But if you can do something once, you can do it again." He handed the sculpture back to Sage who put it away in his backpack.

"As for my course, consider it passed. If you ever decide to go into government, you've got a good friend that can show you the ropes, and I wouldn't be opposed to giving my endorsement of you either. Being an artist isn't for the faint of heart. Might be the hardest damn path of them all, always having to chase the intangible through the tangible. Godspeed son, Godspeed."

Professor Adams extended his hand to Sage, and then to Joaquin. They shook firmly and parted ways. The two friends made their way back out into the hallway.

"What a character, right?" asked Joaquin.

"Yeah, I always liked him. He always seems to be his own person."

"Definitely. It sounded like he was calling you smart and crazy at the same time, huh?"

"He wouldn't be wrong," laughed Sage.

"Ready for History? We've got that simulation exam today. Let's knock that one off the list."

"Lead the way Mr. Leader."

***

The midsection of the Trojan Horse, also known as "the belly," was the most popular location to hold simulation exams and exercises because it had a ton of technology resources and lots of open space. Its official name was the Demonstration Department, and it was composed of four large demonstration rooms called Pods.

Professor Olive Johnson patiently waited for her students to arrive and watched them shuffle in one after the other until Pod 3 was full. Sage and Joaquin made it through the door just in time to procure the last two seats for the 11 o'clock exam.

The two young men put amplifying VR headsets over their heads and logged in. Twenty-four students sat waiting for their exam instructions. The room dimmed and Professor Johnson stood at the front of her lectern, and she looked around the room to ensure every seat was filled and that every student was ready with their headset on.

"Thank you for coming today. This will be your final exam of the semester. It signifies the conclusion of your time in this historical module. History is studied so that our failures of the past may be learned from, and our victories can be reviewed to isolate what worked. We must view it from the big picture perspective of the culture over longer timespans, but equally, we must also view it from the brief, significant moments lived by individuals. For what is a culture or a society if not the result of every individual life in it?"

Professor Johnson pressed a small button on her lectern, and her outfit changed from modern business attire to nineteenth century aristocrat. She pressed another button and the students were transported hundreds of years into the past. Horses pulled wagons down rudimentary streets, and the men and women walked past shops with hand-painted advertisements in the windows. There were no modern vehicles, no portable telecommunication devices, and no electricity — the streets were lit by kerosene lamps. The students were in awe at the world they suddenly found themselves in.

"The time is 10:00pm April 14th, 1865. The place is Ford's Theatre in Washington, D.C. in the United States of America. In 15 minutes Abraham Lincoln, then President of the U.S., will be shot by actor John Wilkes Booth. Your objective is to improve the outcome of this moment in history. You have 20 minutes to complete this exercise. Begin."

Each student experienced the simulation individually. They were on their own. They could not see the direction others decided to go in or what actions they chose to take. Students had to draw upon their knowledge of history to complete the exercise. While many of them slowly inched forward, contemplating plans in their minds and second guessing themselves, Sage knew immediately what to do.

He walked through the arched front entrance to Ford's Theatre and looked in amazement at the building decor and style of dress of those around him. Old photographs of the time period were always black and white, but this experience was in bright, beautiful, vivid color. There was a pleasant energy in the theatre lobby. The men wore suits and the women wore elaborate dresses that must have taken them hours to get into. A small African American boy dressed in a service uniform approached the bewildered history student.

"Do you need help sir?" asked the young boy.

"Yes, how do I get to the balcony seats?"

"Yes sir, I can show you the way. Follow me."

Sage followed the usher past the crowd and up a stairwell. When they reached the top, the young boy pointed and said, "Right over that way sir. Enjoy the show."

"I will, thank you."

Instinctively, Sage reached into his pocket and was surprised to discover two coins from the time period resting at the bottom. He fished them out and gave them both to the usher.

"Thanks sir!" said the boy who left beaming from ear to ear.

Sage was standing on an empty floor. No one was guarding the entrance to the box seats where President Lincoln was sitting. He looked at the timer displayed in the top right corner of his exam screen. It read 14:37:05 which meant he had a little over 14 minutes left, but only about 9 until John Wilkes Booth showed up.

He walked through the doorway and entered President Lincoln's box. He could see the clear figure of the president who was laughing at the show while Mrs. Lincoln gripped his arm. A man noticed him and asked what he wanted.

"I need to talk to Mrs. Lincoln."

"*Mrs.* Lincoln? That's a first. What do you need to tell her?"

"It's a personal matter of the utmost importance."

"What's your name?"

"I'm a family friend. Can you pass a message to her? It won't take more than a minute."

"All right, what's the message?"

"Tell her I have something important to tell her about Willie. Tell her I'll be just outside."

"Okay, I'll tell her."

He walked away, and Sage exited the president's box. Sage sat and waited on a bench along the wall on the other side of the lobby floor. The countdown timer now read 10:17:43. A couple more minutes passed and the First Lady of the United States finally emerged. Mary Todd Lincoln walked towards him, and took a seat beside him on the bench.

"Do we know each other young man? What do you want to tell me about Willie?"

Sage looked at the time and it read 07:48:12. He knew Lincoln would be shot in a few minutes and the exercise would be wrapping soon after.

"You must really miss Willie don't you Mrs. Lincoln?"

"Not a day goes by that I don't think of my boy. Did you know him? He would have been about your age by now."

"I didn't have the pleasure, but I'm sure he was a great guy."

"He brought us a lot of joy, but he could be mischievous too. He used to love pulling all the books down from the shelves. He was a lot like his father. Despite his rambunctious tendencies, Willie was a thoughtful boy."

Sage reached for and held Mrs. Lincoln's hands in his, then gave her a huge hug. He held her in his arms with his head resting on her left shoulder. She welcomed the caring embrace and Sage could feel her body let go of some tension as she relaxed. A tear fell from Mrs. Lincoln's right eye and Sage could feel it land on the top of his head. He glanced up slightly and saw John Wilkes Booth sneaking in through the door to the president's box. His grip on Mrs. Lincoln tightened as he braced for what he knew would come next.

The gunshot sounded and they both looked in its direction.

"What was that?" asked Mrs. Lincoln.

"It was probably part of the play," suggested Sage.

Then screams went off loudly from inside the theater. Mrs. Lincoln got up and rushed to the door to get back to her husband but found it barricaded. She pounded on the door with her fists and yelled, "Let me in!" Sage did not bother to look back as he made his way down the stairs to the main lobby. He exited from the same entrance he first arrived through, and he found himself back on the street looking up at Ford's Theater and listening to the chaos unfold from within.

His countdown clock came to an end and he was once again back in Pod 3 looking at Professor Johnson behind her lectern.

"Thank you for demonstrating your ideas and showing your intellect. I will be reviewing the footage and your choices more closely. You will receive your final grade soon on this simulation exam unless you opt to take an alternate exam later today. Please place your gear in its proper place. You may exit the pod."

Sage looked over at Joaquin who looked like he was struggling. He was physically back in the room, but mentally still in 1865. Sage touched him on the shoulder and Joaquin came out of his trance.

"You okay man?"

"Yeah, wow, that was something."

"Definitely. What happened in your simulation? What did you try to do?"

"I tried to stop John Wilkes Booth from shooting Lincoln. Why? What did you do?"

"I got Mrs. Lincoln outside their box and away from seeing her husband get shot."

"Wait, what? Why did you do that?"

"It improved the outcome."

"How?"

"Lincoln's death becomes something people rally behind and even though the war was pretty much over already, it helped bring an end to that period and allowed people to focus on rebuilding."

"So trying to stop him from getting shot doesn't make a better outcome, and removing Mrs. Lincoln saves her the pain of what she would have had to remember for the rest of her life?"

"Yeah, pretty much."

"Damn Sage, that's pretty good. I'm going to have to show up for another one of these things and ask for a different simulation."

"I'm sure you'll get the next one. I try not to overcomplicate these. She said to improve the outcome. She didn't specify by how much."

"You're right. I'll remember that moving forward."

"Want to grab lunch?"

"I'm starving, let's go."

"Birria tacos?"

"Hell yeah."

Sage walked into his English literature group meet-up on a full stomach. The room could seat thirty but was only about half full. Rebecca, the teaching assistant, led the weekly group discussion on a novel of the professor's choosing. The book they were currently discussing was Mary Shelley's *Frankenstein*. They were supposed to have read two thirds of the book by now, but Sage had only read the first ten pages.

Fortunately, he got through the meet-up without having to contribute any of his own ideas on the book. Any time he was asked, he just responded with a question that someone else eagerly answered. He could always rely on the fact that most people loved the sound of their own voice too much; they would talk forever when prompted. He still didn't get the full significance of the *Frankenstein* story, but he decided to give the movie a watch. The only problem was which version? There were about a hundred of them in the online archives.

Architecture was a breeze. His professor was out of the office so Sage left his design plans on her desk. Her assistant was manning the fort, keeping a close eye on the growing stack of assignments. She knew it was a real possibility someone might try to pull a fast one and switch out a name or pawn someone else's work off as their own. Sage smiled at the assistant in an attempt to help ease her worries. It didn't quite work.

"It's fine, just leave it there. She'll get your work when she returns."

"Thanks. Do you happen to know when she'll be back?"

"She didn't say."

"Okay, no problem. I was only asking because I had a small question. You wouldn't happen to be someone I could ask, would you?"

"Go ahead, what is it?"

"Okay great. Can someone be in the Builders Guild and another guild at the same time? I've never heard of it happening but a friend of mine said it might be a thing. Is it?"

"No, it is definitely not a thing. Everyone knows you can only be in one guild at a time. You can always switch into another guild if you put in the work, but no one can be in two guilds at once. That would defeat the whole point. We're meant to specialize. Everyone doing their individual part gives us the best results for the whole."

"Oh, yeah," Sage said disappointedly.

He quietly left his Architecture professor's office and made his way to his final academic stop of the day: Astronomy. It wasn't the easiest course to study, but the space it was taught in was probably his favorite on campus. The Wells Observatory was located on the very top floor of the Bowl Building. It was called the Bowl Building because of the valley's reputation as being the Salad Bowl of the Nation, but also because the observatory looked like a giant, upside down bowl.

Sage rode the elevator from the lobby to the Astronomy Department, traveling twenty floors up in about that many seconds. He made his way to Professor Greco's office located just outside the main observatory lecture hall. The door to his office was unique because it was curved and rounded with a small half moon shaped stained glass window on top. The glass was a clever contrast of black, white and gray tones all working to create a beautiful moonlike work of art that perfectly complimented the experience of being in the Astronomy Department.

Professor Greco was sitting at his desk when Sage knocked at his moon-themed door. He sat with his feet on his desk going through a stack of photographs of constellations. When Sage walked in, the professor took his feet down, sat up, reached for a small telescope laying on his desk, pointed it at Sage, and adjusted its settings to more properly focus on his student.

He smiled, then said, "Mr. Vector, right on time. Have a seat."

Sage settled down in one of two massive leather office chairs while Professor Greco continued to observe him through his telescope. He remained calm and undeterred while his teacher acted like a planetary probe sent out to the farthest reaches of the galaxy in hopes of finding life there. Greco eventually satisfied himself with his efforts and placed his telescope back on his desk.

"I've been struggling with my scope for days now. I'm not sure if it's a problem with my lens or my vision, but every time I use the thing it seems just a tad bit off. I have an appointment with my optometrist next week, so we'll see. Right now I'm still gathering data. Speaking of which, I have some data for *you*."

Professor Greco looked up Sage's assignment progress on his interface. It took him a couple of seconds to scan through everything. He seemed pleased because his shoulders eased slightly and a slight grin formed with the corners of his mouth. His grin then turned into a wide smile that spread across his face like piano keys.

"You've done well in this course Mr. Vector. Your growth has been steady and your test scores are among the highest I've seen. Science seems like a natural fit for you. Have you considered joining one of its guilds? We need more astronomers, especially with a keen eye like yours."

Sage was thoroughly surprised. He enjoyed his astronomy lessons and studying about the constellations in the night sky, but he never considered actually doing any of that as a career. The idea of joining the Astronomers Guild was on par with telling him to consider being an astronaut or a rocket scientist. They sounded amazing, but completely unreal and nowhere on his radar.

"I'm flattered sir, but I've never considered the sciences. Math isn't one of my strengths and the terminology is probably too advanced for me to follow."

"You know, I used to think the same thing when I was in school."

"You did?"

"Yep, I did. But, you know what made me take the plunge?"

"No sir, what?"

"A girl. Her name was Elizabeth. I took Astronomy because it was required and I was pretty bummed to be taking it, until I saw her sitting there in class. She was the most beautiful thing my eyes had ever seen. Astronomy was the only place I could ever see her. She loved looking up at the stars each night, and her love for them eventually rubbed off on me. It only took one introductory course, and her by my side, to convince me I had to spend my life looking at all of the beauty surrounding me."

"That's pretty romantic professor. What ever happened to Elizabeth? Did you marry her?"

"Elizabeth? No, she moved away the following term. I thought I would be heartbroken, but that first night without her, I looked up at that big, beautiful sky and realized I wasn't alone. The sky was actually more beautiful with Elizabeth gone. I was no longer distracted by what had been so near to me, and now I could send my attention further out — with more focus. I saw things I didn't realize had been there the whole time. The universe is not a mystery to the man who dares look at it. I don't know, but I have a feeling you might be that kind of man too. Am I wrong?"

"No professor, you're not."

Friday Night Rites

Michelangelo Park was situated in the heart of Salinas. It took up one mile in every direction, and a person could walk four miles by circling its perimeter one time around. From up above, it didn't look that much different than the many rows of lettuce and strawberries the region was known for. Flying, one could see similar rows of green plotted throughout the park, the only difference was the splotches of bright colors and the small open gray spaces that looked like punctuations to someone's green words. But when one looked at the park from below, from inside it, all words became obsolete. Beautiful bushes, trees, and lawns created the abundant, vibrant atmosphere of green. The splotches of bright colors were from every imaginable flower on Earth. And the open gray spaces were permanent tributes to mankind's greatest contributors, immortalized forever in the park as stone statues.

Like most people from Salinas, Sage grew up visiting Michelangelo Park. Unlike the visitors that came from all over the world to see the inspiring environment for a day or two, Sage Vector felt an inherent, almost spiritual connection to the place. He came as often as he could, and he walked for as long as his legs would allow him. The statues spoke to something deep inside him. The trees and greenery mixed with the cool, crisp air filled his lungs with a refreshing calmness. As he looked everywhere around him, he felt balanced and whole.

Sage arrived at the park with Zimmer, and the two quickly strolled through the various paths with great familiarity, taking every twist and turn with ease until they reached the park center and stopped. Michelangelo stood twenty feet tall, a paintbrush in his right hand, a hammer and chisel in his left. His stance was confident, and his expression captured the moment when creativity strikes. When one looked up at the statue of Michelangelo, one felt like they were part of a masterpiece in progress.

Sage studied the Michelangelo statue carefully. He looked at it from every angle and could picture it clearly in his mind any time he was away from it. Standing in front of it was probably his favorite place to be in the world. When he was in the proximity of the statue he felt a powerful resurgence, almost as if he was charging up some imaginary battery inside himself. He got something out of every visit. He left feeling lighter and always had an extra bounce in his step for the next several hours.

Today, Sage was feeling in need of some inspiration. His dad, his friends, his professors, everyone seemed to have a different idea of what he should do with his life. He thought he wanted to be an artist, and looking up at the greatest artist of them all, he wanted to rekindle that purpose once again. Sage wanted Michelangelo to work his magic one last time and let him know that what he wanted to do was the right thing. But staring up at him now for the millionth time, it felt different somehow. It was like putting your money into a vending machine that doesn't give you what you want and just takes your money. Maybe he'd taken his hero worship too far and now the juice was gone.

"How does he look?" said an elderly woman standing to the right of Sage and Zimmer. She wore an elegant purple velvet dress with pearls around her neck and huge peacock feather earrings. Her hair was curly black with a hair pin parting it in the middle. She wore big, black sunglasses and had an even bigger smile across her face.

"Powerful, strong and confident. Like Superman if he were an artist. All-knowing? Godlike?" answered Sage.

"Boy, you are too much. Michelangelo was a creator, but *the* Creator? You might be giving him too much credit."

"Yeah, you're probably right," he replied with a little down tone in his voice.

"What's the matter sweetheart? I hope I didn't rain on your parade."

"No ma'am, I guess I rained on it myself before I got here."

"Need someone to talk to about it? I'm a pretty good listener."

"That's really nice of you, but I think that's the problem. I've been talking to too many people about my problem, and in the end I don't come to an easy solution."

"Easy ain't always best. Sounds like you need a bigger problem."

"Huh? What do you mean?"

"Well, first of all, there's nothing wrong with having a problem. Gives us something to occupy our time. Working on it, solving it. The real problem is not moving on to something bigger and better. You get what I mean?"

He thought about it for a second and said, "Yeah, I do. That's actually pretty clever."

"I've been at this stuff awhile. So, what's your bigger problem?"

"Good question. I guess I've been focused on what I'm going to do but haven't thought too much about what it's for. I know what I like and what I don't like. That still leaves a lot of different options. But when I think about the reasons for doing any of them, things do get a bit simpler. At the end of the day, I just want to help people, and I want to make the world as beautiful as it can be."

"That's wonderful. Just remember, beauty is in the eye of the beholder."

"Sure, but when anyone looks at this statue don't you think every one of them would think it was beautiful?"

"Not everyone darling. Some people can't always see — like me."

Sage's heart sank and he froze. He turned and took a closer look at the woman who was looking in the general direction of the Michelangelo statue but not directly at it. He looked again at her big, black sunglasses and glanced down at her right hand gripping a thin metal cane.

"I'm sorry ma'am, I didn't realize..."

"... that I'm blind? Oh, it's ok. It happens sometimes. I get along pretty well not being able to see like most people do."

"If you can't see, why come to this spot with Michelangelo?"

"Oh, me and Michelangelo are old friends. I may not be able to see him with my eyes, but I can feel him. I've seen him with my hands plenty of times. I've got a small replica at home that I'm able to touch. That small statue brings me a lot of happiness because it's the one thing I have that truly reminds me of my husband. He passed a few years ago. He was an artist like him. Painted really elaborate landscapes on these massive canvases, that is until he met me. He became a sculptor just so he could share his art with me."

"That's beautiful."

"Oh, trust me honey, I know. I spent most of my life surrounded by his beauty. And his art was nice too," she laughed. "You see, making the world beautiful doesn't always mean splashing paint or shaping clay. It's the way you communicate with the world around you that matters most. How you make others feel. Especially, how you make yourself feel. Life ain't no race son, it's an adventure. You keep at it no matter what and just enjoy the ride. I better get going. I'm meeting some of my girlfriends for a drink. I hope you figure out the solution to your problem...or not. Either way, you'll be all right. I've got a good feeling about you. Bye now sweetie."

Sage watched the old woman walk away towards the north end of the park and disappear around a giant oak tree. He turned to Zimmer who observed the woman's exit with keen interest. The droid displayed a series of thumbs up emojis across his eye plates.

"Yeah, she was pretty awesome."

"TIME FOR NEXT TARGET."

"Not just yet."

Sage needed to finish what he came to do. He looked at the crowds of people all around him, each person vying for the perfect view of the famous statue of Michelangelo. He took a step back to get an even better view and to get some distance from some of the visitors near him. Because he felt a little self-conscious and wanted to keep his thoughts private, rather than say them out loud, he vocalized them internally, but directed them at Michelangelo.

"It's been a little while, hasn't it? I've been coming to you for years now. You've inspired me and helped me a lot, but it's time I take my own path and live my own life. I don't know if I'll ever make something great like you did. I don't know if what I'll make will be important enough or matter in the big scheme of things. But that isn't why I'm going to do what I'm going to do. I'm going to do it for me. I'm going to do it because I want to do it, and that's all. If it makes a difference to anyone else and makes them happy, that's great. But it won't be why I'm doing it. I want you to know that I respect you. I respect everyone in this park, everyone in this city, my family, my friends, everyone. But I'm done letting everyone have a say in what I do with my life. It's mine. It's probably the only thing that's really ever going to be truly mine. And what I do with it is for me to decide. And I've decided. I'm an artist. I'm a creator. Wish me luck old man."

Sage looked down at Zimmer and said, " Let's get outta here. I've got a game to win."

***

Field ball dominated the attention of the entire city most Friday nights. It was the most popular sport on the planet and every citizen either played it or knew someone that did, but everyone watched. Missing a game was like disconnecting from society. Everyone followed and talked about field ball.

Atlas Arena was the biggest field ball space in the city. The Salinas Stallions used it for professional games but it was also used by the local universities because their games were just as popular. The giant crouched figure of Atlas made up the base and entrance to the main arena. Escalators and stairwells led people up to the giant open globe on top of his shoulders where thousands of seats encircled the lit up field. Tonight, half the stands were filled with mostly green shirts, and the other half, mostly blue ones. The Alisal Trojans were defending their undefeated win streak against the North Salinas Vikings. The air was chilly and more than a few spectators were wrapped in warm, furry blankets representing their team's colors.

Coach Gonia was pacing back and forth across the locker room floor, looking at his watch every thirty seconds. His assistant coaches were just as nervous and kept shifting in their standing positions, adjusting the pressure in one leg to the other. The players were fully dressed in uniform and sat on benches waiting, talking among themselves in low voices and whispers.

"Joaquin!" yelled out Coach Gonia.

"Yeah Coach?"

"What's taking him so long?"

"I don't know coach. He said he was almost here."

"Well, we can't wait any longer. Let's start."

Joaquin turned to his teammates in his loudest voice, "Trojans! Listen up!"

Coach Gonia handed his clipboard to one of his assistants then turned to his players who gave him their undivided attention. Joaquin could feel the tension in the room and hoped their coach could give them the jolt of motivation they needed to win tonight.

"All right boys, this is the big one! This is what we've known was going to happen since the beginning of the season. Those Vikings want to steal our thunder. They want to come for what's ours. We're on top of the mountain right now. Yeah, that view feels amazing, but don't forget how easy it is to fall off the top! We can't give these guys an inch! That field belongs to us tonight! We're not going to let anyone push us around. *We're* the pushers! *We're* the ones that control that ball! What do you say boys? Is that our ball?! Is that our field?!"

"Hell yeah!" they screamed in reply.

"That's what I'm talking about. Joaquin, got anything to add?"

Joaquin stood up. As team captain he was expected to say a few lines to keep the momentum building. He was about to speak when he caught a glimpse of Sage in one of the back lockers changing into his uniform like a man on fire. Joaquin grinned and knew exactly what to say to his teammates.

"All right guys, we want to go out on top. We've worked hard all year for this but the work's not over yet. This isn't the time to coast and think we've got anything in the bag. Every game is a battle, and we know that going in. These guys want to take us down real bad but we're not going to let 'em. You know why? Because they came to play, but we came to work! This is what we do. Like coach said, we don't give them an inch. That entire field is ours. We protect each other, we look out for one another. We know how each other thinks, what the guy next to us will do. We can count on each other being there when it matters most — Isn't that right Sage?"

The players and coaches turned around in relief at the solitary figure of Sage Vector standing behind the last row of them. He was fully dressed in green, with black face paint across his cheeks and under his eyes. He walked slowly towards the front as his teammates slapped his hands or shoulder blades in encouragement. He nodded at his coach and then to Joaquin before he spoke.

He turned to face the entire locker room and felt the energy in it. Sage embraced the moment and knew how to get the team into action. It would only take three words.

"One....more....time." he said with total conviction.

His teammates loved it. "ONE, MORE, TIME!" they shouted.

"ONE, MORE, TIME!" they stood.

"ONE, MORE, TIME!" they jumped.

"ONE, MORE, TIME!" they ran out onto the field.

***

A field ball field is unlike any other field in sports. Instead of being flat, it contains numerous obstacles and barriers. It is a three-dimensionally shaped rectangle, with small, flat sections called peace zones at each end. The huge middle section is the war zone. The war zone is composed of four rocky hills known as "The Rocky Mountains," two placed near both ends of the field closest to the peace zones. Then there's the three big tunnels in the middle of the field, one large one in the center and two smaller ones alongside it. Covering all three tunnels is a huge mound called "The Hilltop." A small, but heavy, round rubber ball is dropped directly above the middle of the field to commence play. The way to score a point is to get the ball into a peace zone. Once someone scores, or if a ball goes out of bounds, a new ball is immediately dropped again from the center of the field and play continues.

The game is non-stop and action-packed. Once a player possesses the ball, he can run with it, or he can hand it off, or roll or bounce it to a teammate. Players are not allowed to throw the ball directly through the air to each other. However, they can get creative with rolling or ricocheting the ball to their teammates. You can lose a point by touching an opposing player in a peace zone, but touching them in the war zone is more than allowed. You just can't hit or kick them, although pushing or wrestling with them is perfectly acceptable and routine. In the event of a tie, the game continues until the next point is scored.

Field ball doesn't have many rules but all of them need enforcing. Enforcers keep watch over the game and make sure none of the rules are broken and that the game runs smoothly, and fairly. Each game is 60 minutes with no breaks and no time outs. Each team starts with ten players on the field and ten substitute players waiting off the field. Any substitutions are permanent for the rest of the game. No player can come back once they leave the game. Players must stay inside the boundaries of the field during play. If a player lands outside the field by accident or by force, he cannot return to the game but his team can replace him with a substitute. If a team finds itself with less than 10 qualified players on the field, then they continue to play with the players they have left.

Strategies vary, but most teams position their ten players in various spots across the field, although there is no requirement to do so. The most common formation is the blanket formation, where a team has one player at every tunnel entrance and one player on each of the hills near the peace zones. In a blanket formation each player is supposed to take responsibility for covering his area, but players quickly adapt as one or more players leave their areas to try to advance the ball and score. There is always an open, vulnerable spot on the field. The most successful teams are either the best at communicating with one another and can adapt to changes quickly, or they are physically strong and dominate the game by muscling the opposing team out of bounds, eliminating enough players to tip the scales in their favor. The two teams playing tonight were representative of these two qualities. The Trojans were smart and quick, and the Vikings were powerful and strong. The entire city of Salinas eagerly awaited seeing which team would be victorious.

Sage looked out into the crowd and couldn't see an empty seat anywhere. Fans were screaming, music was blaring and the flashing lights were never-ending. Joaquin was meeting with the other team captain and the game enforcers. His teammates were bouncing with nervous energy. A few were stretching their arms and legs, and Sage joined them. He took a deep breath and felt the cold air fill his lungs, and then let it out. He watched the steady, slow moving small cloud of his breath move across the field like a quiet storm.

He turned and looked at the crowd of excited fans on the Alisal side of the stadium and heard a few call out his name. He knew his parents were watching from the stands, as well as most everyone he knew in the world. Robin would be sitting there too, probably huddled underneath a green and black blanket, in between a couple of her theater friends. The bright lights made finding her in the crowd nearly impossible, but Sage squinted and tried anyway.

"Sage! It's game time. Let's go!"

He felt the slap of his coach's hand on his shoulder blade, and turned his full attention to the field. His teammates were starting to form around Joaquin, and Coach Gonia walked over to them with Sage right behind.

"All right boys, this is it. We've trained and worked hard for this. This is what we do. This is our field tonight. Let's send those Vikings straight back to Valhalla, what do you say boys?!"

"Trojans, on three!" shouted Joaquin. "One, two, three!"

"TROJANS!!" shouted the team.

The players ran out onto the field fired up and took up their starting positions. Sage joined Joaquin and four of his teammates on the Hilltop along with six opposing players. Each of them manned up, picking a different player to guard. The bright lights beamed down on them like a thousand UFOs. The cold air became unimportant under the heat of the lights and the adrenaline pumping. Looking up, Sage could see the metal chute hovering above. It was filled with dozens of field balls, one resting in the release chamber, ready to drop down upon them at any moment. The stadium was silent and tense as everyone waited for the cannon blast that signaled the start of the game and the dropping of the first ball.

"BOOOOM!"

The ball dropped directly over the center of the dozen players positioned on the Hilltop. Each of them fought their way to the ball by muscling their opponents while the remaining eight players watched keenly from their vantage points atop the Rocky Mountains near the peace zones. Joaquin managed to get to the ball first and the Trojan fans cheered loudly, screaming and stomping wildly. However, their excitement quickly went away when a Viking player slapped the ball out of Joaquin's hands. Sage saw the ball was rolling down the right side of the hill and headed out of bounds, but he decided to take the gamble and chased after it.

The red ball was gaining momentum down the hill when Sage leaped, rolled and dove for it a couple of feet near the field boundary. Several Viking players were headed straight at him hoping to knock him out of bounds and out of the game but Sage didn't bother to look at them. He knew they were coming and was focusing his attention on the nearest peace zone and running towards it as fast as he could. The Rocky Mountains were directly in front of him now. Two of his teammates were trying their best to hold their Viking counterparts away from the path Sage was heading in. He turned to look behind and saw three Vikings hot on his tail, with two of his teammates behind them. One of them was Joaquin with a big smile on his face. Sage looked at Joaquin and nodded. Joaquin dropped back from the chase and waited.

Sage was charging up the middle, in between the two mountain barriers on the field, when one of the Viking defenders got free and headed right at him. He quickly moved the ball out in front of him, extending it towards the oncoming player. The huge Viking with his bright, blue uniform came at Sage like a giant ocean wave about to strike the shore. His eyes were greedily fixated on the red ball in front of him instead of on the player he needed to stop. So when the Viking leapt at the red prize he was too slow to react to Sage bouncing it away from him.

The ball landed in the hands of Sage's teammate. The one who failed to contain the huge Viking was now more than making up for it by taking the ball into the peace zone for the first score of the game. The crowd went wild and the entire stadium lit up in Trojan green.

Sage didn't bother to watch his teammate score. He knew he would, so he immediately ran back towards the center of the field. He saw the new ball drop down to four players on the Hilltop. Three of them were Vikings, with only one Trojan there to stop them, Joaquin. Sage looked out across the field and tried to find his missing teammates. He found two of them at the entrance of the middle tunnel, one seemingly unconscious and the other badly out of breath.

Sage looked down the tunnel and saw two more of his team-mates getting back on their feet on the opposite end. He turned his attention to the player knocked out in front of him.

"Ricardo! Are you all right? We need you man, wake up!"

The young man slowly opened his eyes, squinting, and in a daze.

"Sage?"

"Yeah, it's me. Can you walk?"

He tried lifting himself up but couldn't. Sage turned to the sidelines, looked at his coach and shook his head, letting him know Ricardo was done playing in the game. Coach Gonia let one of the enforcers know they were making a substitution. A couple of paramedics took Ricardo off the field in a stretcher and a new player took his spot on the field just as the stadium erupted once again, except this time it lit up in blue.

Sage was waiting with Joaquin and his teammates on the Hilltop when the third ball dropped. They were evenly matched in numbers this time but the Vikings, in addition to having momentum on their side, overpowered the Trojans. Two green uniforms were hurled off the Hilltop and out of bounds. Before replacements could make their way onto the field, the Vikings were rushing towards the eastern peace zone. Sage and Joaquin were gaining on them but they were running in a protective formation. The ball carrier had two Vikings shielding him on both sides. They were willing to risk leaving the Hilltop mostly undefended to take the lead in the game.

Joaquin called out to his defenders on the mountains, "Stop him!"

The two players struggled to free themselves from the Vikings guarding them. The Alisal team captain could tell their chance of escaping was slim so he turned to Sage and made a quick motion with his arms. It looked like he was shooting an invisible arrow from an invisible bow but his friend knew exactly what it meant.

Sage nodded and the two split up from each other, and charged with all their might into two wide, curving paths. Joaquin on the left, Sage on the right, the two players ran up their corresponding mountains, and used momentum and gravity to leap off of them. Their trajectory put them directly in the center path of the Viking players. Like two cannon balls fired into a troop of charging soldiers, Sage and Joaquin blew up the play and scattered every player involved. The red ball flew out of the hands of the Vikings and bounced towards the unattended peace zone.

While most of the players tried to recompose themselves and adjust to exactly what happened, Joaquin and Sage were racing towards the ball. Joaquin spotted one of the Viking defenders coming towards them. He decided to run towards him and give Sage a chance for the ball and the easy score. No words were necessary to exchange between the two friends; Sage knew what he needed to do. Joaquin got to the Viking and did his best to keep him back despite his overpowering size. Sage reached down and scooped up the ball and rolled with it into the peace zone just before another Viking reached him.

Sage drowned out the cheers, the screaming, the loud music, and even the bright, green lights flashing all around and got back up on his feet and ran. Joaquin and a couple of their teammates were already on the Hilltop. The other team was slow to get back and the Trojans had the advantage now. All of their training clicked into place and they bounce passed the ball in triangle formation around and through the opposing team to score another point.

When the fifth ball dropped, the Vikings were ready with one of their favorite strategies — tunnel trapping. They moved most of their players around the base of the entire Hilltop, and near every tunnel. Six Trojan players stood unguarded on top. Sage gripped the red ball in his hands and waited for Joaquin to direct their next action.

"Marcos, Freddie and Kevin. You're going to block in front wall formation. I'm going to be the catapult. Tomás, you're our cannon ball. Sage, you're back safety. Keep a bird's eye view and step in if needed. This ain't going to be easy. Trojans on three!"

"One, two, three!"

"TROJANS!"

Sage handed the ball to Tomás and stayed back while the rest of them got in formation and started down the hill. From high up he could see the Vikings starting to close in. A few disappeared into the tunnels. A big group was ready and waiting at the foot of the hill when the Trojans reached them. Joaquin timed the moment of impact precisely and shouted, "Now!" a couple of seconds before they collided. Joaquin got down on his hands and knees. Tomás ran onto his back and just as his feet touched, Joaquin lifted him with a quick push. The Trojan flew over the heads of the Vikings, but his left ankle didn't escape their reach. Tomás came down hard while the rest of his team got pushed back into the center tunnel. The ball bounced away and a Viking easily picked it up and ran it into the peace zone.

Tomás made his way back up the Hilltop where Sage waited with the new ball. The rest of their center six were still trapped in the tunnel. They needed their other four players to remain on the mountain ends of the field, so it was only the two of them left to move the ball and try to score. A couple of Vikings were making their way towards them.

"We gonna ping pong it or free the prisoners?" asked Tomás.

Sage looked at the two Vikings running sluggishly towards them, and then at Tomás.

"Why not do both?" he smiled.

"Let's do it man."

They got the ball to one another by bouncing it off the surface of the field. The ricochet back and forth between them was quick, precise, and always took into account where their opponents were. After making it down the hill and past the two Vikings, Sage got near the tunnel where his teammates were trapped. They were held by two Vikings on both ends. Fortunately, the two Vikings nearest Sage had their backs to him and made his next move simple.

With all his might, Sage threw the ball directly at the back of the head of one of the Viking players. It made him fall to the floor, and the other Viking was too startled to keep his attention, or his grip, on his prisoners. In a matter of seconds the Trojan players were all free and running down the field.

Joaquin slapped Sage on the back. "What took you so long?"

Sage laughed, "I was weighed down. Heavy is the head that wears the crown, right? Don't worry, you can have it back." Sage bounce passed the ball to Joaquin who took it all the way to the peace zone and scored one more for Alisal.

The Trojans continued to outsmart and outmaneuver their opponents, and eventually the Vikings changed their strategy. They isolated and outnumbered one Trojan player at a time, pushing them out of bounds and off the field. One by one, the Trojans were eliminated from game play. The crowd booed loudly each time a new player exited the game, but the Vikings continued their aggressive onslaught. It cost the Vikings some points at the start, but they gradually got the Trojans down to five players while keeping all of their own still active.

The North Salinas Vikings took full advantage of their new numerical dominance. They racked up points in no time. The score was tied — 15 to 15. There were only 3 minutes left in the game. The next dropped ball would likely be the last one needed to win. All five Trojan players were on the Hilltop along with six Vikings. There were no Alisal defenders on any of the four mountains. The North Salinas team had a defensive player on all of them.

Joaquin saw the desperation in his team's faces, but he also saw the overconfidence of the other team.

He turned to his teammates and said, "We keep going. It's not over until it's over. We're winning this. Let's do it!" They nodded, and then the ball dropped.

Joaquin touched the ball first with the tip of his fingers and tried to catch it as it fell. He was quickly surrounded by a sea of blue uniforms crashing into him like the violent waves of a sea storm. Sage and the other Trojan players got tossed about in the commotion. Every player battled it out until one escaped with a firm grip on the round, red prize.

Sage wasn't surprised at all when he saw Joaquin running with the ball straight towards the Rocky Mountains with the two awaiting Viking defenders there. The rest of the Viking team was chasing right behind him and the Trojans followed in step. Joaquin was too far ahead for Sage or any of his teammates to catch up to him. There was no time for the team captain to call out a play, and no players to execute one even if there was. He would win or lose this game alone with what he did next.

Joaquin ran full steam ahead and up the middle of the two mountains as the two Vikings closed in on him. The middle valley was the straightest path to the peace zone but it was also the easiest to be stopped in. Joaquin had no other choice, given how close the other players were to his back. He could see the defenders ahead of him, both with a look of greedy delight. He knew each of them wanted to be the one that stopped him. That player would get all the glory.

The two Vikings dove to tackle Joaquin, but he jumped and twisted over them with half an inch of clearance above their outstretched hands. He miraculously landed on his feet and ran the ball another ten yards into the peace zone just as the game clock ran out. He looked back and saw that every player in the game had been right on his heels following him. The Vikings looked down at the ground in defeat, while the remaining Trojans jumped up and down celebrating wildly. They rushed towards their team captain and lifted him up.

Joaquin looked out across the field at the people in the stadium going crazy. He was nearly blinded by the flashing lights, falling confetti, and the sweat running down his face. He heard his name being shouted, "Joaquin! Joaquin! Joaquin!" The feeling was too overwhelming, and he asked the guys to put him back down but they refused. They thought he was being too modest. "Enjoy it! You're the man tonight," they said. The celebration continued and Joaquin was stuck suspended above the ground by his teammates. He looked around for the one person that might help him.

Sage looked up at his best friend with both admiration and sympathy. He knew he deserved to be carried like this but understood it must be embarrassing too. Who wanted to be a living trophy? At the same time, he was inspiring to people. He was an important part of their community and city. Sage smiled at his friend and shouted, "I know." Joaquin grinned, eased the tension in his shoulders and raised his arms and waved his hands to the crowd. They cheered and emotions grew even higher.

The stadium full of people celebrated the game, and would continue to do so well into the night, but Sage Vector would not be one of them. He left the field right away and quickly exited the stadium, hoping he wouldn't be too late to achieve an even bigger win tonight.

LOOK UP IN THE SKY

Zimmer methodically scanned the road ahead, looking for any potential dangers or obstacles. His periphery vision and motion detectors enabled him to react instantly to the environment around him. He discovered a small, jagged rock 20 yards in front and adjusted so smoothly that Sage hardly felt the slight lift to ensure complete clearance over the object. The streets were bursting with life. Talk of tonight's game was very much on the minds of the people of Salinas as they walked, exuberantly smiling and laughing, retelling their favorite moments to one another.

More Trojan flags waved in store fronts, and more green and black clothing appeared on the sidewalks, the closer Zimmer carried his human companion towards the heart of East Salinas. The community was alive and joyful, and the Trojan Horse stood tall, lit green in its full glory. The moonlight paled in comparison to the iconic figure illuminated and growing bigger as Sage made his way towards it.

Sage looked at his watch and knew he had enough time. He pulled his hoodie over his head in an attempt to be less conspicuous as he traveled down Steinbeck Avenue. His eyes peeked out at the people walking along the store fronts, and he got an occasional smile or wave, despite his effort to hide his identity. Finally, he spotted his destination and although it was open for business, the store was one of the few on the street empty of customers. Instead of slipping through the back entrance as he originally planned, Sage hopped off Zimmer and walked right through the front doors of Brave New Books.

The bookstore was one massive maze of shelves spread out across 2,500 square feet in one of the oldest buildings in Salinas. Hector Magaña sat behind the counter of his store reading a leather-bound edition of *A Connecticut Yankee in King Arthur's Court* by Mark Twain. He could hear the door open and close but didn't look up until he got to the end of the page he was on. He flipped the gold tip of the page with his left index finger, read the remaining words of the sentence at the top of the next page of his book, placed the ribbon bookmark in its needed spot, and finally looked up at the face of a young man he'd never seen before.

"Hello. Are you in need of any assistance?" asked the old man.

"Yes, sir. I need some Shakespeare."

"Don't we all," he laughed softly.

Sage could see the twinkle in the man's eyes and knew he possessed great affection for the famous playwright. The old man stopped laughing and could tell there was something different about this teenage boy in front of him. He could see the curiosity in his gaze and found himself admiring his attentiveness.

"Have you read many of his plays?" Sage asked.

"Son, I've read them all. A few of them many, many times over. Are you looking for one in particular?"

"Not exactly. I'm just looking for something different, something I haven't seen before."

"Well, he wrote 38 plays and plenty of poems. You should be able to find what you're looking for in the back. Look for the sign that says DRAMA."

"Thank you."

Sage headed to the back of the store, past dozens of aisles of book shelves, and Hector opened up his book and removed the ribbon from its center. He found the next words he needed in his story, but turned his head towards the young man who was just now reaching the correct section of the store. He turned down the right aisle and Hector Magaña nodded slightly to himself and continued his reading.

The book store was quiet except for the sounds of a John Coltrane recording playing lightly through several speakers in the ceiling. The place was empty. The old man at the front of the store was the only other person in the building. Sage was in complete solitude while he searched for the perfect Shakespeare book to gift Robin. He knew she had *Romeo and Juliet* and a couple of the more popular plays by the writer, but he wondered what lesser known title might make the best addition to her collection. There were two entire shelves filled with Shakespeare books in the Drama section of Brave New Books. One shelf contained paperbacks, and the other shelf contained hardcovers. He knew he wanted to get Robin a nice hardcover edition, so that meant his search was narrowed to one single, but still long, shelf.

There were huge volumes of *The Complete Works of William Shakespeare* but they somehow didn't seem right as a gift. They were too overwhelming and lofty. He didn't want to come across too strong or serious. Sage wanted his gift to create a softer effect, to express he was thoughtful and that he cared. An individual title would suit his needs much better, and so his choices narrowed even further. He wanted something in nice condition, so it couldn't be too tattered or worn. The book he wanted to gift should also be beautiful to look at, and colorful if possible. His eyes finally spotted the right book — *Julius Caesar*.

Like *Romeo and Juliet*, the play was a tragedy. Sage never read it but after some quick research on his interface glasses he learned enough to feel comfortable picking it to gift Robin. The cover was a gorgeous green with silver highlights and the pages were clean and white. It was also fairly light to carry which was convenient for Sage. He was gently tossing the book in his hands to feel its weight, when he happened to spot a different book, one without a title. It was on the highest shelf, in the farthest end on the left. He stared at it for several seconds but didn't know why. His curiosity got the best of him and he put down *Julius Caesar* and reached up to pull the mysterious book down from the shelf.

Right before his fingertips touched the spine, the book shook and emanated a soft glow. Sage tilted his head in disbelief and rubbed his eyes. "I must be too tired. I'm seeing things," he thought to himself. His hands were at his sides and he decided to try again. He reached up once more and his fingertips near the book caused the exact same reaction to it. Sage withdrew his hand and the shaking and glowing stopped. He reached again, and the same reaction occurred. He withdrew and reached again several more times, and each new reach caused the same reaction in the book, while each new withdrawal stopped it.

Sage looked around the store for any possible sign that he was the victim of some unusual prank. There were no people, no hidden cameras, just the same sounds of John Coltrane's saxophone playing through the aisles and aisles of books. Sage's curiosity was at an all-time high as he reached one more time for the strange book on the top shelf.

His fingers finally touched it, then formed a grip around its spine and brought it down. As he held the book, it continued to move and glow. It didn't hurt, in fact it was the exact opposite. Sage felt a gentle flow of energy from the book that slowly filled him with warmth and caused a smile to form across his face. He examined the cover of the book in search of any title or author name. Although the spine lacked any writing, the front cover had four words written across it — *The Book of Space*. There was no author name underneath the title and nothing written on the back of the book. Sage ran his fingers over the words etched in the hard, black leather, and each letter of it glowed brighter as his fingers traveled over them.

Sage took another look around him. He stopped thinking of the book as part of a prank, and instead started thinking of it as something he might get in trouble for having discovered. Fortunately, the book store was still quiet and empty. Sage knew the only other person around was the old man at the front of the store, and he was too far away to see or hear him. Slowly, he opened the book.

Light shot out of *The Book of Space* like a lighthouse on its back. The brightness was tremendous and rushed out of the pages of the book and onto every surface of area around Sage. The intensity of the light continued and he forced himself to confront it. When he looked directly into it he saw pictures and words and symbols form, one into the other, slowly at first, and then faster and faster. An entire universe opened before him as if infinite stories were being born. He gazed, mesmerized, but completely alert and more alive than he had ever felt before. A hunger grew inside of him for what he was seeing and the speed of the pictures and words and symbols grew to meet his hunger. He continued consuming the energy in the light until it vanished suddenly when the book's pages flapped with the speed of an airplane propeller, and the book finally closed shut.

Sage stood firmly with his eyes wider than they'd ever been before, looking at the world around him as if seeing it for the first time. His body felt lighter, like it was made of paper or feathers, but at the same time it felt strong like metal. His attention kept pulling outward onto his environment and he was infatuated with the beauty in everything he looked at. The most commonplace, ordinary things were now rich with detail. The air vents in the ceiling became works of art to his perception. He saw textures in the wall paint that made him giddy. The change he experienced wasn't limited to his sight either. John Coltrane's saxophone playing was a spiritual symphony exalting inside him, and he felt lifted as he followed every note coming from the small speakers.

Suddenly, Sage realized the implications of some simple hidden truth that was now part him, and his head turned to all of the books on the shelf nearby. He grinned and reached for one of them — *A Raisin In The Sun* by Lorraine Hansberry. As soon as his fingers touched the book's spine, a sudden rush of words and images came flooding into him. The whole story came into his consciousness, alive and vivid with full comprehension as if he had written it himself. He felt deeply for the characters and their struggles. Their emotions became part of him and changed the way he looked at things to a marked degree. The joys and the pains would be there permanently, and so would the ideas of the story.

Sage reached for another book, another play — *The Crucible* by Arthur Miller. The Salem Witch Trials in seventeenth century Massachusetts shot into him like a maddening wildfire. He became shocked at the symbolism of the story and what it spoke to about human nature. He found it brilliant and frightening and forever important to remember. Once again, there was no way he could look at the world in the same way.

He lifted his fingers off the book and looked around the store, but this time to make sure no one saw him doing something that might be seen as strange or even crazy. Sage slowly swiped his fingers across an entire shelf of books, wondering what the result would be. He quickly discovered that the transfer of knowledge was exactly the same, only faster as his need adjusted. The very decision to complete a volume by the time his fingers moved to another seemed to make the words and images flood into him to that degree of speed. In less than a minute he had complete conceptual understanding of every volume on the shelf in front of him. It was written in his mind, to be used forever.

Sage felt serenity and peacefulness, but at the same time jubilation and excitement. He looked at the rest of the shelves in front of him, and then looked further at the dozens and dozens of shelves beyond. The knowledge and understanding he could possess here was overwhelming, but he knew he had to make it happen. Suddenly, he remembered Robin and her performance at the amphitheater. He looked at a nearby clock on the wall, momentarily admiring the intricate nature of its craftsmanship and design, but quickly realized he was late. The rest of the books would have to wait for another day. He grabbed *Julius Caesar*, and the book that gave him his wonderful new power, *The Book of Space*, and placed them together under his arm.

Hector was several pages deeper into his book when Sage came up to the counter. He placed the two books in front of the old man and waited. Hector finished reading his last sentence, placed his ribbon back into his book and held it up to Sage.

"Have you ever read this one, young man?" he asked.

Sage took his finger and ran it across the title. The story shot into him. He found it entertaining and quite hilarious.

"*A Connecticut Yankee in King Arthur's Court?* Yeah, I've read it. Mark Twain is a great writer. Really funny too," he laughed.

The old man looked at Sage with a slight confusion in his face. He couldn't quite figure out why, but he suspected the young man knew something he didn't. Sage picked up on this feeling and wanted to put him at ease.

"I had to write a paper on Mark Twain for school. I'm pretty familiar with his work."

"Oh, you did? Well, that's great. He definitely had a big impact on American Literature. *Huckleberry Finn* alone would have cemented the man's legacy. It'd been awhile since I'd read this one. Thought I'd give it another go. You're right, it is pretty funny. Well, what did you end up finding in my little store?"

He picked up the two books in front of him.

"Ah, *Julius Caesar*. Wonderful choice. What's this other one?"

The old man picked up *The Book of Space*. Sage quickly wondered if the same ability he had would suddenly be given to the bookseller. "What if it transfers to him and I lose it?" he thought. Sage watched him closely. When Hector picked up the book and opened it, no light came shooting out, and the old man seemed unchanged.

"Never noticed this one before. But some of these books have been sitting in this store longer than I have. Okay, young man, that'll be ten dollars."

Sage swiped his watch band across the payment screen on the countertop. He grabbed his two purchases and left. The old man remained sitting in his same position, but he didn't reach for his book. Instead, he kept his gaze firmly on the young man just outside his store. He could see him through the glass doors getting onto his robot vehicle. When he was no longer in his sight of vision, Hector said to himself, "Wish I could put my finger on what it is about that young man that's so familiar." He shrugged, then reached for his book and continued reading.

***

The Kazan Amphitheater was only half a mile away. Sage Vector glided towards it with Zimmer lighting the way through the cool California night. As he looked around, the world opened up to him in ways he could never before imagine. The same people and things were there, just like they always had been, except now they were beaming with life. Everything he looked at was rich in extraordinary detail and sharpness of focus. The feeling of lightness he felt before continued and expanded outward. He could see farther, his space was bigger, and the world was transformed into one giant, beautiful spectacle.

The lightness coupled with the cool wind on his face made him feel like he was flying instead of riding down the streets of East Salinas. The Trojan Horse came alive and made him smile a huge smile imagining himself riding on top of it. The joy was overwhelming to Sage but he continued to revel in it, and didn't want it to stop, no matter how addicting it felt. He wondered if the feeling would ever fade away. So far, it only kept growing.

The sky was clear and the stars shined brighter than ever. Sage arrived late to the amphitheater, and the play was well underway. Despite this, he found an empty seat in the far back row and sat down. The entire outdoor theater was surrounded by soft, yellow lights made to look like small fires or torches. The stage was similarly lit, except there were many more lights, including several spotlights. One of the spotlights was shining on Robin as she performed her lines as Juliet, while another highlighted the actor playing Romeo. Both were dressed in Elizabethan costume attire and the backdrops behind them were quite ornate and believable.

Robin was in the middle of the famous balcony scene.

"How camest thou hither, tell me, and wherefore? The orchard walls are high and hard to climb, And the place death, considering who thou art, If any of my kinsmen find thee here."

Romeo was someone Sage didn't recognize, but he found him to be quite good.

"With love's light wings did I o'erperch these walls, For stony limits cannot hold love out, And what love can do, that dares love attempt. Therefore thy kinsmen are no stop to me," he said.

"If they do see thee, they will murder thee," she replied.

"Alack, there lies more peril in thine eye than twenty of their swords. Look thou but sweet, And I am proof against their enmity."

"I would not for the world they saw thee here."

"I have night's cloak to hide me from their eyes — "

Right at that exact moment the night sky above Salinas darkened. Every star was now gone, vanished completely from space. The people in the audience noticed immediately. They were looking up in confusion and wonder, many of them in shock — at their sky without a single star in it. As the truth of the moment sank in, many began talking and pointing and several screamed. The actors on stage were equally distraught, especially Romeo, who wondered if his last line had actually triggered the event. He dropped to his knees and wept, the emotion too much for him. Robin tried to console him but he was locked in to a paralyzed grief.

The stage manager spoke over a microphone, "Tonight's show is cancelled until further notice. We apologize but we are just as confused as you are. Please feel free to stay here if you need to. If traveling home, please do so safely."

Sage watched everything unfold and was now just below the stage waiting for Robin to see him. After talking to a few of her cast mates, she glanced around and saw Sage waving at her. She rushed towards him, hopped down from the stage, and gave him a big hug.

"Thank god you're here. I don't know how to feel about this. The freaking stars in the sky disappeared! And why did they leave the moment Brian said that line?!"

"That's got to be a coincidence. I'm sure the two things aren't connected at all."

"You're probably right, but that's one hell of a big coincidence."

"What was the line again?"

"I have night's cloak to hide me from their eyes — "

"That is pretty strange, but you might be making too big a stretch. I mean, a local actor made the stars disappear? Seems a bit unlikely."

"I know, I know. So what made them vanish?"

"I have no idea."

"Sure you do. You always have ideas, like about everything. Come on Sage, what caused this to happen? You must have a theory or two rolling around in that head of yours. Give me something, because I'm not sure what happens next here. Is the world ending? Did all the other planets in the universe disappear too? Are the stars gone forever, or are they going to come back?"

"Calm down, take a deep breath. It'll be all right."

"How do you know?"

Sage looked right into her big, brown eyes and told her with his, "It's going to be okay." She felt his intention and confidence through the silence and smiled. Her shoulders relaxed, and she reached her arms around him for another hug.

"Thank you for making me feel a little better."

"You're super welcome."

"How are you so tranquil and all zen right now? You really aren't worried about the sky and the stars?"

"Not really. It's weird. I don't know exactly why I'm not too worried about them, but somehow I'm not. I mean, all of the stars are in other galaxies and our planet isn't dependent on them in any way that I know. Now, if the moon disappeared that would be a different story. The moon vanishing would really cause havoc on Earth."

"Oh my god Sage, the moon! I didn't even think of it."

She turned to look for it. "See, it's right there," said Sage, pointing just above her right shoulder. A huge smile spread across her face and she felt calmer.

"Thank god we still have the moon. But, I'm still worried. This is something major. I've never heard of this happening ever. I mean, the stars!? The stars have been around as long as we have. They're always there and now they're not. This is like the biggest thing to ever happen. Don't you think so?"

"Yeah, you're right. This is definitely a big deal. Probably every person in the world is wondering what happened and trying to figure this out, unless..."

"Unless what?"

"Unless this isn't all over the world. What if this only happened here in Salinas, or only in California? How do we know this is everywhere? Maybe the stars are still in the sky in other parts of the globe."

"You're right! Let's find out if it's widespread."

They both put on their interface glasses to see what was being reported. Their newsfeed and inboxes told them right away that it was a global, worldwide event. No one seemed to know how or why it happened. They took their glasses off and looked at each other.

Sage was the first to speak. "It'll be okay. We're still here. We didn't disappear. And eventually we're going to find out what happened."

"What if we don't? What if this is just how things will be from now on? How do we go on with the world like normal when such an important part of it is gone?"

"It'll be hard, but we can do it. It can't be that different from losing a loved one, and people do that all the time. People are pretty tough."

"Yeah, I guess you're right."

Robin smiled and looked up admiringly at Sage, and into his caring eyes. Their faces inched closer to one another. She wondered what he would do if she tried to kiss him. She leaned in a little closer. Sage tried his best to remain where he was because he didn't want to make the first move, but he found himself being pulled towards her. Their eyes looked at each other's lips, and the inevitable movement of their bodies towards one another continued, until it was broken by a familiar voice calling out to them from across the amphitheater.

"Sage! Robin!"

Joaquin ran towards them. A few people in the auditorium recognized him and were momentarily distracted from their recent surprise with another one. He smiled and waved reassuringly at them as he made his way over to his friends. Joaquin gave Sage a big embrace, and a lighter, more respectful hug to Robin.

"This is a big deal. The government, the scientists, everyone is baffled by this. People everywhere are really losing it right now. No one knows how this is possible. I've heard a few insane theories, but the stars disappearing out of the sky is insane too. Do you have any ideas on this one Sage?" asked Joaquin.

"Not really."

"Not really? That means you have an inkling, a small tiny string you can pull, right? What is it man?" replied Joaquin.

Robin chimed in. "Yeah Sage, what did you come up with?"

"Well, it's something you just said that made me just now think of it. You said the stars disappearing is insane. So, any theories about why or how must be insane too. We have to reconsider everything we've known about the universe and how it might work. Either that or..."

"...or what?" asked Joaquin.

"...or the stars didn't disappear at all. We just can't see them for some reason."

Joaquin and Robin were silent, considering what he was suggesting. They looked up at the night sky one more time, and both squinted into it, like they were trying to move some invisible wall blocking out the stars. They quickly realized the futility of the effort and stopped.

"Wait, a minute! I know how to find out if they're still there!" Joaquin said loudly. He put on his interface glasses and searched for what he was looking for. "If they're still there but we can't see them from the Earth, then maybe they can be seen by somebody that's not here."

"Who's not here on the Earth?" asked Robin.

"Astronauts," said Sage.

"Exactly. Now, I should be able to access a live feed from their site. They've got astronauts stationed from the moon all the way to Mars." Joaquin continued searching.

"I don't think they can see them Joaquin," said Sage.

"Why not?"

"Except for the sun, every star is outside our galaxy. All of the astronauts are still within our galaxy. So it's quite possible if something is blocking out the stars it could be blocked for anyone in our entire galaxy, not just for us on Earth."

"Yeah, I think you're right. They all seem to be just as confused as we are," replied Joaquin.

"Wait a minute, what about the sun? It's a star. What if it disappeared too? What if it won't be there in the morning?" asked Robin.

"The sun is still there," said Sage.

"How do you know?"

"Not only would it be all over the news, we'd all be frozen to death by now. No sun, no life."

"Oh, yeah. You're right."

Joaquin took his interface glasses off and put them away in his pocket. He looked around at the people who continued to gather in the amphitheater. Many of them were students, and he could see some of them subtly glancing towards him, looking up from their crouched and huddled positions. They were desperate for answers, and the young leader knew they needed someone to reassure them.

"I'll be right back guys," said Joaquin as he headed towards the amphitheater stage. He found the audio visual team with their interfaces on, sitting in front of the balcony backdrop.

"Hey guys, I need a mic." They all stopped what they were doing, and looked up at the familiar voice with eagerness. "Sure thing Joaquin," they said, almost all at once. It didn't take more than a minute to turn the audio system back on, and to get Joaquin a wireless microphone. A spotlight flipped on and Joaquin found himself center stage looking out at a large crowd of familiar faces.

"My name is Joaquin Malcolm. Many of you know me. I am the student body president at Alisal University, and captain of the field ball team. I know many of you are scared or confused. I feel that way too. It's unsettling to look up and not find what has always been there. We're used to seeing the stars every night. Heck, for some, they're a guide to finding their way back home. Losing your guide, losing a part of your world is hard, really hard. I want to let everyone here know, it's okay to feel what you're feeling. This is a big deal, there's no getting around it.

We may not know too much about this event, but there is one thing I do know. We are alive, we are okay, and we will continue to be okay. The sun is still here, it's shining bright on the other side of the planet, and we'll see it ourselves in the morning. We don't know what happened to the stars, but for all we know, they might come back, or maybe we just can't see them. No matter the situation, we need to stay calm and not panic. The philosopher king, the smartest minds on the planet, scientists, astronomers, astrophysicists, engineers, and more are busy investigating and working on finding answers. There's no need for any of us to get too worried. This event is unheard of, and is definitely going to change things moving forward, but try not to let it change *you*. You are all still the same amazing, resilient, bright, hardworking people I've known my entire life. Let's use this moment to come together for one another. Instead of looking at the loss in the sky, try looking at the win that can be gained tonight and the days moving forward. Be there for each other. Life will always be a challenging and unexpected journey, but it doesn't have to be traveled alone. Look out for one another tonight people. Thank you, and be safe."

Joaquin exited the stage, and walked back towards his friends. He could see a little bit of hope in more of the people's eyes than he saw before as he walked through the rows of people. Some started to stand up and stretch and slowly make their way home. Others were more talkative with who they were with. If the amphitheater space could be considered a room, one might say the energy in it had definitely shifted.

THE PHILOSOPHER'S KINGDOM

A hundred golden buildings shined like giant coins across the mountaintops of Earth City. The sun played and bounced off the walls while the king's guards walked the perimeter and gazed down across at neighboring Kathmandu. The streets and buildings stretched out for miles like a giant mandala, full of life and color. To the east, Mount Everest loomed giant, white and eternal as its cold breath reached across many miles to where the philosopher king stood.

"Your majesty, they're assembled."

"Thank you Ulysses."

The young guard led the king towards the Continental Chamber where his Global Council awaited him. All six members sat in their respective chairs spread throughout the room. The Chamber floor was covered in a beautiful carpet decorated with a large map of the globe, with each continent distinguished by a different color. Each member of the council represented a different continent and sat directly over that part of the map. Antarctica was the only continent on the carpet map without a council member sitting over it. However, the chair that covered it was not like the others, it was much larger. It was the throne reserved for the philosopher king.

"Good morning everyone," he said.

The council members quickly rose from their seats.

"Good morning your majesty," they all replied.

The king sat down over Antarctica, and the council members followed suit and sat in their respective seats. Each waited attentively.

"All right, what information do you have?" he asked.

"My continent's best minds have been working on a couple of theories, both connected to a type of space dust that could be obscuring our ability to see beyond the borders of our galaxy," said the Asian council member.

"Our people have ruled out that possibility your majesty," interrupted the European council member.

"Africa? What do your astrophysicists say? Their authority in these matters is unparalleled," asked the king.

"We ruled out the possibility early on your majesty. We have been exploring other theories centered around mind control and visual optic manipulation," replied the African council member.

"You mean to say we are all implanted with the same delusion that the stars have vanished from the sky? Every single human being on Earth mind controlled?" asked the North American council member.

"What machine or power could do that?" asked South America.

"That is what we are trying to figure out," replied Africa.

"What leads you to believe that we are all being mentally tricked rather than the stars just being physically gone?" asked North America.

"Because there would be remnants or fragments, some pieces of matter or trails of gases left behind to observe, but instead there is nothing — just empty space," replied Africa.

The explanation was accepted by the council members. They nodded slowly to themselves and looked internally, their minds pondering over other potentialities. Ethan Tanaka, the philosopher king, patiently watched them with great interest. It was just under one hour since he first learned about the stars event. He oversaw the immediate call to action of the world's best intellects. He had faith in humanity and knew that there must be a discoverable answer, a rational explanation for what happened. Yet, he kept the slightest part of his mind ready for the possibility that rationality might have no part to play in this. Perhaps God was tired of what he created and wanted them gone. Was Earth next? It was his job to philosophize, but some questions might be better left unasked.

"Does anyone else have other leads we might follow?" asked the king.

The council members were silent.

"Okay, let's address any related problems. What's happening out there?"

"Your majesty, people are afraid. Most schools and businesses have closed. Many are huddled inside their homes scared the Earth might disappear next. People are behaving like it could be the end of the world. How do we address this?" said the European council member.

"We don't know the truth. The people might be right. It really could be the end of the world," said the king. "However, they need to know they are not alone. They need consoling. The stability of the planet depends, like it has for hundreds of years, on the power and reassurance of the throne. I will address the world in one hour. We are bound to discover more about the stars by then, and if not, at the very least I will give the people empathy and compassion, and a friend to go through this with."

"There has been a large increase in the number of reported suicides since the stars disappeared. Your speech will definitely help that situation greatly your majesty," said the South American council member.

"Are there any acts of violence, looting, arson, vandalizing, or the like?" asked the king.

"Very little on my continent," replied Europe. The rest of the council members nodded in agreement. Acts of aggression were rare. War was a thing to be studied in history books, but it was always something the council had to monitor.

"Good. Anything else we should be aware of?" replied the king.

The council members looked around the room at each other and no one had anything further to say. The philosopher king looked at them with gratefulness and dismissed the Global Council. They would gather again every two hours until the crisis was at an end. The king was hopeful, but uncertain that an end was possible. Would the stars magically reappear when the night sky returned to Earth City? It was daytime in his part of the world when the stars vanished. He wondered what it would feel like to experience the phenomenon first hand. Would it bring shock and wonder, or like many talked about, bring an unbearable sadness?

The king left the room and walked towards the great promenade. It stretched for miles along the perimeter and around the mountaintop city. The cold wind hit Ethan Tanaka in his face and body like a stiff bedsheet. However, he also felt the sun on him as he looked out at the city below, full of life. The cars and trucks traveled along straight and curving roads. And white cotton clouds were scattered across the blue sky, moving slowly over everything. The king was closer to the clouds then the people below were. He could almost reach out and touch one, but they were still above him too.

A large thud sounded to his right and the king turned to see what caused it. He saw a little girl lying on the brick pavement holding her knee. As he got closer he could see the knee was scrapped, but not too seriously. The girl was grimacing, her face communicating the sting of the pain she was struggling with. The king looked for the nearest guard.

"George, can you have someone get us a first aid kit?"

"Yes, your majesty," he replied, then left.

The king sat on a bench a couple of feet away from the girl. She started looking around where she fell, as if she was searching for something.

"Can I be of any help?" the king asked her.

"No, it's okay. I'm all right," she said without looking up.

"I understand. Well, I'll be right here if you change your mind."

She heard something familiar in the voice speaking to her, and she finally looked in the direction it was coming from. Her face went pale. She tried to get up off the ground and stand up straight in the presence of her king, but the pain shot through her little body and it was too much for her.

"I'm so embarrassed. I'm sorry, your majesty. I fell and hurt my knee."

"I can see that. No apologizes are needed. What caused your fall?"

The girl looked down, then away. "Nothing, your majesty."

"It's okay. You don't have to be shy. What was it?"

"Well, I was thinking about what everyone has been talking about. How the stars are gone, and when it's nighttime again, that they won't be there anymore. It made me sad because the stars always remind me of my dad. I was looking up at the sky and I guess I wasn't too careful about where I was walking. I lost my balance and fell."

A young woman arrived with a small first aid kit. The king smiled at her and extended his arm out. "Thank you Rebecca, if it's all right I'd like to do it." She nodded, then handed the small box to him.

"Now, young lady if it's okay, I'd like to help you with that scrape before it gets infected. Is that all right?" he asked the injured girl who was looking up at the sky.

"Yes, your majesty. Thank you!"

"You're very welcome. You mentioned something about the sky reminding you of your father?" The king went to work cleaning her knee with cotton gauze.

"My father is in the Engineering Guild. He works on the underground train systems."

"That's quite an important job. Your father must be a very smart man."

"Yes, your majesty, he is. You see, because he spends so much time underground and away from home, when he comes back to us he loves using this telescope of his to look at the sky at night. My brother and I sit outside with him and take turns looking through the eye of the telescope at all of the things my father loves to show us. My mother joins us too when it's not too cold outside, but my brother and I always join my father no matter what the weather is like. We don't get to see him all the time, but when we do, looking up at the stars with him is our favorite thing. Now I'm worried because my father's underground, and when he comes back he won't be able to use his telescope anymore. It makes me sad if what people are saying turns out to be true. Is it true, your majesty?

The king felt a deep ache inside himself and no matter how much he wanted to give this young girl hope, he knew it was more important to be truthful.

"I don't know. We're still trying to figure out an answer to that. If it *is* true, the night sky won't be the same without the stars. Tell me something, what's your favorite thing to see when you're with your father looking through his telescope?"

"Oh, that's easy. Ursa Minor."

"Ursa Minor, that's an interesting choice. Why is that your favorite?"

She was looking up through the clouds as if she could spot where the constellation should be. The king used some medical tape to secure her bandaged area.

"My dad is a big Chicago Bears fan. We travel all over because of my parents' jobs, but our home is in Chicago, in the United States. Anyhow, he loves the Bears and always calls me his Little Bear."

"Now I see. That's quite clever. Ursa Minor means Little Bear."

"Exactly! My dad loves to point at it, and say 'Look baby, there you are, shining pretty bright tonight!,' and it always makes me smile." She looked down at the brick floor. The smile faded from her face and her eyes began to water. The king put his hand gently on her shoulder. She closed her eyes and tried with all of her strength to keep the tears back, but one single drop escaped, and it slowly rolled down her left cheek. The king took a light, blue handkerchief from his pocket, and wiped the tear before it fell further.

"Thank you, your majesty. I know you don't know if the stars will come back, but what do you think the chances are? Fifty, fifty?"

He smiled, then looked up at the clouds hovering near them, "It's hard for me to imagine a sky without anything in it. I think there's a good chance we'll see more there again. Life always seems to find a place to grow. Even if there are no stars, there will always be the space for them. Do you like to draw?"

"Oh, yes! I love to draw animals. My favorite is giraffes. I just love their long necks. It's fun to draw them eating from trees."

"That's wonderful. I love giraffes too. Imagine the world, especially the sky, as one giant piece of drawing paper. With all that space, don't you think someone would draw a star or two? Maybe some planets?"

"Definitely! I would put a billion of them."

"Me too. So I don't think we have too much to worry about, do you? The universe is full of creation. I don't think anything can stop that."

The girl relaxed her shoulders and smiled. She looked up at the sky one more time and said, "I think you're right."

"Mia! Are you all right?! I came as soon as they told me," said a woman dressed in a gray blazer, matching skirt, and black high heels, walking towards the young girl and the king.

"Mom! Yeah, I'm ok. I had some great help," she said, turning to look at the king.

"Oh, your majesty, thank you so much! Mia usually doesn't get hurt, or have accidents. I'm sorry if she caused any trouble."

"None at all, she's a wonderful girl, I doubt she felt much hurt from her fall. She should heal quickly. As for accidents, I like to think there aren't any. Speaking with your daughter today was a real joy."

"That's so nice of you. We're grateful for your kindness," said Mia's mother.

"It's quite all right," he replied, then turned to Mia. "It was really nice talking to you today Mia. I'll do my best to get those stars back if I can. Will you do me a favor?"

"Anything, sure."

"Keep drawing, okay?"

She beamed a big smile, "You got it."

Ethan Tanaka, the philosopher king, walked towards what seemed like an army of his staff who were lined up near the windows of the Alexandria Library Building. His chief of staff, Penelope Singh, stood patiently by with a smile on her face, but he knew in her mind she must be moving a mile a minute, trying to plan for his next meetings in his ever-changing schedule.

"Sorry if I kept you waiting Penelope."

"No, worries, your majesty. Are you ready for your next item?"

"I'm ready, what is it?"

"Your speech to the world. We've written a wonderful address that will put people at ease and make them feel safe. The aim is to neutralize any panic, and build a sense of optimism."

"Thank you Penelope, I'll use it as a guide to refer to, but I'm going to be speaking off the cuff. People need a one to one, heart to heart, real communication. I don't think it's fair to them, in a time like this, to stick to the script. Don't you agree?"

"Yes, your majesty."

"I'm ready when you are, let's go talk to the people."

***

The speech to the world was a success, given the circumstances. Ethan Tanaka looked humanity in the eyes with empathy and compassion. He was careful not to build a sense of false hope, but a genuine one, that no matter what happened next, the people of Earth would face it together. All of the interface surveys pointed to people having a greater confidence about the future, and decreased feelings of fear and panic.

The rest of his schedule was a continuing rotation between check-ins with his Global Council, and one-on-one meetings with some of the planet's top minds. His council continued to chase down or eliminate various theories about how or why the stars were gone. The king listened, asked questions, and tried his best to steer his council in the right directions. He did his best despite a long chain of indirect communication that took time to make its way back to him via the council.

The one-on-one meetings with some of Earth's smartest people, were less complicated and more enjoyable for the king. Every twenty minutes a new genius appeared before him, and the conversations were smooth and productive. Astrophysicists made up the majority of these visiting experts, but there were plenty of other fields represented as well: astronomers, geologists, engineers, astronauts, theologians, philosophers, and even a couple of illusionists. The king explored every possibility with these exceptional intellects, and he was a little more optimistic as each new expert left his office.

The king took a long drink of cold water from the tall glass on his large, wooden desk. He set the glass back down and walked towards his bookshelves. He looked admiringly at them, the memories of each hitting him like the wind outside. Each book reminded him of a different time in his life. He smiled at the copies of *Astro Boy* by Osamu Tezuka that he read when he was a young boy in Japan. Manga comics helped build his early appreciation for art. Next, he looked at his eleven volume set of *The Story of Civilization* by Will and Ariel Durant. He was so proud of himself for reading them all at a crucial point in his life. They gave him a proper scope of his potential purpose. He continued to scan the titles of each shelf, gaining greater comfort from them as he remembered their contents. It was like being surrounded by every friend he ever made, all at once. They gave him power. They made him feel loved.

Penelope came into the room with someone new for him to meet, another expert. "Your majesty, this is Dr. Robert Masters." The man wore a heavy, black suit, with a metallic, black tie that glimmered under the light. He wore a huge unnatural smile across his face.

"I'm pleased to meet you, your majesty," he said, extending his right hand out.

The king smiled, nodded, and reached his hand out to shake. Dr. Masters squeezed the king's hand with a little too much force, and let out a nervous laugh.

"You've got quite the grip Doctor," said the king.

"So do you," laughed Dr. Masters.

Ethan Tanaka motioned with his arm towards the couches in the middle of his office. "Please, have a seat."

The two men sat across from each other on opposite couches and were separated by a single, but elaborate, woven Tibetan rug. The king suddenly noticed, that unlike the other experts of today, Dr. Masters did not bring with him any briefcase, papers, or charts. He was completely empty handed for a meeting with the world's most powerful man.

"What kind of doctor are you, Dr. Masters?" asked the king.

Dr. Masters was looking around the room and seemed to be figuring something out in his mind. He quickly caught himself and turned to face the king once again.

"I have two PhDs. One in Neurology, the other in Psychology."

"That's interesting. How does your background relate to the problem we've been trying to tackle Dr. Masters?"

"Oh, that's quite simple. I believe you're already familiar with the theory I've been focusing on. The idea that the stars are still there, it's just that no one can see them." The doctor let out a tiny giggle.

The king felt uneasy hearing his explanation. "Okay, please continue."

"Well, the theory goes like this. The stars haven't moved one inch from where they're supposed to be. They're still up there in the sky, exactly how they've always been. However, something has happened to every person trying to look at them. They've all been hypnotized to believe the stars are not in the sky."

The doctor's tone was now serious. He looked at the king with blank, unblinking eyes.

"How would that be possible? There is no method or machine capable of something like that."

"Oh yes, there is. Will you allow me the chance to demonstrate how it would work?" He got up from the couch. "Do you mind if I sit next to you? It will make it easier to show you."

The king nodded, "All right, please do."

A playful smile appeared on the doctor's face. Tanaka moved over, making room for the doctor to sit next to him on the couch. Dr. Masters reached into his blazer and pulled out a long, thin piece of rounded metal, similar in shape to a pen. He handed it to the king so he could examine it. Tanaka looked over it carefully but the entire surface was smooth and free of any markings or indentations. The metal felt ordinary and the king handed it back to Masters unimpressed.

"What am I missing Dr. Masters? What does this have to do with hypnosis?"

The doctor laughed. "Everything! It has everything to do with it. This is why the stars are gone." A strange sparkle was in his eyes.

"I'm sorry doctor, but can you give me more detail?" The king looked at him with patience and kindness.

"You're right. I apologize. I get a little excited when it comes to the science. You see, it's new. So new in fact that no one knows about it. But I'm getting ahead of myself. I think it's best I just demonstrate how this little device works."

"Okay, please do."

"See what happens when I hold it like this? Do you see a little red light coming out of the other end of it now? You should be looking right at it, your — majesty," he laughed.

"Yes, I see it."

"You are now under my power of suggestion. I control your thoughts, words and actions. No one but me can undo this. Do you understand?"

"Yes, I do," said the king.

"Very good. You will act calmly, like your usual self. If any-one comes in, you will tell them you need a few more minutes with me. Okay?"

"Okay."

"Great. Ah, this is such a joy Mr. Tanaka. You don't mind if I call you Mr. Tanaka do you? The whole majesty thing just seems pointless now doesn't it?"

"Yes. I don't mind if you call me Mr. Tanaka."

"Splendid. Now, Mr. Tanaka, I'm going to let you in on a little secret. Actually, the biggest secret there's ever been. Would you like to know my little secret Mr. Tanaka?"

"If you would like me to know, yes."

"I would like that Mr. Tanaka. You see, I'm the reason why the world thinks the stars are gone. But they're not gone at all. I just made everyone think they're gone. I did it using the same technology in this little device, only on a much bigger scale and with a bigger device. It took quite awhile to put everything together, but I did it. Years of secret research and development, self funded, I might add, went into this. Do you know how many people I had to control like I'm controlling you right now to make this happen?"

"No, I do not."

"Too many, Tanaka, too many. Getting to the ones in space was a bit tricky, but I figured that out too. It's amazing what you can do with satellites these days. And now, the last phase of my plan is about to begin. You play a very large role. Do you know what your role is Mr. Tanaka?"

"No, I do not."

"You are going to die. I wish I could say I'm sorry about it, but I'd be lying. I need you dead. And do you know what the best part of that is? You're going to do it yourself. After I've left, just as the sun sets, you are going to take a leap right off the side of this mountain. You'll look around, make sure no one is close enough to stop you, and when you've got enough space to clear that perimeter wall, you're going to jump over it. Do you understand Mr. Tanaka?"

"Yes. I am going to jump."

"That's right. When the sun sets."

"When the sun sets."

Dr. Masters got up from the couch and stretched his legs. He took another look around, and his eyes locked on a painting on the wall. Strolling over to it, he said, "It's okay, you can join me. It'll look better if someone comes in."

The king walked over to where Dr. Masters was standing. The doctor looked at the painting in front of him with a mixture of awe and disgust. Ethan Tanaka stood peacefully, waiting for his next command.

"It doesn't surprise me that you have this painting on the wall. He was the first philosopher king. It makes sense. We see his image the most in history books, now don't we?" He turned to look at Tanaka. "I'll bet you're wondering why I'm doing all of this. Well, it's not complicated. It's not about money, I have too much of it, especially now. It's not about fame either. I've lived most of my life practically in the shadows by choice. It actually pains me to be with other people like this. In the end, it's only about power. I have a lot of it already, but the thing with power is that you can never have enough. Am I right? You of all people should understand that."

"I do not agree, but I understand why you would feel this way," answered the king.

"My god, even now, that goodness is still in there. Wow, you really believe in all that stuff don't you? Peace, goodwill to your fellow man, love thy neighbor, blah, blah, blah...blah!"

"Yes. I do believe."

Dr. Masters turned away from him, and considered returning to the couches, but he decided against it. He was nearly done with what he came to do.

"Mr. Tanaka, I'm going to be leaving here soon. What we have talked about will remain a secret deep inside of you. No one will ever know what we have discussed here today. Is that clear?"

"Yes, it is clear."

"Good. What will you do when the sun sets tonight?

"I will jump off the mountain."

"You will make sure you are dead. Is that understood?"

"Yes, I will make sure I am dead."

"You will also make sure no one is near enough to stop you."

"No one will be near enough to stop me."

"Very good. Sadly, I must be going now. I really did enjoy our time together. Don't worry though, I plan on coming back into this room very soon. You won't be here then, will you?"

"No, I will not."

"Oh, I love it. You're quite an agreeable fellow Mr. Tanaka. It's been a pleasure. I'll leave you to your next meetings, and the rest of your — schedule. Goodbye."

Dr. Robert Masters left the room and the door closed quickly behind him. Ethan Tanaka stood looking at the door for sometime after it closed, waiting for it to open again. Penelope came through the door about a minute later with an astrophysicist struggling to keep his charts from slipping out from under his armpits. His nervous energy was familiar to the king, having seen it most of the day, with at least one exception.

His meetings extended, one after the other, as he kept watch through the window, following the movement of the sun with particular interest. His peaceful, friendly demeanor was calming to everyone he met. Each of them left feeling as if they had contributed something to a great cause, none of them aware for one moment that the cause was nothing but an illusion.

When the sun was just about to set, the king told his chief of staff that he needed to step out for some fresh air. He smiled reassuringly at everyone he passed. They felt confident in their king's ability to lead them through this unheard of catastrophe, much in the same way he had lead them for decades. His reign was one of great prosperity. He brought the nations of the world even closer than they had been before, making peace a more solid and tangible thing. No one watching the king would ever suspect he was about to set into motion a plan to overthrow his own power.

The sunlight was fading and a soft orange glow stretched across the horizon. Ethan Tanaka felt the cold wind on his face as he walked along the promenade near the edge of the mountain. He looked up at the sky, wondering if he might catch a glimpse of the stars but there were none to be seen. The king looked to his right, then to his left. The closest person, one of the many royal guards, was about fifty feet away. Without further hesitation or doubt, Earth's eighteenth philosopher king, Ethan Tanaka, hoisted himself onto the rampart wall and jumped from the side of the mountain just as the sun set over Earth City.

The royal guard closest to where the king jumped, ran to the wall and looked over it. They were so high up that all he could see was mist and shadows. He doubted whether he actually saw what he did. This was his king, Ethan Tanaka. How could he possibly end his own life at a critical time like this? The idea was beyond shocking. The image of him jumping kept playing on repeat in the guard's mind. He fell to his knees and felt a sharp pain hit his chest. Breathing was suddenly difficult for him. He fought to compose himself enough to yell out, "Help!"

The king's body was eventually found with the help of several experienced climbers. Due to its condition, a DNA test was needed to verify that the body was in fact the king's. The Global Council met and began implementing the necessary protocols. A new philosopher king would be needed. The search process would take some time, but it never failed to find the right person for the job.

The sky was dark and noticeably lonely over Earth City. A quarter moon was the only celestial shape up above, and its light glowed soft and subdued. Every building in the city was qui- et. People spoke in whispers. Their fear of the future returned

stronger than ever. While they grieved, they also wondered —
"Who would lead them now?"

TROJAN GIFTS

Joaquin Malcolm's head was resting on his crossed arms, that were themselves resting on a large, wooden desk in the Community Communication office on Gomez Street. A thick, wool blanket decorated with geometric Aztec art lay across his back, placed there by the office manager late last night before she left. His friends Sage and Robin were asleep on a neighboring couch. Sage was in a sitting position with his head against a wall, while Robin lay across the rest of the couch, her head on Sage's leg. She had a blanket covering her while Sage managed to keep warm with his jacket. Both were smiling while they slept, but Joaquin had a worried look on his face.

The lights turned on everywhere all at once inside the office building, as they did every morning at 6am. The automatic system also turned on the viewscreens and speakers throughout the office. An image of a local news anchor appeared and his voice traveled to the ears of Joaquin, who suddenly jolted himself upright and turned to look at the screen nearest him.

"...the Global Council is administering kingdom protocols, activating a crown search. The global initiative is already rippling through communities across the planet, as people everywhere are waking up to the news that their king is dead. It has been forty years since the last crown search was undertaken in 2840, when Ethan Tanaka, a then 25 year-old Japanese toy designer was found in the city of Kurashiki. The shocking loss of Tanaka follows the already confusing news story of the disappearance of the stars from the nighttime sky. Last night, reports from all over the world came pouring in claiming that the stars were missing, but as of nearly an hour ago, the stars are now back. Scientists are baffled by the sudden reappearance, and many wonder if the stars might vanish once again, or if they are back permanently. It's safe to say that the last twenty four hours have sent the world into a great deal of uncertainty."

Joaquin stared at the images in front of him, unable to accept the full weight of what the news anchor's words meant. The philosopher king was dead. The stars disappeared but came back. And now a world wide search for a new leader of the world was underway. What could be next?

"The search for the next philosopher king will last exactly one month. As everyone knows, anyone can attempt to fill the position of king. People everywhere are encouraged to test, or re-test over the course of the following weeks. The highest score wins the crown. Contender names are expected to be released at any moment. For those unfamiliar with the contender title, every human being on Earth with a previous test score high enough to qualify to serve as the philosopher king are given the special designation of contender. Any new test takers who score high enough will also be given this rare title. Receiving this designation in itself is a great honor. While it is no guarantee of claiming the ultimate title of king, it is a strong indicator that a person is capable of earning it. However, the decathlon of online tests are available for *anyone* to take, or retake as many times as they would like. Many have taken them before, while in school, or at work, or for guild leadership qualifications. Wait a second, we've just gotten word that the names of all current contenders have been released. We have the list now. There are 218 names on the list. 38 from North America, 11 from California, and one from our local area in the central coast — 16 year-old Joaquin Malcolm of Salinas, California," said the news anchor.

Joaquin was looking at a picture of himself on the viewscreen. He was in shock. Something inside him wanted to scream in excitement, but something else made him feel he should hide. It was too incredible a turn of events to calmly process. His chest tightened and he felt the air more difficult to breathe. He needed to move around, stretch his legs and look outside. He forced himself up and felt the soreness in his arms from sleeping on top of them for hours. His mind was racing and his legs were shaky as he made his way to the door.

The sounds of East Salinas hit his ears, drowning out the voice of the news anchor repeating in his head. Autos were swiftly moving about, making whooshing noises. People were conversing loudly about the king's death. The events of last night's game seemed a distant memory to everyone, when such a short time ago they seemed to be all anyone could talk about. How clueless and isolated they had been in their fleeting, local victory.

"Hey, it's Joaquin!" someone shouted.

An old man lifted his interface glasses, smiling, staring with big, unblinking eyes directly at the young contender. People stopped in their tracks and turned to look at Joaquin. They had a similar excited reaction and everyone rushed towards him. Hands slapped his back, other hands grasped his arms, and some tugged on his shirt. Words shot out of the people like a million tiny bullets, overwhelming the young man, giving him a mix of emotions. His only response was a nervous smile and a simple "thank you."

He looked up and saw his face plastered across a dozen giant viewscreens up and down the street. The crowd of people around him was expanding out in every direction. Joaquin raised his arms high above his head and used them to wave people away, all the time nodding and smiling, letting them know he understood how they felt about the news. Eventually he made his way back into the Community Communication Office, but not before shaking about a hundred hands.

"Joaquin, where did you go?" asked a half-awake Robin.

He didn't know how to respond and turned to look at Sage. His best friend was staring at a viewscreen on the wall, completely transfixed by it. Then he turned to Joaquin.

"Dude," said Sage.

"I know," answered Joaquin.

"What's up with you two? What happened?" asked Robin.

Sage's hands gently turned Robin's head to the news anchor talking. He got up from the couch and walked over to Joaquin. He placed his right hand on his shoulder.

"Are you okay? How you doing with all this?"

"I'm kind of shell shocked to tell you the truth. I went out to get some air and was practically gobbled up. I don't know what to do."

"It's a really, big deal man. You should be proud. You've put in the work, studied hard, and it's paid off. No matter what happens next, you won."

"Yeah, definitely. I'm just trying to make sense of the king's death. Why did it happen right after the stars disappeared? And how did they come back?"

"Who knows? But I'm sure the truth will come out eventually."

"He jumped off the side of the mountain," said Robin.

"What?!" replied Sage and Joaquin at the same time.

"The news says he jumped over the side of the mountain where he lives in Earth City, but no one knows why. A couple of guards saw him jumping but they were too far away to stop him."

"Why would he do that?" questioned Joaquin.

"Maybe he was under too much pressure because of the stars?" suggested Sage.

"I doubt that."

"Why?"

"He was cool as a cucumber. His calm demeanor was legendary. You could scream into his face for hours and the man wouldn't show a hint of being uncomfortable. Don't you remember years ago when they filmed that documentary about him? They showed him doing it. The whole demonstration is online."

"Oh, yeah. I forgot about that. Well, I'm sure there must be a reason he did what he did. It can't be easy being the king."

Joaquin was quiet, reflecting on his comment.

Robin stood up. "Hey, guys, we should get out of here. Last night was hard enough without a billion people coming to kiss the hand of the future king."

"That's not funny Robin. The last thing I need is the image of that many people swarming me," said Joaquin.

"Well, it might not be a billion, but boy is it climbing fast, look!" she pointed to outside the glass doors.

"Dear god," he said.

"You locked the doors behind you, right?" Sage asked Joaquin.

"Um, Robin's right, we've gotta get out of here. Grab your things quick, let's head out the back," answered Joaquin.

The three friends scrambled for their belongings and were in the alleyway in no time. Out of breath, they composed themselves and looked around. No one else was there except for a stray cat watching them, wondering if they might have food.

"Oh man, we walked here last night. How are we going to get through town unseen?" asked Joaquin.

Sage tapped his wrist and said, "Zim, come to my location. The robot came alive, transformed into chariot mode, then glided down several city streets until he zeroed in on Sage's location in the alley. Sage smiled, "Good morning Zim, you're going to be a big help today." He turned to his friends, "Hop on guys, let's get out of here."

Joaquin and Robin joined Sage on his robot. It was a tight squeeze but they managed to hold on comfortably. Fortunately, Sage designed and built Zimmer to hold ten times his weight, so the ride was as smooth as usual. Robin held onto Sage from behind, while Joaquin hid behind them both, trying his best to keep his face from being seen. It didn't take them long to get Joaquin to the one place he was sure to be safe — home.

The Malcolms were an impressive family. Charles Malcolm, Joaquin's father, was the most prominent lawyer in Monterey County. His reputation was legendary. He graduated top of his class from Harvard Law School, his firm was one of the best in the country, he'd argued cases in front of the Supreme Court, and he was on the short list twice to actually serve on the court as a justice. Maria Malcolm, Joaquin's mother, was a marine biologist known internationally for her efforts to protect ocean life. She discovered more than a dozen new species on the ocean's floor, saved twice as many other species from extinction, and Jessica Valentine won an Academy Award for Best Actress portraying her in a movie about her life. Joaquin also had two enormously successful, older siblings. His brother Xavier was the leading scorer in the National Field Ball League. In his sixth season with the Los Angeles Tunnelers, Xavier, or just "X" to his huge fan base, was signed to the biggest sports and licensing deals ever, making him the highest paid athlete in the world. His sister Janet was the CEO of Hyperbolic Hamburgers, a company she started by herself while still in school. She grew it into the largest restaurant chain in the world, using all organic ingredients grown right in the restaurant. It was not only self sustainable and affordable, it was credited with extending the average life span of the people who ate there.

At least a hundred and fifty people were waiting in front of the Malcolm home when Joaquin and his friends approached it. Sage told Zimmer to take him to the back gate. Nervously, he placed his palm on the security plate and the gate opened.

"Want us to come with you?" asked Robin.

"No, I've got this. Thanks for the offer though."

"Joaquin," said Sage.

"What's up?"

"Don't forget about us little people when you're king," he joked.

Joaquin laughed, "I won't, uh what was your name again?" he replied.

Sage and Robin waved goodbye and rode off into the day. Joaquin made his way through the elaborate flower garden in his backyard. He narrowly avoided stumbling into a rose bush full of thorns after dodging several bees gathering near his mother's favorite sunflowers. Finally, he was on the back patio. The floor boards were solid and sturdy, but his body felt shaky as he walked on them. When he got to the large glass door to the main house, he saw his entire family standing on the other side of it, waiting for him there.

Joaquin smiled at them shyly, opened the door, and walked inside.

"Joaquin! What the hell! I mean, what the hell bro! My little brother 'bout to be the king of the world. Congrats, for real!" said Xavier, giving him a huge hug.

"So proud of you baby brother. I mean, your majesty," his sister Janet said giggling, kissing him on the cheek.

"I'm not surprised one bit. You're an amazing young man destined for great things. You're going to help so many people darling," said his mother who squeezed him tightly.

His father was standing the furthest away, a serious look on his face. Joaquin looked up at him, waiting to hear what he might say, knowing his words would resonate the strongest. Charles Malcolm stepped closer to his son and extended his right hand out. Joaquin reached for his hand and shook it. He felt a stronger than usual grip and continued to see a serious look on his dad's face. Their hands pumped several times in an unending silent exchange of looks at one another. Finally, Joaquin's father broke the monotony when a single tear formed around his right eye and fell from his cheek.

He smiled, "Son, you've really done something. For probably the first time in my life, I'm speechless. I don't know what to say. I don't know what anyone can say, except, wow!" He let go of his son's hand, and came in for a big, long embrace.

"Thanks dad. I'm at a loss for words too."

His dad turned to the rest of his family, smiled and gave them a look that told them to join in. Joaquin stood in the center of his family now, and felt the love and admiration flow towards him. He was comforted in knowing he would not face this new journey alone. Family was a powerful force in the world, and he was part of one of the best families to ever do it. After a few minutes of congratulatory hugs and words, the family moved to the living room where they could see a crowd of people in front of the house through the sheer curtains.

"So what do we do about the reporters?" asked Joaquin.

"You give them what they want son," said his father.

"You mean just go out there and talk to them?"

"Exactly. Listen, if you're going to be the king, you've gotta be able to answer any question. You'll need to talk to anybody, at any time. Hell, you've been doing that already most of your life. No need to be afraid, just give them what they want."

Joaquin knew his father was right. Without saying another word, he stood up and walked to the door. His family looked at each other smiling, sharing in the knowledge that Joaquin was ready for the job placed in front of him.

He walked across his family's front lawn to the army of reporters gathered on the sidewalk and spilling out into the street.

What had been a noisy cacophony of inaudible questions just a moment before, quickly died down to a murmur as the young man got closer to them. He stopped and smiled, and what seemed like the entire world, hung on his every word as he spoke his truth from his heart and threw himself into the running for the world's most powerful position.

***

Sage and Robin lay on a blanket over the green grass on top of a hill in Poe Park. They could see the city spread out below them, busy as always and never-ending. Alisal University looked like a bunch of miniature buildings, but the Trojan Horse somehow looked just as big from their far away vantage point. The air was slightly cold, but the clouds were quickly fading away. The sun was shining bright and warming the area more and more with each passing minute.

They were tired from the night before, but kept thinking about all of the people they helped with Joaquin. It was his idea to go to the Community Communication Office. He knew they would know exactly who needed the most help, and they would have plenty of work for them to do. He was right. They made calls, chatted with people online through their interface glasses, and spoke to dozens of people who physically came into the office. It was challenging and rewarding work that made a real impact.

Robin looked up at the sky and asked, "Sage, do you think the stars are really back? Will they be there when the sun goes down, and it's nighttime again?"

"I think so. Maybe they've been there the whole time. Maybe, they weren't gone at all."

"You think so? Then why couldn't we see them?"

"That's the big question that needs to be answered. I'm not sure, but there must be a reason for it. If something can make us stop seeing the stars, that might be more dangerous to us than if the stars actually did disappear."

"You're right! What if we stop seeing other things that are important, like the sun? Can you imagine that? What if we thought it was night all the time, and never day? Would we stop going outside so much? I think a lot of people would be depressed. Don't you think so?"

"Definitely. It's depressing to even think about that, let alone live that every day of your life. Let's hope nothing else goes away. I wouldn't want people to forget the sun, the stars, or anything else that important."

"Agreed."

"Oh man, I'm so bad. I actually did forget something."

"What did you forget? Something big like the sun?"

"Well, maybe not as big as that, but I think it's something you'd like."

He went to his book bag, opened the top, and reached inside. His fingers felt the shape of two books, one was *The Book of Space*, the other *Julius Caesar*. He pulled out *Julius Caesar*, remembering every last detail of the dramatic work by Shakespeare, and handed it to Robin.

"*Julius Caesar*? Sage, is this for me?"

"Of course, who else do I know collecting Shakespeare's books?"

Robin rolled over and put her arms around Sage and kissed him on the cheek. When she lifted her lips she kept her face near his and looked into his eyes. He smiled, and his eyes communicated to her that he liked her in a way that was beyond friendship.

He was nervous and his heart was pounding a mile a minute, but he wanted to take his chance, so he put into spoken words what he was thinking inside.

"Robin, is it okay if I kiss you?"

She smiled and said, "Yes."

He leaned forward and the unimaginable finally occurred. It was like the stars in the sky were definitely back, and blazing just for him. The whole world seemed to expand outward, pushing everything else out of focus. He wanted to live forever in the timeless state of perfection that was this moment.

Robin pulled away slowly, smiled, and slipped her hand over Sage's hand, interlocking her fingers with his. He looked at her, beaming.

"So, what took you so long?" she asked.

He pulled her closer, "I guess I was scared, but I'm not anymore." He kissed her again.

"You were scared of *me*? Why?"

"*Why*? You're — *you*. I've known you my whole life. You're so awesome, and smart. You're talented, and the most beautiful girl I've ever seen. I've liked you forever. I guess I was scared of what would happen if you didn't feel the same way. It'd be worse than losing the stars... for me, in my world."

Robin, kissed him. "You are so sweet. You wanna know something?"

"What?"

"I felt the same way. I've liked you forever too, but was too scared to mess anything up. Didn't you ever wonder why I never had a boyfriend, or why I never took a date to any of the dances?"

"I'm such an idiot, I should have tried saying something sooner."

"No, it's all right. I like how this happened. It's perfect."

Sage let out a small laugh of relief. They kissed again.

"I only have one question, why *Julius Caesar*? Why not Shakespeare's *Sonnets*, or something with romance like *As You Like It*?"

"Friends, Romans, countrymen, lend me your ears!" he replied.

"Oh, you've read it?" asked Robin.

Sage got up onto his feet, and struck a dramatic pose.

"I come to bury Caesar, not to praise him. The evil that men do lives after them. The good is oft interred with their bones. So let it be with Caesar."

Robin sat up, and clapped. "Whoa Sage, that was really good! Did you practice that?"

"No, I guess the play just kinda stuck with me."

"When did you read it?"

"Yesterday."

"Yesterday? Well, I guess it must be fresh in your mind."

"Yep, pretty fresh," he said, glancing at his book bag.

She stood up next to him, her bare toes feeling the movement of the grass beneath the blanket. Her arms reached around him, and she leaned in for another kiss.

"So what other plays can you perform?"

"Oh, I know a few others."

She laughed, "Sounds like you've been studying up."

"The man who has everything figured out is probably a fool," he replied.

"What's that from?"

"*Inherit the Wind*. Have you read it?"

"No, never heard of it. What's it about?"

"Oh, it's really good. It's about this school teacher on trial for teaching evolution in school. It's based on the famous Scopes Monkey Trial back in 1925."

"I think I do remember learning about that. You've got an awesome memory. If you ever wanted to pursue acting, you'd have a bright future in it."

"Sometimes it's like I can see the future stretched out in front of me — just plain as day," he said.

"Sage! What's that from?"

"*A Raisin In The Sun*. Do you know it?"

"I've heard of it, but haven't got to it yet. How can you remember so many lines from plays all of a sudden? You really have been studying."

"Robin, can I tell you something? It's kind of important and I don't even understand what it is, but I figure maybe you can give me your take on the whole thing."

"Of course, what is it?"

"Well, I was at the book store getting you that book and I noticed this strange title that seemed to be calling to me. I mean I felt an attraction to it, like I needed to touch it."

"You trying to make me jealous?" she laughed.

"No, I'm serious. It seemed to want me to open it, so I did."

"Okay, then what happened?"

"It's kind of hard to explain. All of this beautiful light shot out of it everywhere, and I saw a ton of pictures and words. It felt like it was doing something to me, like it was giving me information and power."

"Okay, then what happened?"

"It stopped, and afterwards I touched a different book and all of the knowledge of that book came to me all at once. It was as if I read the book, maybe even wrote it, within a split second. All the ideas just went right into me with total understanding."

"Sage, stop it! You're messing with me. That's not cool."

He looked confused. "I'm telling you the truth."

"You're good. I can't believe I missed seeing this side of you before. You really are a good actor. Why would you play with me like this?"

"Play with you? I'm not — "

"You know my passion is acting, and drama. You purposefully learned those lines to impress me, and to trick me." She held up the *Julius Caesar* book, waving it in front of him. "This isn't just some story to me. This isn't entertainment to keep from being bored. This is life, and ideas, and the power of human beings to connect to one another on a higher level. This is artistry and everything beautiful about the world. Why would you mock it? Do you think it's a joke? I'm so mad right now, I can't even think. I'm leaving!"

"Robin no, wait! You've got this all wrong. Let me explain."

"I'm tired Sage. Last night took a lot out of me, and sleeping on that hard couch didn't do enough. I don't have the mental energy to play games right now. I'm calling for a ride to meet me down by the park entrance. After I've had time to rest, and to think, you can try to explain then. I don't know for the life of me how you're going to do it, but I'll be all ears. And you won't have to ask any Romans for theirs... goodbye!" She tossed the copy of *Julius Caesar* at his feet.

She stormed off and Sage watched her walk down the hill while she called for a ride with her interface glasses. When she got to the bottom, he sat back down on the blanket and watched her wait at the entrance until an auto glided up and carried her away.

He turned to Zimmer and said "Zim, what do you do when a girl gets mad at you?"

The robot's eyes lit up, then displayed "GIFT, GIFT, GIFT, GIFT."

"Damn, you're smart. You've given me a great idea."

He stood up and folded the blanket. Then he gathered his things, including the copy of *Julius Caesar* which he placed back in his book bag alongside *The Book of Space*. He then pulled the strange book out of his bag to examine it more carefully. It looked just like it did when he took it out last. There wasn't any writing except for the title on the front cover. No symbols or brands were etched into it either. And all of the pages were blank. Even though no light was shooting out of it, and no strange images, words, or symbols were dancing in front of him, he knew the book was still working its magic on him. Every time he held it he could feel an energy coursing through him, stronger each time he did so. He wondered if he shouldn't just have it right next to him all the time. Regardless, he knew he needed to keep it. He was drawn to it, or maybe the book was drawn to him.

"Zim, we're going back to the bookstore. Transform to chariot mode."

He arrived at Brave New Books earlier than the last time he visited. The owner, Hector Magaña, greeted him behind his copy of *A Connecticut Yankee In King Arthur's Court* and pointed him in the direction of the Romance section. Sage wanted to know everything he could about the subject.

After reading every single book in the Romance section, Sage was more confused than ever. He walked back to Hector and asked him for a different recommendation.

"What kind of book talks about what to do when a girl is mad at you?" he asked the old man.

Hector stared at him for a moment, then laughed louder than Sage ever heard anyone laugh before. Eventually, his laughing stopped and he looked at Sage with empathy.

"Sorry, son. It's been awhile since anyone said something like that in front of me. What you're looking for is in the Self-Help section, under Relationships."

"Awesome, thanks!"

He made his way down the aisles until he found the right section. He immediately started touching every book he could find on the subjects of relationships and love. His face was beaming with the newfound information he now possessed. It was like he was a relationship expert and understood what countless PhDs and professionals did. He was confident he could resolve what happened with Robin, as well as any other relationship issue that might pop up with her, or anyone else for that matter. It was all really quite simple now. It was so simple that Sage let out a huge laugh, much like the one Hector let out when he asked him for help earlier. He wondered if the book store owner knew what he now did, and if that's why he laughed.

His whole body felt light, like it always did when he read a new book now. His perception was keener, his space bigger, and he was always happier. He looked at a nearby clock to see the time: 3pm. The store didn't close until much later. He looked around at the many aisles of books and wondered how long it would take him to read them all. He decided it didn't matter. The rewards were too great, and he just needed to start.

Sage walked to the very back aisle, in the farthest corner of the store. It was here that he would begin systematically reading every book in the store. The aisle in the back, in the farthest corner of the store just happened to be the Art section, and Sage lit up like a sky full of fireworks before he even touched a single book near him. When he did, he became a man possessed. He was like a machine built to never stop. Each new book was a revelation, leaving him feeling like God must have felt when he first looked at nothing, but knowing he could make everything from it. He went from book to book, aisle by aisle, until every drop of knowledge in the building was his to carry away with him.

He walked over to Hector when he was done. He placed one book onto the counter to buy: *The Princess Bride* by William Goldman. Hector looked down at it, then up at Sage.

"Say, you look different son. What have you been reading back there?"

He smiled and said, "Everything."

Barbarian at the Gate

The sun was shining brightly through Sage's window. Zimmer was inside his room monitoring the activity of the outside world, but keeping most of his attention on his human companion. Normally, at this time he would wake Sage from his sleep with loud music, but today was different because he was already out of bed. In fact, the fifteen year old hadn't touched his bed all night. It was the first time Zimmer observed him going without sleep. Strangely, there wasn't a sign of tiredness, like redness of his eyes, or slowing of his heart beat at all. Instead it was the exact opposite, he was bursting with energy. Zimmer couldn't help but notice one other, notable difference happening in front of him. Nearly every part of Sage's room was covered in paintings, drawings, designs, and sculptures.

Sage was shuffling his feet in a whimsical dancelike movement while listening to Tony Bennett's *Steppin' Out* album. He was also putting some last brush strokes on an 18x24 stretched canvas resting on an easel in front of him. The painting was an impressionistic landscape of the Salinas Valley, in mostly vivid greens and browns. White clouds swirled in the bluest of skies, and the orange beams of the sun created a surreal, magical effect. The painting was practically a masterpiece, but what made it even more impressive was the fact that Sage made the paint he used from scratch using local plants and minerals. He also built the wooden easel he was using, and stretched his own canvas onto a frame he constructed by hand. The painting was only one of many leaning against or hanging on the walls of his room.

The drawings that were scattered about were even more abundant than the paintings. However, there were only half a dozen sculptures because Sage wanted to make them bigger and bigger, and eventually ran out of room. This also forced Zimmer into a tight corner, and he wondered if he might be painted next.

Suddenly, the door to his room burst open. His sister Sara was standing there with her nose up high.

"What's that smell?" she asked, then took in the entire scene in front of her. Sage put the finishing touch on his painting, then set his brush down and shuffled his feet, tap dancing his way over to his sister. Her eyes were wide and her pupils moved like two metronomes, as she looked at the transformation of her brother's room.

"Sage, what have you been doing in here? Did you rob a museum or something?"

He let out a big, amused laugh. "That's a good one sis! Nope, I made all of this."

"No you didn't. I've never seen you draw more than a stick figure. Seriously, where did you get all of this?"

"Sara, seriously, this is all me. What do you think?"

"You jokester! Stop messing around, or I'm going to call the police."

"Why would you do that?"

"Sage, these are obviously works from some museum collection. Did you get them from the Alisal archives or something?"

"No. Sis, I honestly made these. Look, I even signed my name on each of them." He took a painting that was leaning against the wall nearest Sara and handed it to her. Look, my name's right there. Be careful though, the paint's still a little wet."

She held the painting in front of her, then looked at the bottom right corner and saw her brother's name clear as day. She recognized his signature. Then, she set the painting back down and felt the dampness of half dried paint on both of her hands.

"What the hell is going on Sage? How is this possible? Have you been hiding this talent from us your whole life?"

"No, not exactly. I've been interested in art for awhile now, but only recently started taking it seriously."

"Recently, huh? You're such a liar. I'm going to tell mom and dad." She turned to walk away, but did so slowly. She wanted to give her brother a chance to stop her. She knew he wasn't telling her the truth, and she might still get it out of him. But instead, he walked right past her, turned around and said, "It's okay, I'll tell them myself."

Sage walked hurriedly down the hall towards the kitchen, saw that it was empty, and then headed to the living room. Both of his parents were sitting together there drinking coffee.

"Mom, dad, there's something I have to tell you."

They looked up from their cups. His mother said, "Of course Sage, what is it?" Sara came from behind him, and slipped into one of the empty chairs, then said, "Sorry, but I've gotta hear this." Her parents were suspicious now. His dad looked him over, then noticed his hands.

"Sage, why are your hands dirty? Have you been painting?"

"Yeah dad, I have. It's part of what I want to tell both of you. You see, for awhile I've been struggling with choosing a path for myself now that school is wrapping up. Dad, I know you want me to go into the Builder's Guild, and even though the tests pointed to it, I couldn't shake the feeling that maybe there was another path for me to take. I've been interested in art for a long time, but I never thought I could really do it. I didn't know where to start, and there were other options that seemed to be better at the time, so I never committed to actually learning it. My curiosity about art died, until I took some courses in school that reignited my interest. I've been studying it a lot recently, trying to see if it was something I could actually do, and if I was any good at it."

"And are you dear?" asked his mother.

"Yeah, mom. I'm actually pretty good. Ask Sara, she's seen my work." Everyone in the family turned to look at her.

"Yep, he's great! He's probably an artistic genius! Are you satisfied?" she answered annoyedly. Her parents looked confused, like they were missing something important.

"Don't blame Sara, she just found out a few minutes ago. Dad, I respect what you do, and I'm sure I would have a great life building like you, but there's something inside me that absolutely loves making art. The two aren't that different when you really think about it. Both involve creating something new that never existed before. One is practical, but the other is essential, at least to me. That's why I'm choosing to take a different path, and become an artist. I hope you both will respect my decision, and support it. There, that's it. You know, it really wasn't as hard as I thought it would be. I feel pretty good right now."

His mother stood up, walked over, and gave him a big hug, and a kiss on the cheek, then said, "You will be a great artist, my son. You have my full support."

"Thank you mom."

His father didn't move from where he sat. Instead, he looked at his son for a long time, until he pointed at a spot near him, and said, "Sage, have a seat." His son nervously sat down.

"I want to tell you a story. It's something I've never told anyone, not even your mother knows this about me. When I was around your age, maybe 14 or 15, I was really into Conan the Barbarian. Have you ever heard of him? He was a fantasy character, a really strong, and powerful guy. Anyhow, I used to sit reading his stories for hours. Your grandfather used to be a pretty tough, serious man, and I was always afraid of him. When I discovered Conan, I realized he was stronger than my dad. I guess I thought he could protect me from him if I needed him to. It was all in my imagination, of course, but the more I read, the more I started to learn from his example. He was brave, when I wasn't. He wielded power, when I couldn't. I really idolized the character, and I wanted to be him. I'm sure you've experienced something similar at some point, right?"

"Sure dad, I felt like that about Superman."

"Yep, I remember that! You used to run around the house with a towel tied around your neck. You really thought you could fly if you just believed hard enough. I explained to you that Superman was from another planet, and that's why he had powers, but you didn't care. You thought you would eventually fly, when you got older. I'll never forget taking you to the hospital after you climbed up on the roof and jumped. I wish that broken arm would have stopped you, but nope, you just focused on developing your heat vision instead. Remember, you used to stare at your sister, asking her if she felt burnt?"

Sage laughed, and Sara frowned slightly.

"Okay, back to my story. So, I read every Conan book I could get my hands on, but one day my parents surprised me with some Conan comic books. I didn't even know they existed. What had been mostly in my imagination, was now in the real world. I could see Conan in a totally new and exciting way. It made me fall in love with comic book art. I tried drawing it every chance I got. A big callus developed on the side of my middle finger, in the spot where the pencil rested on it. That little spot hurt sometimes, but I didn't care. I drew the pictures I saw in the books, and tried drawing some of my own too. I wasn't half bad either."

"What happened? Why did you stop?" asked Sage.

"You're grandpa got hurt, and he couldn't work anymore. It destroyed him. My father was the toughest person I'd ever met, but he fell apart almost immediately when we brought him back home. He looked around, sunk into his old chair, and didn't speak to anyone for a week. The next time he did, it was to ask my mother for a drink. I think you know the rest, when it comes to your grandfather."

"Yeah dad, you don't have to go into that part," said Sage.

"Thanks son, it's always a hard one for me. Well, the guys at the guild had their eyes on me for years. Just like you, I grew up around them. I knew practically everything there was to know about being a builder. So when my old man passed away so suddenly, they offered me a place among them. I've been there ever since. I don't regret becoming a builder. It helped me take care of my mother, and I needed the support of those old timers back then. My father was my whole world, and watching him destroy himself nearly destroyed *me*. No, I'm grateful for what I became, but from time to time I often think about Conan, and those drawings, and what course my life might have taken if my father never got hurt."

"Damon, you never told me you could draw," said his wife.

"Honey, it's not something I like thinking about. Plus, I didn't want you to think I was unhappy with my life. I may have had a rocky start, but it's been smooth sailing since I found you." She came closer to him. He leaned in and kissed her.

"Well, it's been pretty nice from where I've been sitting too," she said.

"All right, you two, why don't you get a room?" said Sara with a pretended look of disgust on her face that quickly turned to a grin.

Damon Vector finally rose from his seat. "Sage, I love you. I've only ever wanted what's best for you, but only you can know what that is. If that means joining the Artists Guild, I think that's great. You have my full support son."

He opened his arms, and Sage walked into them. The big embrace was overdue and they both felt relief from it. After letting go, Damon Vector looked at his son and said, "So, is your sister the only one that gets to see what you've created?"

Sage smiled. "Everything's in my room, if you want to see what I've made so far."

"Lead the way son, I can't wait to see your art."

***

The Mark Twain Lecture Hall was filled to capacity. Security guards stood in front of every entrance and exit. The steel and glass building often held its doors wide open as a sign of inclusion and open dialogue, but today was anything but normal. The famous Flags of the World were spread around the building like a ring around Saturn, but they were all at half-mast, in honor of Ethan Tanaka's passing. Tonight's ticketed event was an exclusive evening with one of the most famous people on the planet at the moment: Crown Contender Joaquin Malcolm.

It'd been only one day since news of the king's death spread throughout the world. The list of contenders started with a couple hundred names, but it was now cut in half, because many of the people on it declined to wear the crown. This wasn't unusual, because every search for the crown, going back to the first one, always had many decline the chance to be king. Some simply didn't want the responsibility, some didn't trust themselves to do a good enough job at it, and others were just too happy and content with their current lifestyle. The remaining contenders were the serious ones, those willing to devote their entire life to the service of mankind.

The lecture attendees were all in their seats, except for those without tickets who managed to convince someone to let them stand in the back, and a handful of lucky people who got to stand and watch from backstage. Sage and Robin were such people. They were even luckier, because rather than stand backstage, they were given stools to sit on while some of the others around them were forced to stand.

Sage looked at Robin and smiled. She tried to keep a poker face, staring straight ahead towards the stage, but her eyes peeked at him ever so slightly, and she couldn't help engaging with him.

"Why are you smiling?"

"You know why."

She smiled, but tried to keep it back. "Why don't you tell me anyway?"

"You're so beautiful. I can't help it."

"There you go again! You can't do that Sage."

"I can't do what?"

"Play games with me."

"I'm not playing games with you. I'm sorry if I made you think I was. Can you just forget about yesterday, and give us a fresh, new start?"

"Us? What are you implying?"

"I want to be with you, officially. Wait a minute, I have something for you."

He reached into his book bag, and pulled out *The Princess Bride*.

"Let's leave *Julius Caesar* in the past where it belongs. This may not be a ring, but in a lot of ways I think it's better." He handed her the book.

Robin moved her fingers across the title and felt them fall inside the grooves of the letters. The gift made her feel at ease. She turned to Sage, this time looking him directly in his eyes.

"Okay. A fresh, new start. I guess I'm sorry too. I was exhausted yesterday, and when you started talking about...honestly, I can barely remember what you were trying to say. The whole thing is a bit of a blur now."

"Do you remember the really good thing that happened yesterday?" he asked.

She looked at his lips. "Yeah, I remember," she said smiling.

He moved a little closer to her. "Good, me too."

"Sage, you better not break my heart."

"I won't break your heart. Do you know how I know I won't?"

"No, how do you know?"

"*You* wouldn't break mine. Thanks for giving me another chance."

She moved a little closer to him.

"You're welcome."

Sage was moving in for a kiss to seal the deal when the lights flickered. Professor Adams walked out to the podium at the front right of the stage and tapped the microphone.

"Welcome to today's event. I'm your host Professor Kendrick Adams, faculty here at Alisal University, in the Government Department. We have the unique pleasure, and honor, to hear from one of the brightest minds this fine university has ever produced, and who may just be the brightest mind in the entire world. Please give a warm welcome to Alisal's very own, Joaquin Malcolm!"

The whole audience stood up, cheering as loudly as any audience ever cheered. Their hands applauded loudly and their feet stomped on the floor. The entire hall shook with enthusiasm, and the energy electrified the young crown contender as he walked out on stage, waving and smiling. He pumped his fist in the air and jumped off the ground a little before sitting down next to Professor Adams.

It took several minutes for the audience to settle down enough for Professor Adams to ask Joaquin his first question.

"Mr. Malcolm, the last 24 hours have changed the world. How have they changed your life in particular?" asked his professor.

"Well, I've always felt a natural tendency to help others in a leadership position. My father has worked in the field of law my whole life, so you can kind of say, I was born into it. But at the same time, I knew I needed to know everything I could about organizing people, managing them, and providing leadership at every point of society. We are never islands, by ourselves. All of us belong together, not only for our greater survival, but because it just feels right. When I found out about the king's death, I was truly sad because Tanaka was a hero to me. When I learned I was selected as a contender, I was overwhelmed by the weight and scale of the task ahead for whoever wears the crown next. But I know in times like these, the planet needs someone that can rise to the call and get the job done. This world has given me so much, and I have a duty to do what I can to help make it better. That's why I decided to pursue the crown."

The audience stood up again, and roared and clapped even louder than before.

"That's really great Joaquin. As you know, the stars event occurred just before the king's passing. We know he was working on the issue up until his death. What are *your* thoughts on the stars? Are they back for good? Why do you think they vanished? And if you win the crown, what actions would you take on this subject?"

"Well, Professor Adams, I think the king was on the right track by meeting with the world's top minds. I'm not sure how many of them are actively meeting or working together, but I would make sure they communicate and coordinate with one anther frequently. I'm not sure why the stars vanished. Some say they didn't vanish at all, that we were just prevented from seeing them for awhile. Either of those circumstances are scary for the people of Earth. This is probably the biggest mystery in the history of the world. One thing I know about mysteries though, is that they can usually be solved. If I become the next philosopher king, I'll solve it."

People in the audience stomped loudly. They clapped until their hands stung. They were beyond proud of their local hero.

"That's great Joaquin. Besides the stars, what other areas would you like to focus on as king?"

"I'm a firm believer in the power of education. There are still parts of the world that technology has yet to really make an impact in. I'd like to see some of those areas brought up to speed. They have unique perspectives that are invaluable. Imagine what some of their minds might bring to our guilds? What ideas we can learn by integrating their knowledge into ours? I would encourage all the peoples of the world to join together, so we get as close to 100 percent societal participation as possible. We are stronger together, I would like to work to bring us even closer."

"Very well stated. I wonder where you fall on the issue of galaxy exploration."

"I'm for it. I think it's an important endeavor to understanding the universe. Not to mention, all of the inspiration it provides to people everywhere."

"But what about the cost? Some suggest the price is too high, that those resources might be better spent here on Earth."

"The cost *is* high, but that goes for anything worth pursuing."

"Very true. Well Joaquin, why don't we get a few questions from the audience? I'm sure they've got some good ones."

"Sounds great."

"All right, we've got someone in the audience with a question. Please, go ahead. Make sure to speak loudly into the microphone so we can hear you."

A young boy put his mouth close to the microphone and his heavy breathing was heard throughout the hall just before he asked his question.

"Joaquin, if you become king, will you still play field ball?" he asked.

Some in the audience laughed, many cheered, but all were genuinely interested in the answer Joaquin would give.

"I love field ball. I'll be a Trojan for life. I'm just not sure it'll be the best use of my time to play while king. But, I might play the occasional game here and there, especially if it's with my teammates. Aren't they the best? If any of them are here, please stand up so we can clap for you."

Several members of the team stood up, included Sage, and everyone acknowledged them with a huge round of cheers.

"Okay, who else has a question?"

An elderly woman walked up to the microphone.

"I live downtown in a senior center. I got into an argument with my best friend, that used to share a room with me there. Don't worry, she apologized. She knew I was right, and she was wrong. Why she thought the Titanic was only a movie, I'll never know, but I digress. Every time I have to go see her, I have to take three different buses to get there, then another three to get back. My question is, can you make just one bus take me? Thank you."

"Mrs. Henry, thank you for your question, but like I've told you at the last five events, you don't need to take three buses, because there is a free shuttle that can take you straight there. All you need to do is call the number on the card I gave you," said Professor Adams.

"I want the future king to drive me," she said.

"I'm sorry Mrs. Henry, that's not how it works — " said Adams.

Joaquin interrupted him. "Mrs. Henry, I'd love to take you. We'll meet up after the event. How does that sound?"

"Oh, that would be lovely. I knew you would help me. Thank you dear."

"Okay, we've got time for one more question. Who's next?"

"That would be me," said a man with too big a smile on his face.

"Go ahead sir."

"Thank you. It's an honor to speak to such an... important person in the lives of everyone here. We know that the king jumped to his death while pursuing the truth behind the... stars event. Aren't you worried that you might meet a similar fate? I mean, the philosopher king is supposed to be the... greatest thinking mind on the planet. If his mind led him to a decision to jump to his death, what makes you think your mind will faire any better?"

The people in the audience were silent. A few of them started booing the man that asked this awkward, slimy question.

"BOOOOOOOOOOOOO!!!!!!!"

"Please, everyone, let's keep this respectable. It's quite all right. He has a valid question. Joaquin? Want to give him your answer?" said Professor Adams.

"Sure. I won't pretend to know the reasons why the king jumped. Perhaps they were good, or maybe they were bad. Either way, we have no way of knowing those reasons at this time. When it comes to the philosopher king, I personally feel he must have had a good reason to do what he did. Would the same automatically happen to me? I don't think so. I'm a different person in different circumstances. I do know I trust my mind. If a person doesn't trust themselves, they might as well cash in their chips, and quit whatever game their playing. And I plan to play this game as long as I can. Does that answer your question Mr......?"

"Masters. Well, I'm a doctor, so technically Dr. Masters."

"Good to meet you Dr. Masters. What are you a doctor of?"

"Neurology, and Psychology."

"Interesting subjects. Perhaps I can pick your brain after the event."

"Oh, sure! I'd love to pick yours too!" he said with a big Cheshire Cat grin.

"All right everyone, that's all the time we have for tonight's event. Mr. Malcolm here is quite in demand now. I'm sure he has many more questions to answer from the press that are waiting for him backstage. Please be careful on your way out. Goodbye."

Sage turned to Robin, "Well, that didn't take too long."

"The longer part happens next. Poor Joaquin. He's going to be answering questions for the rest of his life."

"Well, that's part of the job. If anyone can do it though, it's him. Hey, do you want to get out of here and go do something?"

Robin smiled excitedly, "Sure, but do what?"

"Anything, I'll let you choose. We can go anywhere your heart desires."

"That sounds lovely. I think I have a location in mind."

"Great, where's that?"

"Well, there's this old movie playing at this little theater I love going to."

"Sounds perfect."

"Don't you want to know what movie it is?"

"It doesn't matter. If you're interested in it, I'm sure I will be too. Let's go. We can slip out the back. We can catch up with Joaquin later."

Joaquin wasn't alone. His family was with him as he spoke to the countless reporters in attendance. They stood behind him proudly, nodding in agreement when he said something wise, and laughed when he delivered a witty punchline. The entire time, Joaquin felt more alive than he ever had in his life. This new role fit him like a glove. It was everything he trained for without knowing it. He always knew political office was his calling, but pictured himself in Congress, or possibly a Governor, and if he were really blessed, maybe one day President. Never in his wildest dreams, did he imagine himself as the philosopher king. And now, here he was preparing for the biggest job anyone could ever have. He was truly proud of himself for what he was doing, and the looks on people's faces only further validated that he was on the right path in his life.

When the press were finished with their questions, Joaquin spoke to people he was told he should speak to, shaking their hands with genuine affection. He was happy to know them. He was smart enough not to make promises he couldn't keep, and never spoke negatively about anyone's ideas when they presented them to him. Charm was one of his best gifts, and he dished it out constantly. People couldn't get enough of what he had to say. He was the man of the moment, and he would continue to strike while his iron remained hot.

Joaquin's family encouraged him to come with them to their favorite restaurant for dinner, but he said he was going to stay a little longer, and that he would meet them there later. They said their goodbyes and Joaquin went back to work. He shook more hands, smiled more smiles, and breathed in the atmosphere of the never-ending accolades. He eventually retired to a private room they assigned to him as a dressing room, although he didn't need it to change his clothes in. Instead, he flopped himself down into a large, comfortable leather chair, and took a big drink of water. He was tired but content, and still smiling.

A knock sounded at his door. One of the security guards opened it slightly, looked at him and said, "Mr. Malcom, there's a Dr. Masters asking to see you. He said you wanted to pick his brain? Want me to send him in?"

"Oh, yes. I remember him. Go ahead, send him in."

He closed the door. A minute later it opened again, and Dr. Masters walked in. His eyes were a little red, as if he were tired or had a couple of drinks. The same big smile was spread out, practically across his entire face. He reached his hand out and Joaquin took it.

"Thank you for seeing me. I know you're a busy man."

"It's quite all right Dr. Masters. I was just wrapping up, so your timing is perfect. Won't you have a seat?"

"Thank you Joaquin. Is it okay that I call you that?," he asked, then sat down not bothering to hear his reply.

"Sure, Joaquin is fine."

"I know you wanted to pick *my* brain, but I'm really here to pick *yours*," he said through his unnerving smile.

"Okay, go ahead."

Dr. Masters reached into his pocket and pulled out his small, metal rod.

"I'm going to do it with this. Do you see a little red light coming out of it?"

"Yes."

"Perfect. Here's the deal Joaquin. There's a white, transport truck waiting one block to the West of this building. You can't miss it. It'll be the one with a zebra painted on both sides. When you see it, you're going to get in the back and sit down until it reaches your final destination. You see, I'm sending you away on a vacation of sorts. You'll be gone about one month. You won't be seeing your family during that time. No need to bring any additional clothes, you won't need to pack. You'll be well taken care of where you're going. I'm in charge of you now. Isn't that nice?"

"Yes, it's nice."

"I'm glad you think so. Obviously, you won't remember why you're obeying my every command, you'll just do it. If I say jump, you jump. Got it?"

"I got it."

"Terrific. I know you want to be the king, but I've got other plans for you. And don't worry, you'll have lots of fun where you're going. You'll have a lot of friends there too."

He looked around the room as if he was trying to find some invisible thing in it.

"Ah, one last thing! I'm going to leave, and it'll be as if I was never here. You're going to be a clever, charming boy, and do and say whatever you need to in order to get to the white truck with the zebra. You will not raise any suspicions. You will be calm, and cool. Your top priority is to get into the back of the white truck. Okay?"

"Okay."

"Splendid. See you in the funny papers, my boy!"

Dr. Masters left the room, and Joaquin began formulating a plan to sneak away from everyone, especially his security. He opened a closet and saw there were several coats and hats. He put one of each under his right arm, and walked out of the room. One of his security detail was there.

"The doctor forgot his coat and hat. I'm just going to get these to him. Can you stand guard at the door until I come right back? I don't want anyone in there with my stuff. Is that okay?"

"I got you. Do what you gotta do."

"Thanks! I'll be right back."

Joaquin slipped into a bathroom around the corner. It was empty. He went into one of the stalls and put the coat and hat on. He knew the building well because of the many lectures he attended here over the years. One of the side exits was only twenty feet away. He left the building without anyone noticing. The white truck was a short walk. When he saw it, he went right up to the back door, opened it, got inside, and closed it shut. There was nothing inside but a bucket seat with a belt strap. Joaquin sat down and strapped himself in. Then, he closed his eyes and fell asleep, just as the truck's wheels began to move.

WHEN THE WIND BLOWS

Joaquin's family knew there was something wrong as they sat at the restaurant, waiting too long for him to arrive. When their calls went unanswered, they waited longer, and eventually left. Upon getting home, his family half expected him to be there, and when he wasn't they contacted the Security Guild. They didn't know where he was either. One of Charles Malcolm's friends in the guild let him in on the fact that Joaquin's disappearance wasn't an isolated case. Dozens of contenders from all over the world had been reported missing in the last several hours. The Malcolm family stayed up all night making calls, searching for any information that might lead to Joaquin's whereabouts, but they didn't find anything useful.

A gray sky blanketed the Salinas Valley the morning the news hit. Dark clouds cast enormous shadows over homes and the air was thick with a cold moisture. The streets were quiet and less busy. People chose to stay indoors, having looked at the sky and predicted it was going to rain. But the larger reason for so many staying home today was the uneasiness and fear they felt from the news on their viewscreens. Contenders were missing, and it was uncertain whether they were still alive or not. Many of the remaining contenders announced their departure from the competition, no longer wanting to be considered for the crown. This brought further speculation that perhaps the reason so many contenders were missing, was because someone was manipulating the contest. Heavy attention was now on the few remaining contenders. If any of them should win the crown now, it was doubtful the world would follow them. It became crucial to the survival of the entire governmental system that the missing contenders be found, or the planet would risk destroying what took centuries to build.

Sage Vector was asleep in his bed, unaware of the dozens of missed call alerts on his interface. Zimmer waited patiently for him to wake, having tried unsuccessfully to do so with three alarms that his human friend quickly turned off. He returned to his sleep, leaving the robot with nothing to do but monitor the surrounding camera feeds for movement. A group of four suddenly appeared in front of the Vector residence and Zimmer could easily make each of them out. They were the Malcolm family, minus their youngest.

Charles Malcolm pressed the door bell and waited for someone to answer. Victoria Vector smiled warmly at the Malcolms, inviting them in. They sat down in the living room and explained the reason for their visit. The news of Joaquin's disappearance and the circumstances surrounding the other contenders was news to Sage's mother. She often didn't check her newsfeed so early in the day, opting instead to listen to an audiobook each morning. The Malcolms explained their interest in talking to Sage. Because he was close to their son, they thought he might have some useful information. They'd been unsuccessful reaching him through his interface.

"You know, he rarely uses it. Some young people have their glasses on all day, but Sage manages to forget his too often. He probably hasn't looked at it since yesterday. He's in his room sleeping. I'll go get him," said Victoria.

"That would be great Mrs. Vector. We've been so worried and any help Sage might be could really turn things around," replied Charles.

"Of course, I'll be right back with him."

Victoria Vector walked the short distance to her son's room and knocked on his door. "Sage? You've got visitors. Are you still asleep?"

The tired, young man shifted slightly, then lifted his head slowly. "Mom?"

"Yes, darling, it's me. You have visitors. Get dressed, and come out to the living room. It's important."

Sage jumped out of bed, threw on his clothes from last night, and walked directly to the living room. He was startled when he saw the Malcolms. They were hardly all together like this. Their work took them to so many different parts of the country, and even the world, that holidays were often a challenge to pull off. Joaquin often told him how proud he was of his family, but how he wished he could see them all together more often. So, when Sage first looked at Joaquin's family, it didn't occur to him right away that Joaquin wasn't with them. It took him a second or two to look around the room for him, and when he didn't see him, he knew something was seriously wrong.

"Where's Joaquin?" he asked.

"We were hoping you could help us figure that out Sage," replied Charles.

"When was the last time you saw him dear? We were with him at Twain Hall, and he was supposed to meet us for dinner, but he never showed up," said Joaquin's mother Maria.

"I was at the event watching him from backstage, but I didn't get a chance to talk to him. When it was over I waved goodbye and left. I knew he was going to be busy, and I figured I would catch up with him later."

"Did he call you or try to contact you since then?" asked Charles.

"I haven't looked at it since yesterday, but let me check." Sage went to his room, dug out his interface glasses, and scrolled through his piled up messages. He walked to the living room as he got caught up with his feed. He stumbled on a news story headline that almost made him lose his balance. He quickly took his glasses off, then looked around sympathetically into the faces of the Malcolm family.

"Someone took him? And took other contenders too?" he asked.

"We don't know for sure what happened, but it looks that way," said Charles.

"So he didn't try to contact you?" asked Maria.

"No, Mrs. Malcolm. I'm sorry," replied Sage.

"Thanks for checking. Did he seem okay to you? Recently, I mean. Did he show any signs that something might be wrong? Or maybe that someone was after him?"

"No, nothing like that. He looked happy, like he always does. In fact, he looked happier than I've ever seen him. I think the whole contender thing brought out more of him than anyone ever got to see. He's been in his element. He was made to be king. He didn't have a problem in the world. He was on top of it. I'm sure there were people that were jealous or didn't like him, but I never met any of them. I never saw anyone stalking, or creeping around either. Wait a minute, isn't he given a personal security detail, because he's a contender?"

"Yes, son. There was one posted right outside his dressing room, and two others in the building. But none of them know how he could have been taken from inside the Hall facilities. They think it happened outside, away from campus," said Charles.

"Have any witnesses come forward in any of the other disappearances? Are there any clues that might lead to who could have done this?" asked Sage.

"So far, no. The most likely culprit is one of the remaining contenders. It makes sense, because they have the most to gain from something like this. We're just hoping Joaquin is all right, wherever he is. I've got to believe he's still alive. The contest lasts another few weeks, whoever did this might be keeping the missing contenders until it's over."

"What if the person that took him is one of the missing contenders?" asked Sage.

"Wait, what? Oh, damn. That's definitely worth considering," replied Charles.

"What is honey?" asked Maria.

"Sage thinks one of the missing contenders could be the person that took the others. If true, it would be a pretty smart way to escape suspicion."

"But what would they have to gain?" asked Janet.

"Who knows? But whoever did this is smart as hell and has a lot of resources," replied her father.

An idea suddenly struck Sage, but he wasn't sure if he should share it with the Malcolms, and probably not with his mother either, who was all ears and taking in the whole situation too.

"What is it Sage? I can tell somethin's rollin' aroun' in that head o' yours," asked Joaquin's brother Xavier.

"It's a crazy idea, and a total long shot, but..."

"But what man? Out with it bro. Everything's already crazy, it can't get any worse," said Xavier.

"...what if I try passing the tests and become a contender? Then the same people might try to take *me*. When they do, the authorities can track and follow me right to them. I can help free Joaquin and the others."

The Malcolms looked at each other to make sure the others heard what they just did. Then, knowing they each heard him correctly, started talking to Sage a mile a minute, all at once.

"You can't be serious, you know how hard those tests are to score that high on?!" asked Joaquin's sister Janet.

"Oh, no! Sage, you'll just be getting yourself in danger too!" said Maria Malcolm.

"Bro! That's nuts for real man! What are you gonna do? You think you're Batman or something?" said Xavier.

"Sage, what makes you so sure they would even take you? They didn't take all of the contenders. What if doing it just makes you another suspect? You can ruin your reputation for the rest of your life!" said Charles.

Victoria Vector stood up, and shouted down all of them.

"Quiet! He can do it! He *will* do it! He can save Joaquin! I know he can!"

The entire room was silent, stunned by the shocking words coming out of the always pleasant Mrs. Vector. She looked at them all and knew they were listening, so she continued.

"I love my son. I would never want to even imagine him getting hurt, or doing something so dangerous, let alone encourage him to actually do so, but I also know what he's capable of when he sets his mind to something." She turned to her son and said, "Sage, it doesn't matter what any of us say about it, does it? You're going to do this aren't you?"

Sage looked at her and nodded.

Mrs. Vector turned to speak to the Malcolms again. "You see? I know my son. His father and I raised him to care about his friends, to do anything for the people he loves. He's grown up with Joaquin, he's like a brother to him. Of course he wants to help him. Part of me wishes he wouldn't even think of trying to do it, but most of me is too proud of him. I've seen what my son can do, and I think he should at least try, because it'll be a whole lot worse if he doesn't. There, I've said my two cents."

Charles Malcolm stood up. "Sage, my son is lucky to have a friend like you, but I can't let you be the only one that tries this. I've taken those tests many times, but I'll take them again and try until the clock runs out."

"Hell, me too pops. I've taken them, but I might as well try too. It's a good plan Sage. You're a real one," said Xavier.

Janet didn't want to be left out either and spoke up, "I've probably got the best chance out of all of you, so you know I'm not sitting this one out."

"That goes for me too. I've never taken the tests, so who knows, maybe I've got a shot just like any of you," said Maria.

"I've actually been taking them since yesterday. I thought it would be fun to see how I did," said Victoria.

"Mom, you are something else," said Sage.

"She sure is," said Joaquin's dad. "So, we've at least got a hail mary kind of plan to work on for now. Let's all stay in touch with each other. If any of us passes and becomes a contender, our name will become public immediately, so it's best to be ready. I'll let my government contacts know what we're up to, just in case. They'll probably laugh at me when I tell them, but I don't care. If it takes moving a mountain, or finding a needle in a haystack, I'd do it for my son. Thank you Sage. And thank you Mrs. Vector. We'll talk more soon."

The Malcolm family left Victoria Vector alone with her son. She held his hand and smiled, trying to hold back a few tears. Sage leaned on her shoulder, like he did when he was a kid sitting next to her on a long road trip. He would fall asleep next to her almost instantly every time. Today, it was just the opposite. He knew he needed to jump into action to implement his plan and help Joaquin, but he also wanted to take a moment and cherish the awesomeness it was to be the son of Victoria Vector.

"Sage?"

"Yeah, mom?"

"Maybe we don't tell your sister or your dad about all of this. Not until we know you're actually named a contender."

"You think it'll actually be me? Why not one of the Malcolms? They're all super smart."

"I just have a feeling, that's all. You're super smart too. Look at all of those paintings you were able to whip up! You're bigger than you realize. That's why I trust you'll be able to save your friend. And if he ends up as the new king, you might just save the world too!"

"Thanks for the encouragement mom. I should probably get to it now."

"Any time. Go help your friend."

Sage grabbed his interface glasses and put them in his pocket. He lifted his book bag over his shoulder and felt the weight of *The Book of Space* resting at the bottom of it. Zimmer watched him with great interest as he leapt over the piles of books, stacks of drawings, and the rest of the clutter that was his room. Eventually, he had what he needed, and turned to his mechanical sidekick.

"All right Zim, let's get going." A minute later they were gliding down Steinbeck Avenue, heading for the John Appleseed Memorial Library. He messaged Robin as they traveled, telling her to meet him at the front entrance of the massive university library. His message ended with, "I want to show you something."

***

Robin Vasquez stood near the front steps to the Appleseed Library with her copy of *The Princess Bride* that Sage gave to her. She was reading it when a light drizzle began to fall. She closed the book and placed it in her bag before it could get ruined. Then she took out her small, black umbrella, opened it, and sheltered herself from the light rain. Several other students were doing the same. A few started to walk faster, or even ran towards their next destination.

The overall campus was thinned out, lacking the busy vibe it usually possessed. The sun was completely hidden by the numerous, gray clouds, and there were no birds flying among the trees. Robin continued to wait, scanning the area every couple of minutes in hopes of spotting Sage.

He was right on time, riding in on Zimmer like one of those old cowboy movies like *The Lone Ranger* or *Zorro*. There was an intensity to Sage that Robin couldn't quite identify. He leapt off Zimmer, pulled her closely and gave her a quick kiss on the lips, then smiled. His intensity turned to calmness and Robin felt herself at ease, but at the same time excited for what Sage wanted to show her.

"Well?" she asked.

"Oh, right. Sorry, I just got lost in your eyes for a moment. They're so vivid today. It must be the change in lighting because of the weather pattern." He looked up at the gray clouds, admiring their new activity.

"Weather pattern? It's raining. What's up with you today? There's something different. Does it have it do with what you're going to show me?"

Sage kept looking up at the sky.

"I can see things with more clarity lately. It's almost like I can be the things I see, and occupy their space. Does that sound crazy?"

"No, that's kind of amazing. What brought that on?"

He reached for her left hand, and slipped his fingers over hers, locking them together. "Come with me. I'll show you."

Sage led Robin through the tall, wooden doors to the massive library. The large stained glass windows let in a kaleidoscope of colors that cast brilliant shadows on the floor, desks, and countless book shelves. The place was practically empty with so many students having opted to stay home today because of the weather. Sage and Robin took one of the six library elevators up to the top floor of the building, famously known as the "Tree Top."

The entire top floor of the library was constructed with windows for walls, giving the feeling that you were floating in the sky, or perched high up in a tree. There were many book shelves in the middle of the floor and several big, comfortable, leather chairs facing the windows. The Tree Top was a favorite study location for students because of the escape it offered. The views were breathtaking, and the entire floor was built for quiet isolation, and studious focus.

Today, the top floor was completely empty. Sage and Robin took seats next to each other on two of the comfortable, leather chairs. They both looked out at the world below them, as well as the one all around. East Salinas looked small from so high up. A few people were walking with their umbrellas above them. They looked like small, mostly black dots moving across a game board like chess pieces. Cars and trucks were a bit bigger, and they moved faster. And all around them was the gray sky, with its dreary clouds, constantly crying.

"Sage, what did you want to show me? If it's what the campus looks like when it's raining, trust me, I've seen it plenty of times."

"No, it's something you've never seen before. Actually, I don't think anyone's ever seen it. Maybe you can help me figure out why that is."

"Okay, go ahead..."

"All right, wait right where you are. I just need to grab something first."

He walked over to the nearest book shelf, and grabbed the first book within his reach. Robin could see he didn't spend any time thinking about which book he wanted to pull, he just pulled a random title. He walked back to her and gave her the book.

She took it, reading the title out loud: *"Dialogue Concerning the Two Chief World Systems* by Galileo Galilei. I don't get it, do you want me to read it?"

"Not exactly. Just ask me anything you want about it."

"Anything, huh? Okay, I'm game." She flipped it open. "What year was it published?"

"1632."

"Okay, what language was it originally written in?"

"Italian."

"Who's it dedicated to?"

"Fernando II de' Medici, Grand Duke of Tuscany."

"You're memory is amazing. When did you read this?"

"I'll tell you in a minute. Ask me some more questions about the book."

"Okay, what's it about?"

"It's a comparison of the Copernican system to the Ptolemaic system. Basically, it goes over Copernicus' theory that the Earth and other planets revolve around the sun, and not the other way around, like the Ptolemaic system professed."

"Wow, that sounds interesting. Okay, one more question..." She flipped further into the book, and spotted a name. "Who's Salviati?" she asked.

"Salviati, is one of two philosophers in the book. He argues in favor of the Copernican theory, and he takes Galileo's side in the book. The other philosopher is Simplicio, who argues the Ptolemaic side of things. His name is meant to imply he is simple minded. Then there's the layman, Sagredo, who listens to each philosopher make their case and tries to decide which is right."

"Sage, when did you read this? I didn't know you knew so much about science."

"Listen, I don't want you to think I'm playing a game, or trying to trick you when I say this. It's the honest truth, and why we're here."

"Okay, go ahead..."

"I read that book today, just now, when I got it from the shelf."

"That's impossible! You didn't even open the cover! You must have read it awhile ago, for a science class you took or something."

"I know it sounds impossible, but hundreds of years ago people thought it was impossible that the Earth revolved around the sun, and now look at what they believe. Sometimes we don't understand something, until we do."

Robin was truly confused. There was an upset feeling she was fighting hard to suppress. She didn't want to explode and tell Sage what a jerk he was being for lying to her. Instead, she tried hard to imagine the possibility that he might be telling her the truth. It was painfully difficult, because she didn't want to look foolish and be tricked into something embarrassing.

"Sage, what you're talking about sounds like magic. Do you know how hard it would be to accept? That someone can read a book by just touching it?"

"Yep, I know. I didn't believe it myself at first. But I think I can prove it to you."

"Okay, how?"

"Do you believe I read the book in your hands? Regardless of when you think I might have read it?"

"Yes, I think you did read this."

"Okay, great. I want you to do the exact same thing, except with another book. I want you to ask me anything about it, like you just did. But this time, you pick the book, and all you have to do is let me touch it for a brief second."

"I don't know."

"Robin, do you see how many books there are on this floor alone? You pick the book this time. Or do you think I've read them all already?"

"Okay, you've got a point, I'm game. Let's see what you can do."

She walked over to the same shelf that Sage found the Galileo book and put it back. Then she looked for a book she was sure he couldn't have possibly read. She spotted an old set, grabbed one of the volumes from it, and extended it out to Sage. He touched it, and smiled.

"Oh, you read it, did you?"

"Yep."

"Okay, let's test you on it. This is… *Naturalis Historia* by Pliny the Elder? This is really old, you're in trouble. When was this book published?"

"AD 77, in Latin."

"Wow, you actually got that right. What is it about?"

"It's actually about a lot of different things, mostly the natural world through the lens of an ancient Roman. Pliny takes a viewpoint of nature that describes it as divine, and he often talks about it in relation to humans. This volume focuses on plants, with a heavy emphasis on their medicinal value to people. It would have been a really excellent guide for those living centuries ago, to help them identify nature they could put to use in their daily life."

Robin closed the book and put it back on the shelf. She walked over to another part of the library, pulled out a new book, and handed it to Sage, who touched it and again smiled.

"*The Wright Brothers* by David McCullough. When was it published?"

"2015. It's the story of Orville and Wilbur Wright who were early aviation pioneers. They were the first to conquer the skies with a successful airplane flight over the sand dunes of Kitty Hawk, North Carolina on December 17, 1903."

Robin put the book back, grabbed another one, and Sage touched it. She asked him questions, and he answered them. She repeated this ten more times, eventually accepting the startling truth. Robin walked unsteadily back to the leather chairs and sat down. She looked out through the huge windows at the world below. The city looked even smaller now, but the sky was a little less gray.

Sage sat down next to Robin. "Do you need me to get you some water?" he asked.

"No, why do you ask?"

"Well, you look a little out of sorts."

"Hmmmm, I wonder why?"

"So, you're okay?"

"Yeah, I just need a minute to gather my thoughts. This is too incredible. I can't quite wrap my head around what this means."

"Means about what?"

"Exactly. I don't know what it means! Did you somehow unlock a secret, hidden human ability that we all possess, or is it an isolated incident? Is it a permanent ability, or a temporary one? What will the world look like if everyone someday can learn like you can? Imagine the things people will be able to do, to build, to make!"

"You're absolutely right. I wish everyone could feel what it's like to understand so much, and to see the world with an enlightened mind. My space is so much bigger now. The world is one giant, amazing marvel I never get tired of looking at. I'd love to have more people experience it."

"Wait a minute, so everything you were trying to tell me on the hill..."

"Yeah, it was exactly how I told you. I reached for this book, light shot out, and the next thing I know, I have this ability."

"I'm sorry I didn't believe you. It just sounded like you were messing with me."

"I would never do that. I care about you too much to ever hurt you, or to play those kind of games."

"I know that now. Do you forgive me?"

"Of course."

"Wait, I have to know something. It's been a couple of days that you've had this ability. How many books have you read so far?"

"You've been to Brave New Books before, right?"

"Yeah. How many did you read there?"

"All of them."

"What? Seriously?"

"Yeah, it took me about an hour, but I went through every aisle, and touched every book on every shelf."

"Oh my god! You must feel amazing! How does it feel to know that much?"

"You're right, I do feel amazing. In fact, it gets better each day. After I've read a book, its knowledge becomes part of me. I gain total comprehensive understanding of it. That understanding expands as I find new ways to apply what I've learned. It's strange, I used to avoid reading books because I thought they were too long to get through, but now they're my favorite thing to find. They've opened up the entire world to me. It's funny. The whole world has been here this whole time, but I wasn't really seeing it clearly. Now, details are inescapable. I admire everything I see. It's all so beautiful. Even the things I used to think were ugly now look pleasant, and important."

"That sounds so lovely!"

"It is," he said, then smiled.

"Sage, so this book that you touched, the one that gave you this ability, where is it now?"

"I have it with me, in my book bag. Want to see it?"

"Oh my god! Of course, yes!"

Sage reached into his book bag and brought out *The Book of Space*. He handed it to Robin who cradled it, then she placed it on her lap. She grabbed the top right corner of the cover with her fingers and slowly opened the book up. No light shot up, and no images, words, or symbols flickered. Robin flipped through the blank, empty pages disappointedly.

"Nothing happened, right?" asked Sage.

"No, same old me," she replied.

"I kind of knew it wouldn't work again so easily."

"What made you think that?"

"Well, because if this book gave the ability to anyone that opened it, the whole world would know about it by now."

"You're right. It must be selective. What if it only works on one person at a time? And when that person dies the book can give the ability to a new person?"

"Yeah, it could work like that. I just don't have any way of knowing for sure. But I'm sure the answer is out there somewhere. That reminds me of something. The other reason I needed to come to the library."

"What's that?"

"Joaquin."

"What about him? Did something happen?"

"You haven't looked at your news feed, have you?"

"No. Sage, tell me. What happened?"

"He's missing. Along with most of the other contenders."

Robin looked scared. Her body tightened and her legs were squeezed together while she waited for Sage to tell her more.

"I think he's been taken in an attempt to manipulate the Crown Search. It's possible he's being held with the other contenders until the contest is over but no one really knows for sure. I met with his family this morning and came up with a plan of sorts."

"A plan for what?"

"To get him back."

"What? How? Do you know who has him?"

"Not a clue, but I do know what they want."

"What? To be king?"

"Yes, that's ultimately what they want. But, before they get it they need something else — contenders."

"Okay, and..."

"And I'm going to become a contender."

"What!? Are you crazy? Why would that help? Unless you also want to..."

"Yep, I am going to get taken too. It'll be a set up, a trap. They'll come for me and when they do, the Security Guild, the Police

Guild, and the entire government will follow where they take me. It's the best way to find Joaquin and get him back."

"Sage, what if they hurt you, or even kill you?"

"It's a risk I have to take. Joaquin is my best friend. I've known him my whole life. I can't just sit by and do nothing when I know there's something I can do that might save him. I have this amazing gift, why not use it? If it's not for helping people, what good is it? I know you don't want me to get hurt, but trust me, I've thought a lot about this since the idea came to me. I have to do it."

"This is huge. If you hadn't shown me what you could do, I would say your chances were impossible, because it's like something out of a spy thriller. But having seen it with my own eyes, maybe you're right. It does kind of make sense. I'm sure you can pass the tests, especially if you touch every book in this library. That's why you're here, right?"

"Right."

"Well Sage, you better get to it. When do you plan to take the tests?"

"As soon as I'm done here. Hopefully in a couple of hours."

"I better leave and let you get to it. Will I see you again before the news hits?"

"Sure, meet me at Twain Hall later. If this goes the way I think it will, that's where the media will be. I can call you when I've passed the tests."

Robin went to Sage. She put her arms around him, and leaned her head against his chest. He put his arms around her.

"You need to come back to me. It would be horrible to lose you now, just when we're at the start of this. Bring Joaquin back, but make sure you come back too. Deal?"

"You've got it. I don't think there's too much that can go wrong. I know too much, and I'm about to know so much more."

"Well, make sure you go through the Self Defense section twice, okay?"

"Don't worry, they had a nice section of that at the book store. I know 34 fighting styles. I just haven't had a reason to use any of them yet."

"Well, I hope you don't get a reason to, but it does make me feel better."

"I'll come back to you. You're the best book I've ever read."

"You sweet talker. You know exactly what to say. Okay, I'm going now. Don't forget to call me the moment you're done."

"I won't."

Robin left, and Sage went to work. He touched every book on the Tree Top, reading them all in twenty minutes. The floor below, the seventh, was devoted primarily to History, and it took him thirty-five minutes to complete. The sixth floor was a mixture of Art and Philosophy, and took him twenty-eight minutes. Sage continued moving down, floor by floor, until he reached the lower level, one floor below the first floor. The basement level contained books on Agriculture. It had an entire section celebrating the Salinas Valley and California's rich history of growing so much of the world's produce. Sage took pleasure in knowing that he could grow life from what he now knew. He imagined an even greener world, filled with taller trees, richer soil, and a more diverse ecosystem that worked in harmony to support all life.

It was hard for Sage to remain totally focused on Joaquin and passing the tests needed when so many wonderful ideas were racing through him. He felt the need to run, to climb a mountain, to sing, to dance, to drive fast down a highway, to roll in the grass, to dive in the ocean, to laugh with his friends, to have a meal with his family, to write, to paint — to make something. He felt like the embodiment of joy, and wondered when the smile on his face would finally fade. His creative energy was euphoric but needed to be tabled for the time being.

Sage walked to the elevator, marveling at how the doors opened. He stepped inside, pushed a button, and was lifted effortlessly back to the Tree Top where he began his time here today with Robin. He found a comfortable seat looking out at East Salinas through the wall-sized windows on the west side of the building's top floor. He rested his book bag against his chair, took out his interface glasses, and accessed the Crown Search testing platform. Sage spotted the large START button and tapped on it. The smile on his face grew just a little bit bigger.

cherry flavored hall

Maria Malcolm was in her kitchen sprinkling white sea salt on the salmon on her stovetop. A tray of neatly cut, steamed bell peppers and onions sat next to a large plate filled with hot almond flour tortillas. Mrs. Malcolm used a stainless steel spatula to transfer her salmon fillets onto a separate tray. Every part of dinner was ready for consumption, so she moved everything to the large oak table in the dining room. Before calling her family to sit, she set out the plates, napkins, silverware, and condiments. Maria looked at her immaculate dinner table and finally felt satisfied. She hit the dinner alarm button on her wrist watch and a pleasant musical chime echoed throughout the house. One minute later the Malcolm family was sitting together to eat fish tacos.

Mr. Malcolm stared at his empty dinner plate as if he were picturing something on top of it other than food. A puzzled expression sat across his face. He lifted his right arm, then his right index finger, and began tracing shapes on the surface of the plate. He was lost in a problem he couldn't solve.

Xavier's elbows were resting on the table, his palms covering most of his face, while he massaged his eye lids. When he lifted his hands away from his face, his eyes looked tired and red. He opened his mouth wide and let out a huge yawn. When his breath was fully exhaled, he shook his head rapidly from side to side, then looked down in disappointment. He then slapped himself in the face a couple of times, but the painful effort didn't result in the effect he was hoping for, so he finally lay his head down.

Janet had her interface glasses on at the dinner table. Her head moved from side to side, and her fingers extended outward, making selections in the air. She was fully engaged in one of the qualifying tests. Her mother watched her with great interest while her food sat, barely touched. Maria's husband, and then her son, joined her in watching Janet's reactions as she competed. Although they couldn't see what she was working on, they looked on with hope. Each of them had failed miserably all day, with scores nowhere near what was needed to become a contender. Perhaps Janet was going to break through their streak of bad luck and do what none of them so far had been able to — score high enough.

"Damn! I was so close!" shouted Janet. She slammed her interface glasses down hard onto the table in front of her, then buried her head under her arms. After a few moments, she lifted her head back up, tears running down her face. Her mother got up from the table to stand next to her, and she wiped her tears with a napkin.

"You tried your best Janet, don't be too hard on yourself. It's a nearly impossible task. Hardly anyone in the world can pass these tests. They're designed with an algorithm geared towards finding particular qualities in decision making and thought process. We'd practically have to become different people to pass these tests. It's asking a lot. Don't beat yourself up. All we can do is try again."

"I know, you're right mom."

"Why don't you have something to eat. It'll give you a pick me up. We can all use some nourishment right about now."

Her father spoke, "Sweetheart, your mother's right. All we can do is try. I'm so amazed Joaquin was able to pass, and score high enough to be a contender. He did something remarkable. I've been impressed by him his whole life, but I'm impressed by him on a whole other level now. We've got one smart boy in our family. And you know what? That's a testament to everyone sitting at this table. He may be the youngest, but he became the wisest, by learning from all of us."

"You're right dad. We just gotta keep it moving. Joaquin's super smart. He's probably doing fine. Who knows, maybe he found a way to escape, and is already heading back here as we speak," she replied.

"That's the spirit, I like that! We should all be thinking positive outcomes, because there's probably a million ways this ends up a happy ending," said Mr. Malcolm.

"Yeah, I like that sis. I can see him outsmarting those fools. Shoot, I don't know what we're worried about. If they took all the contenders, they bit off more than they can chew. All they have to do is talk to each other and coordinate a plan. They're literally the smartest humans alive. They should run circles around whoever's got them," said Xavier.

"I think you're right dear," said Maria. "Joaquin is brilliant, and every one of the contenders is a certified genius. Their minds make them capable of surviving and thriving in any environment. We should hear from them in no time."

"Wait, what if they have them locked up in separate areas where they can't communicate with one another?" asked Janet.

The Malcolms considered this, and they remained quiet for a long time.

"There's still a chance though, right?" suggested Xavier.

"Yes, of course son," replied Charles.

"I think so too," Maria chimed in.

Janet sat in silence, putting a piece of salmon into her tortilla. Next, she used her fork to put some veggies on top. She grabbed a bottle of hot sauce, and shook the bottle so its contents came shooting out like tiny bullets. She looked down at her taco, seemingly riddled in red bullet holes. Janet shrugged then took a big bite.

Half an hour later, the two Malcolm men were back to their test taking efforts. The women sat in the back garden drinking Chai tea. The evening was cold and they both wore thick jackets. On a night like this they would normally drink their tea inside, but they needed the fresh air. Most of their day was spent online with their interface glasses on, and that level of introversion needed to be countered with some extroversion. It didn't matter that light rain was coming down, they were protected by a large, outdoor canopy. They also had something besides their thick jackets to combat the cold with — a small, weatherproof, electric heater.

"Mom, what if Joaquin doesn't make it back? What if they kill him and the other contenders?"

"Janet! You should know better. Some things are better left as only thoughts, rather than spoken words. Words have a chance to became real. Be careful which ones you choose," replied Maria.

"Mom, I'm just being realistic. Kidnappings are rare. This particular one is global in scope and will shape things on the planet for decades to come. I'm sorry if I can't keep my optimism level high enough. I just want to prepare for the worse, just in case. If things don't go the way we want, what do we do then?"

"We do the same thing we're doing now — something. We keep moving, keep living, and never let anyone stop us from trying to help each other, from trying to live the best way we can, for one another. Your brother is a survivor. He knows how to thrive, and how to win. We have no reason to think he won't do the same in this situation. Isn't that right?"

"Yes, mom. You're right. I just get so worried about him. It seems like yesterday I was babysitting him. I remember taking Joaquin to the playground down the street, and he'd fight like hell to stay there as long as possible. He'd make such a fuss, but I just waited until he tired himself out, then I'd put him in his stroller and wheel him back with no problem. It was so hard taking care of him, and so easy at the same time."

"Trust me, I know exactly what you mean. And just like then, he's going to fight like hell. He'll find a way to outlast whoever has him. He's Joaquin."

They laughed out loud, smiled contentedly, and felt the most relief they'd felt since hearing the news that their youngest family member was gone. There was nothing to do but wait, or go online and try to compete for the crown. So far, their strategy to rescue Joaquin was increasingly frustrating. But regardless, the battle needed to be fought.

Janet was glad to have this time with her mother. She knew she could be a better daughter. She was just so caught up with work, and it was difficult to talk longer like they were doing now. The moment she learned her little brother was in the running to be king, she dropped everything. She wondered if she could make her time away from work even longer, because it felt so good to be back home with everyone she loved most in the world.

"He did it! He did it!" Xavier came bounding out of the house shouting.

"Joaquin!? Is he back!?" asked his sister Janet.

Xavier was out of breath. He was too excited. He put both of his hands on his head, trying to get the blood flowing from his arms towards his racing heart.

"Sage! Sage did it! He's a contender!"

Janet and her mother both jumped, screamed, and shouted, "Yes!!!"

Charles Malcolm ended his call, then walked outside. He tucked his glasses into his pocket and joined the rest of his family. Everyone was still reveling in the excitement of the news.

"The boy did it. I guess Joaquin and him are cut from the same cloth. It makes sense. They've hung out together so much, they're bound to think the same about things. But even still, what an accomplishment!" said Charles.

"Did you speak with Sage?" asked Maria.

"No dear, not yet. I couldn't get through to him. I spoke with my contact at the Security Guild. They're getting a team in place to safeguard and track Sage's every movement. He's confident we'll be able to find Joaquin."

"That's excellent news!" replied Maria.

"Dad, we should go talk to Sage. We should congratulate him, and tell him how grateful we are for what he's doing," said Janet.

"I agree, and we will. There's only one problem. We don't know where the boy is. Let's all of us make some calls, and see if we can't find him," said Charles.

"Okay, sounds like a plan," said his daughter.

The Malcolms went into action, filled with more excitement than they'd felt since learning Joaquin was named a contender. Hope was alive and well within each of them. They were confident they would get Joaquin back home safely. His best friend had actually accomplished the impossible task of scoring high enough on the decathlon of tests. What made it truly remarkable was how quickly he was able to accomplish the target. Sage managed to beat the tests with the precision of a clock maker, or better yet, a nuclear bomb dismantler.

The Malcolms owed a lot to Sage, and they were going to make sure they did everything in their power to provide back up support for the young man attempting an even bigger, impossible task. The next one would be the real test. He was going to attempt to rescue his best friend and dozens of the world's smartest people, from an organization, or person, capable of taking people from all over the world without leaving a trace. Did Sage stand a chance against them? Or would he just be one more missing person?

***

Sage was in the same dressing room Joaquin used when he spoke at Twain Hall. He was sitting on a couch with his arms around Robin, trying to console her. She was shaking and crying the moment she walked into the room to meet Sage. Even though she knew what he had been trying to do, a part of her thought it was unlikely he would actually pull it off. It wasn't very real a few hours ago, but now it was too real. He did exactly what he told her he was going to do. The seriousness of the moment overwhelmed her. She wanted to support Sage, but at the same time, she didn't want anything bad to happen to him. Robin knew too many dramas, especially tragedies, that ended in someone's downfall. She liked reading about tragedies, but didn't want to live through one.

Sage tried to console her. "It's going to be okay, really. If you knew what I know, you wouldn't worry. Have faith, and believe in what I'm telling you. Trust me when I say — I know. I have total confidence I can make it through whatever happens next. It doesn't matter that I don't know who did this, or where they might take me. All that matters is that I'm prepared for anything, because I know practically everything. Any subject in the world is in my mind for instant use. You were there, you saw how it works. Robin, I read every book in the building. There's no way they can stop me. My mind is too strong."

"I know, I keep forgetting. It's still hard to process. Okay, I'll trust what you're telling me. I'm sure everything will work out like you say."

"It will. Listen, my parents and sister should be here soon. I'm sure the Malcolms will want to see me too. I want you to keep everything you know about my ability a secret from all of them, from everybody. You're the only one I've told. There's not enough time to tell my family, or the Malcolms, without them thinking I'm crazy. When I get back, I'll tell them, and even show them, but for now I want to keep this just between you and me. Is that cool?"

"Sure Sage, I guess that makes sense. It's not an easy thing to explain to somebody in a short period of time. I won't tell a soul."

"You're the best, thank you. Now, the Malcolms and my mom know about the plan to help Joaquin, but I'm not sure if my dad or my sister know yet. Don't be surprised if they need to get caught up. I'd like to tell them if they don't already know."

"Okay, no problem."

"Cool. I still don't know if the people that took Joaquin and the others will try to take me. This whole thing is a big roll of the dice. I've spoken with the government, the police, and the Security Guild. They're going to have eyes on me the entire time. They're also going to place trackers inside my clothing and shoes. There's no way the authorities don't find me. I'm going to lead them right to Joaquin. The plan is solid. I don't see how it could fail."

"It does sound pretty legit. I just hope you don't get hurt."

"I can take care of myself exceptionally well. I'm up to 88 fighting styles now. I also know survival tactics, hunting, trapping, and even guerrilla warfare. I could build a makeshift weapon out of practically anything."

"Don't put those ideas out there for my imagination to run wild with. I don't want to picture you in some jungle fighting for your survival. I've read *Robinson Crusoe*, he didn't have an easy time on that island."

Sage laughed, "He faced challenges, but eventually got free. It's a good book. I read it today, along with more of Daniel Dafoe's works. "

"I'll bet you did. Fine, I'm going to stop worrying."

"Awesome. I think you'll find it easier that way."

A knock pounded on the dressing room door. The security guard opened it, and peeked inside. "Mr. Vector, your family is here."

Sage stood up. "Send them in."

His mom, dad, and sister rushed towards Sage, drowning him in one giant bear hug.

"Son, we just found out the news! Your sister was the first to see it. You know she's online more than me or your mother ever are. How did this happen? I thought you were going to be an artist, but now you might be king!?" asked his dad.

Sage looked at his mom, and she gave him a look to let him know she hadn't told him anything about his reasons for wanting to be a contender.

"Well..."

"Sage! I'm so proud of you! My feed has been blowing up like crazy since the news hit! All my friends are so jelly. I said duh, yeah he's super smart, and I helped tutor him practically his whole life. I mean, I could have taken the tests, but I never wanted to be king or queen, you know? Do you mind if I take a quick selfie with you brother?" asked Sara.

"Uh, sure," said Sage.

"Awesomeness. Okay, one, two, three, say 'kiiiiiiing!' Oh, okay that works. Thanks Sage."

"So, dad. There's something I've got to tell you. You may want to sit down for this. Oh, sorry I forgot to say something sooner, but this is Robin. Robin, this is my family."

"Hi everyone! It's good to meet you!" replied Robin.

"It's good to meet you too!" said his mother.

"I'm Damon, a pleasure to meet you Robin," said his father.

"So Robin, are you guys together now, or what?" asked Sara.

Robin looked at Sage who encouraged her with a look to go ahead and answer how she pleased.

"Yeah, we are. It just kind of happened."

"Uh, huh. So my brother is basically going to rule the world, and now you want on that train? Is that what you mean?"

"Sara! No, it's not like that at all," said Sage.

"Sage, it's okay. I can answer her," said Robin. "Sara, I've liked your brother for a long time, and he's liked me back just as long. A couple of days ago we both got the courage to let each other know. This whole king thing happened after. I think he can tell you more details about that."

"Okay, sorry Robin. It's just that we're a pretty powerful family now, and I've gotta protect it. No hard feelings. Just doing my job," said Sara.

"It's all good," said Robin.

"Well, now that that's all settled, there's something I need to tell you guys. Please, have a seat," said Sage.

They all sat down.

"So, you know Joaquin is missing, right?"

"Yeah, we heard this morning. We've been worried about him, along with the others. The whole world has them in their thoughts right now. You must be going through hell son. I know he is your best friend," said his father.

"The news definitely hit me like a ton of bricks. But I've been busy trying to make it right. And I have a plan."

"A plan to do what?" asked his father.

"I'm going to find Joaquin, and bring him back home. And the others that were taken too. That's why I wanted to become a contender."

"I don't understand. What do you mean?"

"I entered the contest in the hopes the same people that took Joaquin might try to take me too."

"What!? Why would you do that!? That's nuts! What if they kill you!?" replied Damon Vector, visibly shaken.

"Dad listen, I've thought this through and the plan is practically fool proof. The authorities, the government, practically every security agency in the country is helping to monitor and track me. We're setting the ultimate trap. I'm going to lead everyone we've got right to Joaquin and the others."

Damon Vector ran the plan through his mind, considered it in whole, then broke it down into pieces, trying to find all the ways his son might get hurt. There were plenty of risks, but ultimately he knew it wasn't all that crazy of a plan. Plus, he knew how his son felt about Joaquin. Their friendship was a rare one, built on years of experiences, and mutual trust. He knew his son would move forward with his plan, no matter what anyone told him, even his father.

"Okay mijo. I know it's dangerous, but so are lots of things. I can see you're committed to doing this. Hell, I'd probably do the same damn thing if I were in your shoes. But, there's one thing I don't understand."

"What's that dad?"

"How in the world did you pass those tests? I know you're really smart, but how did you pass them?"

Sage looked at Robin who was wearing her best poker face, then back to his father. "The tests are designed to find a specific range of characteristics. They're not necessarily looking for the highest IQ person. Character, ethics, morality, problem solving, and critical thinking play a much bigger role in passing the tests. Philosophy is basically the study of asking the right questions about life, and knowing enough about the world, and our place in it, to come up with optimum solutions and answers. I may not be the biggest bookworm, at least not until recently, but I've spent most of my life thinking about the world around me, and how I can maneuver through it the best."

"Son, we're so proud of you. We know you're going to do great things," said Victoria Vector.

"Your mom's right. I've always known you were going to be a better man than me. It was always my wish that you would achieve something great, and you've done it. I'm beyond proud Sage," said his father.

"I don't know why everybody's so surprised. I knew he could do it. He *is* my brother, and he learned from the best," said Sara.

"I couldn't have done this without everyone here. So, thank you guys. You're all the best."

There was a loud knock on the door. The security guard popped his head in.

"I've got the Malcolm family asking to see you? Should I send them in?"

"Yes, please. Thank you."

The Malcolms walked into the dressing room. They went immediately to Sage and gave him a big embrace. Maria Malcolm kissed him on both cheeks, Charles shook his hand tightly, Janet left tears on his shirt, and Xavier went through a series of hand slaps, back pats, and fist bumps. Sage was overwhelmed by the affection coming from the teary eyed family.

"We are so grateful to you son," said Charles.

"You don't know what this means to us," said Maria.

"I know you're going to lead them right to him," said Janet.

"You scored when our team needed you kid, much respect," said Xavier.

The Vector family made room for the Malcolm family to sit with them. Sage stood, too full of energy, and too locked in to the moment.

"So, Sage how did you do it? All four of us tried all day to pass those tests, with no luck. Janet came the closest, and even she was still miles away from passing. What was your secret?" asked Charles.

"Well, Mr. Malcolm, I guess I just hung out with Joaquin so much, some of his luck just rubbed off on me."

"You see! I told you all, didn't I? Two birds of a feather flock together. I knew that must be the reason," Charles replied.

"However you did it Sage, we're just glad you did. You gave us some real hope today. Now we have a real shot of getting our boy back. Thank you again. You're such a good friend, and a good person," said Maria Malcolm.

"I know Joaquin would have done the same for me. It was an easy choice to make. But now comes the trickier part."

"Don't worry, my contacts in the government let me know they have practically every man they've got working on this sting operation. Every available resource, from undercover operatives, to high tech equipment, is being utilized right now to help you succeed. Satellites, surveillance, the latest tracking, all of it will be pointing in your direction. Whoever comes for you will have the whole world coming for *them*." said Charles.

"Thanks for helping coordinate all of that Mr. Malcolm. I'm confident I'll be safe. There's no way we don't find Joaquin and the others."

Another loud knock came at the door. The security guard opened it wide this time. A group of Security Guild officers dressed in black, military uniforms walked in. Their leader was a man in his forties with gray hair, built like a tank, and a name tag that said: FORTISTA.

"Mr. Vector. I'm Senior Officer Fortista with the Royal Protection Unit of the Security Guild, North America. We're here to escort you to the press conference where you'll answer a few questions. When that's done my team will take you to a secure location where we will outfit you for surveillance and tracking. Don't worry, we'll have eyes on you the entire time you're in the building. You can say goodbye to your family and friends now.

You might not have time to see them again before this all goes down."

"Okay, thank you officer."

Sage's family, the Malcolms, and Robin, got up and went to Sage. Few words were spoken. They'd said everything there was to say already. They hugged him tightly one last time, sending their best thoughts forward into him: "He would come back with Joaquin." "The others would make it back too." "It was all going to go smoothly."

"Okay everybody, this is it. Goodbye," said Sage.

He started walking towards the security team.

"Wait!"

Sage turned around, and Robin jumped into his arms one last time and gave him a huge kiss on the lips. They both looked a little embarrassed but smiled at one another, then nodded. "Don't worry, I'll come back to you soon," he whispered in her ear.

He walked down the hall towards the stage, the security team covering him from every side. There were lots of people waving and shouting at him as he walked. He recognized many of them, but most he didn't. The security guards struggled to keep them all back. Their rifles were a good enough deterrent, but as the amount of people grew, it became harder and harder to keep people away from Sage. Their excitement was palpable and their voices grew louder.

"You did it! Go, Sage!"

"Salinas back on top baby!"

"All the way to Earth City!"

"Go Trojans! Alisal, represent!"

"All right Sage! You can do it!"

He arrived back stage in one piece, and tried to concentrate on what the organizers were telling him, but it was hard to drown out the voices still echoing in his head. The organizers led him towards the front of the stage. His security team fell back, but spread out and kept watch. There were another hundred government officials and security officers located around the perimeter of the hall and interspersed in the crowd.

Sage looked past the bright lights and saw how many people there actually were in attendance. Not only was every seat in the house filled, but there wasn't a place to stand either. The aisles, from front to back, had people in them packed like sardines. It reminded Sage of old photographs of early mass transit trains in places like New York City, or New Delhi. The noise was even worse. The shouting and cheering was deafening.

Someone nudged him to the podium, and when he stood up, the entire hall went into a fever pitch. He tapped on the microphone to test it, but couldn't hear anything. He lowered his mouth to it, "Hello, is this mic on?" He couldn't tell. A reporter was standing just below him, in front of another microphone. Sage could see his lips moving, but because of the crowd, he couldn't hear him. The reporter tried again when he saw Sage shaking his head, pointing to his ears to let him know he couldn't hear him. No matter how many times they tried, or how long they waited for the crowd to calm down, it was more of the same.

The people grew frustrated with not being able to hear Sage through the speaker system. The technical team tried to solve the problem, but it wasn't a technical issue. Their efforts only made the matter worse by confusing the people into believing it was anything other than their own excitement that was causing the problem. Only hours ago, many of these same people were worried and scared, unsure of the future, and thinking the world as they knew it might soon be over. Now these same people looked nervously at the chaos around them in the hall and began to lash out.

Some of the men standing nearest the walls started hitting them, pounding out their frustration and hoped to get others to join in. This pounding made several women scream, which set off a chain reaction for many of the children in attendance to scream too. People shouted at each other to calm down, but none did. One man threw a punch intended for another man, but it accidentally landed on a third man. Their fighting grew into something bigger.

Sage remained at the podium watching the scene unfold like an out of control wildfire on a windy day. He shouted into his microphone, but it made no difference. The people couldn't hear him, and they were no longer looking at him either. They were too busy looking at the wild behavior all around them.

The reporter that tried to ask Sage a question earlier walked away from his spot in front of the microphone, and went to talk to a colleague with a video camera. The two of them were trying to capture what appeared to be the new big story of the night. All but one reporter were busy doing the same. A young female reporter wearing glasses walked up to the now freed up microphone.

Sage watched the female reporter with curiosity. He wondered what she was going to do differently. She started speaking into the microphone. Once again, he couldn't hear what was being said through the microphone, so he focused on her mouth and read her lips, making out two words — I'm sorry.

The reporter reached into her small purse, took out an even smaller gun, and began firing shots at Sage. He instinctively dove for cover behind the podium. His security team rushed towards him. A police officer tackled the shooter to the ground. Her gun fell out of her hand and lay on the ground. Another officer came over and secured the weapon.

Officer Fortista's men were huddled tightly over Sage, protecting him from any other possible attack. The senior officer looked the young man over. "You've been hit. We need to get you out of here. Can you walk?"

Sage looked down at his legs and moved them. "Yes."

"Okay, we're going to get you up." Then, to his men, "All right boys, we're going to keep a shell formation around him the whole time. Stay alert. Let's get him off this stage."

Fortista helped Sage get up to walk. "Keep low," he told him. There was blood coming down his left shoulder and also from his abdomen. The floor near the podium was spattered in red. People were shouting and screaming but Sage couldn't see them. All he could see was the ground as the security team blocked out the rest. He shuffled his feet, stayed low, and was soon outside the building.

An ambulance with medics was waiting there. The officers helped get Sage onto a gurney. "They'll patch you right up kid. Don't worry, we'll be right behind you the whole way," said Fortista.

"Okay, thank you."

The doors of the ambulance closed. Sage's injuries were being attended to by two of the three medics in the vehicle. The third medic was sitting in the back whistling.

Sage recognized the tune.

"That's *Singin' In The Rain*, isn't it?" he asked.

"Why, yes it is." He stood up, and looked over the work the medics had done. Turning to them he said, "Good job, he should bounce back quickly. Did you get the bullets out?"

"There was only one to remove, but we got it. The other one went through clean."

"Splendid," he replied.

"Sage, you're one lucky boy. As a reward, I've got a nice lollipop for you. I hope you like Cherry."

He reached into his pocket, and took out a small, metal rod.

"Do you see a red light? Red, like cherries. You do like cherries don't you?"

"Yes, red like cherries."

"Splendid."

La casa Grande

Hearst Castle sat atop La Cuesta Encantada, or "The Enchanted Hill," as it had for hundreds of years. Originally constructed in the early 1900's, the castle estate remained one of the great architectural achievements of mankind. It wasn't as famous as The Great Pyramids in Egypt, or as tall as the Burj Khalifa in Dubai, but instead it made it's mark with its overwhelming beauty. The lavish estate was filled with priceless art from all over the world, pristine gardens, an outdoor Greek pool, an indoor Roman pool, tennis courts, and so much more splendor. In its early days, it was host to legendary parties with Hollywood A-listers, famous politicians, and powerful businessmen. It looks today, much like it did back in those days, many centuries ago. And just like they did back then, today's guests fall in love with the beauty of Hearst Castle and never want to leave it.

A cool breeze blew through the open window into the guest room where Sage slept. It carried the smell of the mineral rich, salty sea, and a faint hint of dry grass. The coolness of the air felt pleasant against his face, but the smell of it made him curious and caused him to stir. He suddenly realized he wasn't in Salinas. The events of yesterday were jumbled in his mind, but his basic purpose came back to him like a tidal wave when he remembered Joaquin. He opened his eyes and sat up in bed.

He looked around and took in his new surroundings. There were two elaborate beds, each with posts, and fancy headboards.

A huge fireplace was on the opposite side of the room, and on each side of the fireplace was a separate bathroom. The whole room was covered in art, and a beautiful, large rug covered the floor beneath the beds and furniture. Sage's mind was racing. He identified many of the art styles and time periods represented in the artwork and tapestries. They were hundreds of years old, some more than a millennium old. He felt transported back in time, but he knew the art wasn't from any one period. Someone carefully curated and designed the room he was in. Whoever it was had exquisite taste, and way too much money.

Sage tried moving himself off the bed, and for the first time felt the soreness in his shoulder and his midsection. There were bandages over both areas, and although he hurt, he realized he could still get around with a little, extra effort. There were slippers on the floor, next to his bed, and he tried them on. The material felt wonderful on the bottom of his feet. He wiggled his toes and felt the same sensation on the top of his feet. He shuffled himself around the impressive room, looking at each painting and all of the decor. Suddenly, he thought to look up and was amazed at the beautiful craftsmanship of the ceiling. Every inch of space in the room he was in was masterfully executed to bring about wonderment and awe. Sage felt like a kid in a candy store and was trying to enjoy every last bit of what was around him.

The sound of a voice outside reached Sage's ears. It was male, younger like him. He couldn't quite make out what the voice was saying from where he was, so he walked towards the doorway and shouted, "Hello!? Is anyone there!?"

Sage heard steps coming closer, and finally a young man a little younger than himself, appeared in the doorway. He was wearing a gray and purple tunic with brown leather sandals. His hair was dark black, his skin brown, and his face communicated kindness as he smiled at Sage.

"Hey, you're awake! How are you feeling?" he asked.

"Surprisingly good. Where am I? Is this some kind of hospital?"

The boy laughed, "No, this is definitely not a hospital. But if you need a doctor or a nurse, they have them here."

"What is this place?"

"Hearst Castle. San Simeon, California."

"Really? I remember reading about it. This is it, huh?"

"Yes, it's remarkable isn't it? The walls are made of reinforced concrete. It's amazing the place has survived so long. It's nearly a thousand years old. I never heard of it before coming here. But it sounds like you already know it?"

"Yes, it's as old as you say. It was built by a very rich and powerful media tycoon. He lived here, controlling a vast media empire from it. Celebrities and all sorts of powerful people spent time here. It's supposed to have some of the world's greatest art built into its design. Now this room I'm in makes more sense. For a minute I thought I was dreaming."

"No, we're both wide awake. This place is real."

"I'm sorry, I didn't introduce myself. My name is Sage. What's your name?"

"Sage, what a great name. Mine is Siddhartha. I'm from India, how about you?"

"I'm from California, not too far from here, more than a couple hours drive north."

"That's very close. You've never visited this place before?"

"No, it's been privately owned for centuries now. It used to be owned and managed by the State of California, but a trillionaire forced their hand and took it over. Can you imagine? People used to be able to visit and take tours of this place."

"Well, while we are here we can take a tour anytime we like. Although, it might be best to rest a bit more before venturing out. You must be hungry. What do you like? They make everything here, and it's always delicious."

"I could use a little something. Maybe some fruit?"

Siddhartha walked over to a table, and picked up an old fashioned telephone with buttons on it. He pushed one of them and waited.

"Yes, hello? This is Siddhartha, can you please bring my roommate Sage a platter of fruit? Okay great, thank you."

He put the phone back on the table. "It will be here shortly. The service here is excellent."

"I've never seen such an old phone before. It's interesting to look at. People actually held that in their hand while they talked to someone. They must have kept their conversations short, or their arms would get too tired."

"I know! It's such an odd feeling when I use it, but it's a lot of fun too. It makes me feel like I've traveled back in time. This whole place is like one giant time capsule, or museum."

"You're right about that. I mean, H.G. Wells would have loved a situation like this."

"Ah, *The Time Machine*, written in 1895. Good reference. What about this one? Do you know Marty McFly?"

"The name sounds familiar, but I don't think I do. Is he an author?"

Siddhartha was amused by this and laughed. "No, he is a character in one of the most famous time travel movies of all time: *Back To The Future*. Marty is a student who accidentally takes a time machine thirty years into the past, when his parents were his age. Marty spends the rest of the movie trying to get back to the future. It's quite an entertaining movie."

"I haven't seen too many movies. I mostly read."

"Me too, me too. But I do have a soft spot for cinema. My father is a film producer in India. America has Hollywood, but we have Bollywood. I sort of grew up there, so I couldn't help watching movies."

Just then a man appeared at the open door.

"I have that fruit platter you ordered Siddhartha. Oh, hello Sage! I'm glad to meet you. Here, let me place this down on the table, and I'll shake your hand."

The large silver tray he set down was filled with every imaginable fruit someone might want to eat. The various fruits were cut with precision and arranged in a colorful, inviting manner. The man extended his hand out to Sage. His smile was filled with admiration and excitement. Sage took his hand and shook it.

"We're excited to have you as our guest. If you need anything at all, please just pick up that phone and ask. We can get you most anything. I better head back to the kitchen now. We're working on a new dessert, and I don't want to miss the chance to try it. It's been a pleasure meeting you Sage, goodbye now!"

"Goodbye!" replied Sage, as the man walked away as quickly as he came.

"I didn't even catch his name. Who was that?"

"You know, he never told me either. How strange, I never thought to ask him. I just know him as the man who brings me anything I want. Just earlier, he brought me my favorite chocolates from Switzerland. Oh, and he brought me a beautiful leather edition of Charlie Chaplin's *My Autobiography*. I'm a huge fan of his films, so I wanted to learn more about his personal story. I heard he used to stay here at the castle, maybe the book mentions it."

"Can I see it?"

Siddhartha handed the book to Sage. He felt the beautiful texture of the cover, admired the shiny, gold gilded pages, and flipped the book open to see some of the photographs inside."

"Wow, what a life. I think you'll like this story."

"Have you read this book?"

"Yes, it's wonderful, and inspiring. He played an integral part at the beginning of filmmaking. He was the first international movie star. And he did it all by making people laugh."

"That's exactly right! He also knows how to pull on your heart strings. His movies have so much emotion. It's impressive how he was able to do what he did at a time when pictures were silent. We should ask to see one of his films. They have a movie theater here. All the guests are supposed to watch a movie together each night after dinner. Isn't that nice? Last night we watched *The Wizard of Oz!*

"Wow, this place really does have everything. Siddhartha, can I ask you a question?"

"Of course, my friend. What is it?"

"Are you a contender?"

Siddhartha's face became serious for the first time. He looked over his shoulder, then around the room. After a long pause, he finally replied.

"Why don't you have some fruit? Then I can give you a tour and fill you in."

Sage picked up on his subtle choice of words and said, "Okay, sounds good."

"Great, I'll let you eat. There's also a pitcher of water and glasses. I'm sure you can use some hydration after your long sleep."

"How long have I been out?"

Siddhartha looked uncomfortable again, then said, "The strawberries are my favorite, but don't forget to try the watermelon. I'm going to step out for a few minutes. When I come back I'll give you the tour, and catch you up. Okay?"

Sage nodded, and his new friend walked away. He turned his attention to the fruit platter. He picked up a strawberry and sniffed it. There didn't seem to be anything added, but he cautiously licked it with the tip of his tongue to know for sure. Satisfied, he stuffed the strawberry into his mouth and hoped for the best. He could tell as soon as he swallowed the strawberry that it was the best one he'd ever tasted. He ate them all, then moved on to the next fruit, and then the next one, until he was full. Each fruit was equally delicious and the best he'd ever had.

The pitcher of water was immaculately clean, and so clear, he almost didn't want to disturb its perfection. But he lifted the pitcher and poured himself a glass. He could tell it was pure and rich in minerals. It was most likely from a nearby natural spring. It was also the best he'd ever had.

Siddhartha came back soon after he was finished. Sage was just outside of their room, in the hallway, looking out at the breathtaking view of the surrounding mountains. He felt at peace, and strength was starting to come back to the parts of himself that were injured.

"Wow, you look better already! How did you like the fruit? Was it the best you'd ever had?"

"Yeah, how'd you know?"

"That's how everything is here. You'll see. Are you ready for the grand tour?"

"Let's do it."

"Okay, great. So this floor is mostly guest rooms, and there are a lot of them too. There's a whole row of guest rooms here, and another similar set of guest rooms on the other side of the building. They call it La Casa Grande, or "The Big House," and it *is* pretty big, you'll see."

"Who else is staying here?"

"Oh, lots of people. Don't worry, you'll meet the rest of the guys soon. Oh, and the rest of the girls too. They stay on the other side though, in those other guest rooms."

"Are they all our age?"

Siddhartha laughed, then said, "No, but wouldn't that be fun!? They're all different ages, and from different parts of the world."

They walked past several other rooms that looked very similar to theirs, but each was decorated with unique art. Next, they came to a spiral staircase at the end of the hallway. Sage looked down the narrow stairwell and hesitated.

"Oh, no. Are you able to make your way down these?" asked Siddhartha.

Sage grabbed the curved metal handrail, then placed his right foot on the first step going down. He felt a little discomfort, but he knew he could make it down.

"I'll be okay. It's only one flight down, right?"

"Yes, I'm just going to show you around the grounds a bit. Let me know if you need any help. Just take your time," replied Siddhartha.

Sage found it interesting how the narrow, spiraling stairs were so solid after so many centuries. The craftsmanship that went into this place was truly impressive. Finally, they made it to a wooden door that led outside. When it opened, the sunlight came through golden and bright. The blue sky was perfect, but somehow paled in comparison to the perfection below it.

The world outside the main building was the perfect balance between nature and art. Gorgeous trees, vibrant flowers, and lush greenery encircled the two young men as they walked across beautiful, handcrafted tiles, and marveled at timeless statues. It reminded Sage of Michelangelo Park back in Salinas, only better. The artwork on the castle grounds was centuries old and transported one back in time. Statues laid about like hidden treasures, or religious alters for people to worship at. And everywhere you looked was Mother Nature in all her glory, cultivated to a level of brilliance that would have made the Garden of Eden jealous.

They walked to the front of La Casa Grande and Sage was enraptured. The Spanish art and gothic decor was overwhelming. He gazed at the Madonna and child, the wild men, and their ornate details in wonder. The large wrought-iron door stood before him like the gateway to another world, one that was transformative, yet frightening.

"This is incredible," Sage told Siddhartha.

"I know what you mean. Wait until you see the pools."

They walked a little further, passing more and more amazing landscaping and architecture. The castle was more than one giant building, it was a series of buildings, each a marvel in its own right. Sage couldn't help but be curious about them all, and he wanted to stare at them forever, to go into each and explore every inch of what must be inside. He hoped he would get the chance to satisfy his curiosity with his time here, but knew it was unlikely he would get the chance to learn everything he wanted to know about this incredible place.

They turned a corner and he saw the bluest blue water, surrounded by Greek pillars and carved stone. Once again, he felt transported to a different time and place, one entirely fantastical and sublime. It was something out of a fairytale, or classic Hollywood picture, equal parts heaven and paradise. There were about a dozen people swimming in the pool below, and several others lounging around it.

"This is the Neptune Pool. Isn't it spectacular?" asked Siddhartha.

"It's amazing. I've never seen a more beautiful place to swim in my life. My god, you can see the ocean from here too," replied Sage.

The Pacific Ocean was an almost afterthought for someone at Hearst Castle. It was gorgeous to look at, and made many of the views truly special, but at the same time it could also fade into the background. On most days, the ocean took its place as one more beautiful thing to look at while at the estate, always competing with the grandeur of the castle, the beauty of its gardens, and the unforgettable art that was everywhere. The ocean was not a far trip away, but most guests of the castle preferred swimming in the waters of the Neptune Pool, not only because of its convenience, but because of its epic beauty.

Sage and Siddhartha made their way down several steps, past the statue of The Birth of Venus, and made their way underneath one of the colonnades. The shade was refreshing under the temple-like structure, and the view of the Pacific Ocean to the left, and the Neptune Pool to the right, made them feel like they were on some sort of magical, floating island.

There were people laying and sitting about, most of them wearing interface glasses, and moving their arms and hands in the air in front of them. A young woman, a little older than them was stretching on a yoga mat, a relaxing smile forming on her face as she looked up at the two new visitors to the pool.

"Hi," she said. "I'm Ayanna. Did you two just get here?"

"My name is Siddhartha, and this is Sage. We have been here since yesterday, but Sage has been recovering from an injury, so it is his first time out."

"Oh, no," she replied. "What kind of injury? Can I take a look? I'm a first year doctor."

Sage couldn't help but notice Ayanna's beauty. Her body was as fit as he'd ever seen on anyone, and there didn't appear to be a single wrinkle, mark, or blemish anywhere on her. The young woman's skin glowed, and there was an energy about her that was both calming and electrifying.

"I'm not quite sure what happened. I have two bandages, one on my stomach, the other on my shoulder. Maybe you can check them for me?"

Ayanna smiled. "Take a seat. I'm happy to take a look."

He sat on a nearby chair and she examined his bandages.

"I'm going to press down gently, let me know if you feel any discomfort when I do, okay?"

"Okay."

She pressed down on his shoulder injury slightly, then with a little more pressure. "This one doesn't seem too bad, right?" she asked. "No, it's just a little sore," he replied.

"Okay, I'm going to lift it up and take a look." She slowly lifted the taped bandage and got a better look at what was underneath. "Okay, this doesn't look too bad. It's going to heal in no time. Let's see the other one now."

Ayanna put some slight pressure on Sage's abdomen. While she examined him, he couldn't help but look at her. She was probably the most beautiful girl he'd ever seen in his life. Her body was so close to his that it made him feel a little guilty being so intimate with a girl other than Robin. He forced himself to turn his head to the left, and he gazed out at the ocean.

"Now I'm going to take a look under the bandage," she said.

"Okay," he replied.

"Well, this one is deeper and will take a bit longer to heal. But I don't think you have anything to worry about. Whoever handled your injuries knew what they were doing. If you don't mind me asking, who shot you? You don't look like somebody someone would want to take a shot at."

"I was shot!?" asked Sage. "Are you sure?"

"Yep, you were definitely shot by a couple of bullets. It's unusual to see in this day and age, but these things do still happen. I've studied these types of injuries pretty intensively."

"I didn't know I was shot. I don't remember it at all."

"Well, I wouldn't worry. It's not uncommon for memories to be suppressed after a traumatic event. Just give it some time, I'm sure it will come back to you. So where are you from Sage?"

"I'm from Salinas, here in California. What about you?"

"That's awesome! I love Salinas, it's really beautiful there. I'm from Los Angeles, near Hollywood."

"You know, Siddhartha is like your distant cousin, he's from Bollywood, in India."

Ayanna, turned to Siddhartha who was smiling, and a little embarrassed, not knowing he was going to be put on the spot so suddenly.

"Oh, yeah? That's so awesome, dude. I haven't seen many Indian pictures, only the *Apu Trilogy* by Satyajit Ray. Are you a fan of American movies?"

"Oh, yes. My favorites are all from America. I am currently going through a silent film phase in my movie viewing. I very much admire the beginning era of filmmaking. Buster Keaton and Charlie Chaplin are my favorites at the moment."

"I love Chaplin! You know he used to come here, back when this place was just built? He must have swum in this same pool."

"I know, it's so exciting. The castle is so magical."

"Ayanna, why are we here?" asked Sage.

Her smile faded, and she looked at Siddhartha for help in answering the question, but he was equally at a loss for words. Ayanna struggled to find the right answer. Finally, she said, "I think we're here to help him." She pointed to a young man about Sage's age. He was wearing golden swim trunks, laughing and sitting on the shoulders of an old woman, while he used a big, red foam bat to hit another swimmer across from him who was sitting on the shoulders of an old man. The other swimmer wore blue and orange trunks and was trying to defend himself against the red foam bat with an equally sized yellow one. He seemed afraid of the young man in the gold trunks, and so did the old man whose shoulders he sat on. Both the old man and the old woman were struggling beneath the weight of the two people they held up in the water.

"You can do it Martin!" shouted the swimmer in the gold trunks, "Just hold him up a little longer! I want to be the reason he falls!" He took another big swing at his opponent, landing a terrible hit to his skull. The man in the blue and orange trunks came toppling down, taking Martin with him.

"Ha! We did it Beth! You strong, old witch! I told you we could beat Julian and your husband! Okay, I want to get off now. Kneel down in the water so I can get off your bony shoulders!"

The old woman dunked down into the water and let the young man in the gold trunks swim off of her. When she resurfaced, she looked at her husband with red eyes. He was rubbing his left shoulder, tears falling from his face.

"Martin! Are you okay, dear?" she said as she swam over to him.

"Yes, Beth, I'll be all right. My shoulder hurts, is all."

"I knew this was going to happen. That shoulder hasn't been the same since your surgery last year. I'll take you to see one of the doctors."

"Yes, dear. And how about you?"

"My shoulders feel bruised. I could use a look over myself."

The older couple struggled to get out of the pool, but did so. Ayanna quickly went to them, and escorted them in the direction of the doctors. Sage and Siddhartha watched them walk away slowly up the marble steps, surrounded by gorgeous pointed Italian Cypress trees.

The young man in the gold trunks walked over to a man reclining and reading a book in one of the lounge chairs. The man was in his mid 50's, with graying hair, wore thick, black reading glasses, and was without a shirt, soaking up sun rays. The young man in the gold trunks cast a shadow over the man, blocking out the sun. The man reading in the chair looked up nervously at his unexpected visitor.

"Well?" said the young man in the gold trunks.

"Well...what?" replied the older man.

"Get out of my chair. This one's mine."

"I'm sorry, I didn't see anyone using it. It was empty when I got here."

"Get up!!" screamed the young man. The older man complied, and scrambled up out of the reclined chair. The younger man grabbed him, clenching a bunch of his skin near his collar bone tightly.

"Do you see all of this?" said the young man, indicating the entire castle estate with his left hand.

"Ouch, yes! I see it!"

"It's all mine. So the next time you see that I want something anywhere on this damn mountain, or anywhere I just happen to be for that matter, do yourself a favor, and move the hell out of my way. Got it!?"

"Yes, Robert."

"Who told you it was okay to call me by my first name!? It's Mr. Masters, or Mr. Robert Masters, the second. Don't let me catch you slipping again. Now get the hell out of here! Damn peasant."

The man walked away dejectedly towards the main house, loosely gripping his book. It slipped out of his hand onto the floor, and jarred his attention. He suddenly realized he was without the rest of his things. His shirt, sandals and a small bottle of sun block were on a towel near the chair he left behind. As he turned around, considering whether to risk retrieving his belongings, he saw Robert pick them all up in one giant bundle and hurl them over the railing at some far away trees. Then, he wiped his hands on his shorts, as if touching the items left him dirty or diseased. He lay his head back in the lounge chair, and closed his eyes. A couple of seconds later, he opened them again, shook his head violently, leapt out of the chair, then picked it up with both hands and hurled it over the railing too. He let out a wild scream, "AHHHHHHHHHH!!!!! Damn, dirty peasants!!," then stormed off.

The shirtless man looked away, and he continued his journey back to the main house. Sage, Siddhartha, and the others at the pool were quiet, taking in the incident, and trying to make sense of it. No one wanted to speak first, as if their doing so would call unneeded attention to themselves. The atmosphere had shifted, and no one dared try to shift it back just yet.

"Who the hell is that guy?" asked Sage.

"That's Robert Masters Jr." answered Siddhartha in a low voice.

"Does his family own the place or something?"

"I think so, yes. His father is Dr. Robert Masters. You'll see him around."

"Siddhartha, why are we here? What is all this?"

His roommate looked around, then spoke in a low voice, "We're here to help Robert Jr. pass the tests."

"Which tests?" asked Sage.

"The crown qualifiers. The decathlon. We're here to help make him king."

"What!? Why would we do that? That's not right. It's completely unethical."

"I want to do it. We all do," said Siddhartha.

"What!? Why!?"

Siddhartha looked confused. "I'm not exactly sure, but I want to help him win. Everyone feels the same way. It's kind of nice being on a team for once. Are you going to join us?"

"No. I'm not going to help that maniac get anywhere near the crown. Him, in charge of the whole world? No way. I'm shocked you, or anyone else would want to help him win."

Siddhartha looked confused, then the confusion went away, and he smiled. "No, I definitely want to help him win. It's very important that I help him."

"Why?"

"You know, I'm not sure. I guess, I just feel it deep inside. It's the best thing for me to do. Otherwise..." He drifted off in his own thoughts.

"Otherwise, what?" asked Sage.

Siddhartha smiled. "Hey Sage, did you know they have a movie theater in the big house?"

"Yeah, you told me that earlier."

"Maybe we can watch a film later tonight. They might not have as many movies as I have at home, but that's okay. I don't mind if it's one I've already seen either. I can watch a movie again and again. Can't you?"

"Uh, yeah, sure. Siddhartha, are you okay?"

He was staring at the water in the swimming pool. It was empty now. Everyone had slipped away after Robert threw the chair over the railing. The water was clear and Siddhartha was staring at the black geometric designs on the bottom of the pool. He watched them blur ever so slightly as the water drifted lazily back and forth over them. Sage clapped his hands loudly together in front of Siddhartha's face and his friend became alert once again.

"Oh, hey Sage. The pool is beautiful isn't it? The time just goes by so fast. Hey, where did everyone go?"

"I don't know. Where do you think they could be?"

"Well, they could be anywhere on the estate. Playing tennis, going for a walk, resting, reading in the library, or talking to Dr. Masters."

"How do I find Dr. Masters?"

Siddhartha looked up towards La Casa Grande, "Oh, look! He's right there!"

Sage lifted his head in the direction he was looking. He saw a middle aged man wearing a black suit, with a shiny, black tie. He had a huge smile on his face, and it looked like he was laughing at a joke. The man turned, revealing someone else was with him. He put his arm around him, and the two walked away. The other person with Dr. Masters was Joaquin Malcolm.

Animals at Dinner

Sage walked towards the steps leading back to the buildings as fast as he could, but the pain from his injuries slowed him down. His abdomen hurt badly, and his shoulder was more aggravated than before. Despite this, he knew he had to get to Joaquin. The pain grew worse with each step he took. By the time he was at the top, he was out of breath and sweating. He looked everywhere around him but couldn't see where Dr. Masters and Joaquin had gone. Defeated, he staggered over to a nearby bench to recuperate.

"Sage!" called out Siddhartha, "You took off so fast! I don't know how you did that without…" He looked at his friend who was bleeding from his midsection. "We've got to get you medical attention. Stay here, I'll get someone!"

Siddhartha ran to get help. Fortunately, he ran into Ayanna on her way back from helping the elderly couple from the pool. When they got to Sage he was unconscious, laying across the marble bench with both arms flailed outwards, the blood trickling from his soaked bandage. With the help of a couple of nurses from the nearby medical office, they got Sage on a gurney and transported him to one of the two doctors on the estate staff. Dr. Denton applied some topical medicine, fixed up his stitches, and monitored his vitals. After several hours he was transported back to his room.

Sage heard a familiar voice carrying on a conversation with someone which caused him to wake. He opened his eyes and saw Siddhartha speaking with Dr. Masters. He recognized the doctor from his devilish smile from before. The two of them were laughing together, as if sharing a joke with one another. Both were unaware that Sage was awake and he stayed as quiet as he could so he could listen to their unfiltered conversation and perhaps learn something new about his situation on this private estate.

"...that's the way it is with healing. You've got to give it more time than you want. Otherwise things get messy, and sometimes worse."

"I thought you were a psychologist. Have you worked with patients with physical injuries as well?"

"Boy, I have seen everything there is to see. I doubt there are many medical doctors, or emergency care physicians that have seen the amount of blood I have. My scrubs can bare witness. They tell the tale. Have to replace the damn things so often is the problem. Why, the other day, I got a few drops on my shirt! It wasn't a major operation or anything mind you, just the latest casualty caused by my nose."

"Your nose, doctor?"

"Yes, my nose. The thing has a propensity to bleed ever so often. It's a wonder I keep the thing around anymore. But what's the alternative? Walk around looking like an exposed skeleton every day of my life? Ha! Might be okay on Halloween...but what about the other days!?" replied Dr. Masters, laughing.

"Dr. Masters, you've got a great sense of humor."

"I'm glad you recognize it Siddhartha. You're a funny boy too, if I must say."

"You think so?"

"No, not at all." Dr. Masters wore a deadly, serious look on his face, and became silent. Siddhartha felt afraid and unsure of what to do or say.

"Ha! I'm just playing with you boy! You're a riot! You know how to take a joke, truly!"

"Ha, ha! Dr. Masters, you're too much! You really got me that time. Say, Dr. Masters, sir… will Sage be able to help your son like the rest of us, if he's still recuperating? Wouldn't he be better at home resting? He told me he doesn't live far from here."

Dr. Masters wore an expression of disgust, as if he were asked to do something unthinkably repulsive. "Siddhartha, you're a young man, but sometimes your ignorance baffles me. You're supposed to be bright. Why can't you see what's right in front of you?"

"What do you mean Dr. Masters? What am I not seeing?"

"The big picture, my boy. The big picture. Hmm…did you hear that?"

"No, what did you hear Dr. Masters?"

"I believe I heard Jason downstairs with a tray. Why don't you go see if he needs any help?"

"Yes, Dr. Masters, right away. Goodbye."

"Goodbye…" Siddhartha left, and Dr. Masters said, under his breath, "…and good riddance, you annoying little brat."

He stood up, stretched his arms out, and paced around the room. He was staring at a tapestry, confused by its meaning, but the feeling of it pleased him. Then he walked over to Sage's bed and stood over the young man.

"Sage? Are you ready to wake up? I've got a whole lot of people waiting to meet you boy."

The young man turned slightly in bed, and pretended to wake for the first time. He opened his eyes slowly and looked up. A huge grin greeted him.

"There he is. Welcome to Shangri-la," said Dr. Masters.

"We're in Tibet?" replied Sage.

"Smart boy, you made that connection. No, unfortunately. At least not yet that is," he replied, laughing to himself.

"Where am I?"

"You're in San Simeon, at Hearst Castle."

"Oh, that's right. Who are you?"

"I'm Dr. Robert Masters."

"How did I get here Dr. Masters?"

"You don't remember? You volunteered to come and help us with our special project. You're here to help my son Robert Jr."

"Help him with what?"

"You don't remember any of this?" Dr. Masters was honestly surprised.

Sage thought it best to lie. "Oh, yes, now I remember. I'm here to help him with the tests."

"Yes, that's right! You're all here to help him with the tests. Together we're going to achieve the highest scores anyone has ever received on these tests. Isn't that fun!?"

"Oh, yes. I can't wait. When do I get to start?"

"I love your spirit. Well, as soon as you feel up for it."

"I'm a bit hungry. May I start after dinner?"

"Why, yes, you certainly may! We're going to be gathering for dinner in the refectory. If you're up for it, we'd love to see you there. Don't worry about the stairs, you can take the elevator down. It's just a short walk."

"There's an elevator?"

"Oh, no one told you, did they? Yes, I know it's an old building, but they managed to sneak in a few technological conveniences back in the day. Speaking of which, there is a telephone here in your room. You can use it to get anything you need, including getting help downstairs, refreshing your bandages, a late night snack, anything at all. Isn't that nice?"

"Yes, sir. Thank you."

"Doctor."

"I'm sorry?"

"I'm a doctor. You should address me as... *Dr.* Masters."

"Oh, right. Thank you, *Dr.* Masters."

"Very good. You're a quick learner. We like that around here. All right, I'll leave you now. Dinner is at 6pm. If you need something to do in the mean time, the library is just down the hall. Oh, I know some of you brought your own books with you, but the library is filled with so many more. But, I did take the liberty of obtaining some of your personal effects before you arrived. You'll find them in the top drawer of that dresser over there. Well, see you soon Mr. Vector."

"Goodbye, Dr. Masters."

Sage waited in bed for the sound of the doctor's footsteps to fade, then he slowly sat up. The pain was definitely still there, but tolerable. He put his feet on the floor and walked over to the dresser Dr. Masters had mentioned. He grabbed the handle of the top drawer and opened it. Inside was his book bag. The contents of his bag were exactly as they had been the last time he saw it. He could tell right away the thing he was most concerned about was still in his possession — *The Book of Space.* Sage knew that whoever looked through his things was clueless about its power, otherwise it wouldn't still be in his book bag. They probably saw the blank pages and assumed it was an unused sketch book.

He put the book back in his bag and closed the drawer. He walked to the adjoining bathroom, splashed some water on his face, and looked in the mirror. From now on, he had to be fully alert, and extra careful about what he said, and who he spoke with. There was something odd about everything Dr. Masters told him. His entire reason for being here made no sense to him at all. He was determined to get to the bottom of everything, but until he did, he needed to be smart with the moves he made. He would play along for now, and do what was asked or suggested to him.

Sage walked to the front door of his guest room and peered out into the hallway. It was empty. He could wait for Siddhartha to return but decided it best to venture out on his own. The library was on the same floor and he knew he could find it easy enough.

At the end of the hallway was the same spiral staircase he used from before, but just around the corner from it was a lobby area. The wooden ceiling and paneling was exquisite. There were two entrance ways to another larger area and Sage walked towards the one closest to him. As soon as he took his first step in its direction he knew he had found the library.

The library was unlike any Sage had ever seen. It was yet again another time capsule, transporting him to a different era. The Spanish influences were unmistakable, but so were the Greek vases, and Roman art. A huge Italian table sat in the middle of the room, and a large limestone fireplace graced the wall between the two entry ways. Books lined the walls, but not ordinary ones, these books were practically ancient. They sat on thick, dark, wooden shelves protected by thin, metal grate overlays, an extra protective measure to help preserve the delicate volumes. The enormous wooden ceiling had an impressive geometric design that covered the entire library. It looked like a hundred small portals to other worlds hovering above the heads of any that sat in the many chairs scattered about.

Presently, there was one person sitting in a chair in one of the corners, but Sage couldn't quite make out who it might be. They had their back to him and all he could see from his position was a head of short dark hair with interface glasses over their ears. The rest of them was hidden behind the back of a chair. Sage walked to the other side of the library to give the person a bit of privacy while he examined the many books all around him.

Sage started touching the books closest to him. He began what was now becoming his regular process to tackle the reading of a huge collection of books. He started on the top left of a section and worked his way right, then down to the shelf below, and went left to right again. All it took was the tip of his finger making contact with each book for the information to pour into him instantly. His understanding of the material was always complete, thorough and enlightening. The more books he read, the faster the process seemed to go. To the unaware, casual observer, Sage appeared to be skimming book titles, never finding one that was interesting enough to pull from a shelf. But the entire time Sage touched those titles, he was enhancing his understanding of the world, of his fellow man, and achieving a level of learning that might take a normal man several lifetimes to accomplish. He was doing it in minutes.

The books Sage read were priceless. They were unlike any of the books from Brave New Books, or even from the Appleseed Library. The books in this library were older, so their perspectives were colored by experiences of life from much different times. They contained many of the same subjects Sage was already familiar with, but their unique points of view gave him a more nuanced understanding of those subjects. He was nearly done with two thirds of the collection when the other occupant of the library rose from their chair and turned to look at Sage moving his fingers across a row of books.

"Who are you?" he asked.

Sage turned around, smiling instinctively, but quickly changed his face to have a more serious look. He now knew who was in the room with him, it was Robert Masters Jr., and he looked on the verge of hitting something.

"My name is Sage. I hope I didn't disturb you. Your father encouraged me to come here."

"He did? So you know who I am? And why you're here?"

"Of course. You're Mr. Robert Masters, the Second. I'm here to help you score high on the crown qualifiers. How has it been going?"

Robert's shoulders relaxed, and he smiled genuinely at Sage.

"Well, it's been disappointing because so little progress has been made. My father says to be patient because it's only been a couple of days, and that we have nearly an entire month left, but he doesn't know how badly I want this. I should be on the contender list by now! We've got dozens of you here! I don't know why it's so hard to do!"

The anger was spreading throughout Robert's body. Sage could practically see the veins bulging on his forearms and neck. He walked over to Robert slowly and put his hand on his shoulder.

"It's going to be okay. I'm going to help you become a contender by the morning. And then I'm going to help you score high enough to win the whole thing. Sound good?"

Robert looked at him skeptically. "What makes you think you can deliver on those kind of promises? We've got a whole bunch of you working on this, and so far no one has been able to do that. You're all too weak mentally. My father says you need time to adjust from the..."

"From the what?"

"Oh, never mind! I'm getting out of here! You stay, and read some of these books. Maybe you're not as brain dead as some of the others. But I've still got my eye on you. Remember that."

"I won't let you down Mr. Masters."

Sage waited for Robert to fully leave the library before letting his propped up smile return to a more genuine one. He was excited to finish reading all of the books in the library collection and went back to touching them. A few minutes later he was done. He took a seat on a nearby couch, thinking about the new knowledge swirling around in his head, and let it all linger there for awhile. He looked up at some of the Greek vases that stood on top of the wooden paneling. They were on top of every book case, and stretched out, in one large peripheral boundary across the entire library. He observed several of the human figures painted on the sides of the vases, and wondered what the men that made the vases would think of their art existing today, so far into the future, in a place like this. Would they be pleased? Or would they be upset that their work belonged to such an evil man and his monster of a son? Sage was reminded of his own art. He wanted desperately to return to making it. He wanted to be at home, sketching and painting, with Zimmer projecting old movies on the wall, or blasting hip hop music through his speakers. He wanted to be with Robin on that hilltop in Poe Park. He wanted to run out on the field with his teammates one more time. He even missed seeing his sister's impatient feet under the bathroom door, and hearing his mother's voice remind him one more time not to forget his interface glasses.

"That's what I need — my glasses," he said to himself.

Sage got up, left the library, and walked back to his room. He opened the drawer that held his book bag, and found his interface glasses inside. He put them on and tried accessing his contacts. They were disabled, along with everything else, except for a unique portal that led to the crown qualifier tests. Sage took the glasses off, but slipped them in his pocket. He knew he would be asked to use them later.

It was a short time until dinner and Sage thought it best to rest for a few moments, so he laid down in his bed. He closed his eyes and tried to remember the events that led him to this place. Ayanna said he'd been shot, but he still couldn't remember anything about it. The last thing he remembered was seeing his family, the Malcolms, and Robin. He knew he was a contender, and that the others at the castle were probably contenders too, but he didn't understand why they wanted to help Robert Masters, let alone for something so vitally important as the Crown Search. He searched through his memory for any clues and asked himself the question over and over again, "What could cause so many highly intelligent people to follow the wishes of a mad man?"

After several minutes of deep thought, Sage came up with a possible answer. It must be some kind of mind control, or hypnosis. From what he knew about these subjects, it was highly unlikely that the individuals at the castle were missing long enough to be so thoroughly brainwashed or indoctrinated into such blind obedience. He also knew that only a small portion of the population was susceptible to hypnosis, so it was hard to believe that so many highly intelligent people were defenseless against such a cheap parlor trick.

Sage knew he was on the right track, but he would need to discover more facts before he could pinpoint the true cause of the insanity he was seeing around him. He was certain tonight's dinner would prove to be fruitful when it came to uncovering more of the truth. Sage got up from his bed, freshened up in the bathroom, and changed into a new set of clothes. Fortunately, his room was stocked with clean, ironed clothing in his size. When he was ready to leave, Sage awkwardly picked up the telephone by his bedside. He heard a voice on the other end say, "Hello?"

"This is Sage Vector, on the second floor. How do I get to the refectory for dinner?"

He was given instructions, then he hung up. With his right hand he felt his chest to make sure his interface glasses were still in his coat pocket. Satisfied, he left his room once more. This time, he knew exactly where he was headed.

***

The refectory was located on the first floor of La Casa Grande, right in the heart of the building. Like the library, it had an impressive ceiling, but the room was much taller, and grander.

There were Gothic tapestries hanging along the walls, and both sides of the room featured 15th century Spanish choir stalls. An immense, long wooden table took the center position of the room, decorated with antique silverware, and thick, wooden chairs with cloth backs.

Most of the chairs were filled with guests. Dr. Masters and his son Robert were seated in the center, one right across from the other. Sage spotted an empty chair and walked towards it. Siddhartha was sitting next to the chair and smiled at him. Dr. Masters noticed Sage for the first time, and motioned for him to sit down. Many of the eyes around the room landed on the newest visitor to the dinner table, and Sage simply smiled at everyone, and nodded.

"Sage! You're out of bed, that's great!" said Siddhartha.

"Thanks! I'm feeling much better. I appreciate your help earlier," replied Sage.

"Oh, it was nothing. Anyone would have done the same. Pretty amazing place to have dinner, isn't it?"

"It's beautiful, like something out of a movie."

"Exactly! It makes me feel like an old film star. Chaplin might have sat in my seat!"

"I'm sure he must have come here many times, so the chances of that are pretty good. Say, have you seen Ayanna? I'd love to thank her too. The medical office told me what you both did to help me. But, I don't see her here."

"Hmmm, that's strange. She should be here. Most of us are. But then again, it's not mandatory or anything. Maybe she has a special diet and eats in her room, or someplace else. I wouldn't be surprised. She looks the type. Me? I'll eat anything that looks delicious, and this place is stock full of deliciousness."

Dr. Masters stood up, then cleared his throat. He looked around the room to make sure everyone was giving him their undivided attention. Sage made sure to join the others in looking directly at Dr. Masters, and he forced a smile on his face.

"Welcome to our little abode. Robert and I are pleased to have you here. Many of you have come from all points across the globe for one purpose. You are all believers! You believe that my son Robert deserves to be king. It truly humbles my heart to see how many of you have volunteered your time to make sure he sits on that planetary throne in Earth City. You are all heroes of the highest order, so bravo! Before we eat, I wanted to make a quick announcement. There is one of you that deserves high praise for their commitment to our cause. One person who has sacrificed so much in his short time here, and is dedicated to the task at hand. We should all be inspired by his devotion. Give a strong applause to — Mr. Joaquin Malcolm!"

From one side of the room, Joaquin entered like a military soldier. He waved his hand in the air, smiling at the dinner guests, then walked over to Dr. Masters and shook his hand effusively. Next, he leaned in and hugged Dr. Masters like a father. Robert stood up and Joaquin gave him an enthusiastic high five, then the two of them hugged each other. The entire time every guest at the dinner table clapped and smiled. Sage's hands were beginning to sting, and his forced smile was beginning to slip just as Dr. Masters motioned for them to sit down. He offered his chair to Joaquin, who seemed moved by the gesture and reluctantly took his seat.

"This young man has been working tirelessly at the tests since he's gotten here. I've had to force the boy to take his glasses off from time to time so he can get some sunlight or take a drink of water. He was kind enough to join us here tonight. I'm going to step out, but he has some important words of inspiration he'd like to share. Joaquin, you've got the full attention of everyone here."

Dr. Masters walked out of the refectory. Joaquin got up from his chair and looked around the room. His eyes met Sage's, and he seemed to not recognize his best friend, but Sage saw the slightest twinkle in his eyes that made him feel his friend still remembered him.

"Friends, we are here for one reason, and one reason alone. You, like I do, believe that this gentleman deserves to be our philosopher king! You have volunteered for this, now it's time to fight for this! Some of you have been plugging away, others are about to. We only have a few short weeks to get Robert the highest possible scores on all ten tests of the crown qualifiers. Each of you have passed the test before, but we need to ensure that our friend not only passes, but scores higher than any of us. Fortunately, Dr. Masters found a way for the highest of our scores, on each of our tests, to find their way into his son's interface account. So all you have to do, is test as much as possible while you are here. You can take breaks when needed, but every minute spent testing helps ensure our friend gets the highest score of anyone here. I know I'll do my part. I hope you will do yours." Joaquin looked at Sage.

Robert stood up, shook Joaquin's hand, hugged him again, then said a few words of his own.

"All right, let's not make a big deal out of this. Joaquin is setting the example to follow. Everyone here should be testing day and night until this contest is over. You should all want me to win this thing real bad. If I don't, there will be unimaginable consequences. The Earth is in trouble without me, especially the people you know back home. You don't want anything happening to them, right?"

"No!" shouted the dinner guests.

"Good! That's what I like to see, a unified front. You're my army. I need you to win this war, okay!?" he screamed.

"Okay!"

"Now eat your dinner, you animals," he said laughing, then walked out of the room.

Four waiters came in carrying large, silver trays of food and placed them on the long, center table. They lifted the lids to the trays, revealing a wide assortment of tantalizing meats. There was every cut of beef, pork and chicken imaginable. Several smaller trays arrived with piping hot seasoned potatoes and steamed vegetables. Last came baskets of freshly baked, buttery biscuits. The waiters stood by the tapestries along the walls and watched the guests shovel food into their mouths like they'd just discovered this place after escaping famine in a desert.

Sage looked at the spectacle of gluttony around him and felt sick to his stomach. Everyone in the room was oblivious to one another, and completely fixated on the plate in front of them. Sage tapped Siddhartha on the shoulder.

"What's up?" said Siddhartha, through a mouth full of meat.

"My stomach hurts. I'm going back to the room to rest."

"Okay. Too bad though, this is one of the best meals yet!"

"I know, it looks delicious. I'll have to wait for the next one. See you later!"

"Okay, feel better my friend!"

Sage got up from his chair, and several guests turned to look at him with curious eyes, their mouths still working hard to chew the meat in them. He started walking towards the exit when he heard a familiar voice behind him.

"Hey, leaving so soon!?" It was Joaquin, holding a large drumstick in his right hand like a policeman's nightstick.

"Yeah, my stomach is a bit off right now. How's everything going Joaquin?"

"Everything's great. They told me you passed the tests too, then volunteered. We could sure use your help. Robert is a great guy. He deserves to rule."

"Joaquin, what makes you so sure?"

He looked at his friend like he'd just stabbed him through the heart.

"He's an incredible leader. Sage, he's going to be the next philosopher king. We have to help him or else..."

"Or else what? Don't you see what's really going on? Take a look around. This isn't right. Why are you helping them? They've got everyone under their control somehow. Joaquin! You've got to wake up from this! We need to find a way out and get help!"

A blank look was on Joaquin's face. He heard the words his best friend spoke to him, but they failed to penetrate the spell that was cast in his unconsciousness. His face turned angry.

"Fine! We don't need your help Sage. We've got a whole army here. These are the brightest people on the planet. We're going to get Robert the scores he needs to secure his spot at the top of the contest. When this month is over, he *will* be the new king. You'll regret not helping us. I feel sorry for you. You had so much potential. But I guess I'm not that surprised. It was always hard for you to make up your mind, wasn't it? Go handle your little tummy ache. I've got important things to do here. See you around."

Sage was speechless. His heart sank as he watched his best friend walk away. He'd never said such hurtful things to him in his whole life. Sage felt like bursting out in a loud scream but kept the emotion inside. His eyes began to water. He quickly left the refectory and found himself in another art-filled room. There was a nearby couch and he took a seat to compose himself. He knew the words Joaquin spoke were not his own. They were a computation, the effects of whatever implanted commands were inside his mind. Sage took a deep breath, then exhaled. He stood up from the couch and walked a little further, just past the room he was in.

There were voices coming from the next room. They were accompanied by the sounds of something striking loudly into something else. Sage stood by quietly, and listened. He made out two familiar voices.

"It's taking too long! Why haven't they scored high enough for me to be a contender!"

"I've told you this before son. The effects of the device are temporarily dulling them. Right now, they're not their usual selves. They're not going to be as bright as we want them to be at the beginning. It takes tremendous mental skill to pass those tests. Every last one them has passed them before, and they'll pass them again. We just need to give them time to adjust. Their analytical abilities will return shortly. There's plenty of time. The important thing isn't that you become a contender, the important thing is that you become king! So, please, for the love of god, stop questioning the process. Everything is working exactly how I planned it to." Dr. Masters plopped several billiard balls into place in a triangle rack on the pool table in front of him. He made sure the balls were straight, and ready to be hit, then removed the triangle.

His son Robert aimed at the balls with his pool stick, and hit the white billiard ball in front of him hard, sending it flying, and ultimately scattered the balls chaotically across the table.

"I'm tired of waiting! What am I supposed to do while these book worms stare in their glasses all day!?

"Why don't you do what you always do? Partake in something physical. Go for a run, ride one of your ATVs through the hills, swim in the ocean, or maybe just find something to hit, and keep hitting it until you can't hit it anymore, then come back the next day, and do it all over again."

"I'm tired of that! I want something more! I want to use my brain."

"You mean your mind."

"You know what I mean! I'm tired of always being behind. I know I'm not a doctor like you, and I haven't read all those books in your office, but I know I'm smart, just in a different way. I know I can learn some of the stuff these nerds know. We've got the best ones here. Why can't I have them teach me? Then, I can pass the tests on my own!"

"Go right ahead son! See where that gets you. I've hired the greatest instructors, the best tutors, paid for every course available to man, and you're still as thick headed as the day you were born! I'm only glad your mother isn't alive to see the lengths I have to go in order to make you happy."

"Screw you! Why don't you just make me a zombie too, huh? Go ahead, take that little pen out of your pocket and make me happy dad! Do it! You'll be doing both of us a favor! I'm sick of this!"

"*You're* sick of this!? I'm the one taking the stars out of the god damn sky for you!! And why?! Because someone says, it's the only way they'll ever be bigger than their old man! It's the only way to prove I really love you, right?! Well, here we are my secure son, right in the middle of your every dream come true. And now, you say, it's not enough!"

Robert slammed the pool stick in his hands over his knees, cracking it in half. He threw the pieces on the floor, at the feet of his father.

"You think these things were ever enough?! I want more than things! I want to walk down the street like a normal person, and have somebody see me, and say, hey, there goes Robert, he's a great guy! But they don't! And you want to know why?"

"Okay, why son?"

"That's just it, right there! I'm your son! You're like this giant shadow over me my whole life. *I'm* supposed to shine bright! *I'm* the sun! But here you come, something bigger, something darker, blocking me out, like a giant eclipse! My world's too dark and too cold with you standing in front of me. It's time you got behind me for once. The crown makes that happen. You'll have to listen to me then, everyone will."

"I hope you're right son. God knows everything else hasn't worked. No amount of toys ever made you happy."

"Toys? I've got enough for the whole world to play with. I want something no one can touch, not even you."

"You want to be smarter? Is that right?"

"Yeah! I want to know more than I do."

"Why, for heaven's sakes, don't you pick up a book then?"

"You know why! They never made any sense to me. I just look at the pages and my mind goes blank."

"You must have finished one at some point. I remember you read *Tom Sawyer* when you were younger. What about that?"

"I lied. I couldn't get past the first page."

"It wasn't as bad as all that, was it?"

"Don't you remember? You paid for all the teachers and tutors, but you also paid for them to keep passing me. I didn't learn anything worth knowing, except what money could do, and power. I've got enough money. You know what I need now dad."

"The same thing *I* need son. Don't worry, let these guests of ours do all the work. There's plenty of time for learning later. You may not be book smart, but you're smart enough."

"I'm going to get out of here. I'm going hit a few balls on the tennis court. Sorry about the pool stick."

"Think nothing of it. I've broken much worse."

Sage slipped away before Robert could see him. He watched the young man storm out, and wondered what to do about the troubled kid, but his father was the bigger problem at the moment. He thought about the pen he carried in his pocket. It must be how he was able to control everyone. Sage needed to get a hold of it, or find something that could stop it. There had to be a way to discover the technology Dr. Masters was using, study it, then stop it. He suddenly realized what he needed to do.

space meets energy

age was outside standing in front of La Casa Grande, looking out at the greenery and statues. The Pacific Ocean was in the far distance to his left, but he couldn't see it this time of day. A beautiful California night covered the castle estate and the stars were shining, as they were supposed to do. To add to their luminance, were dozens of light poles with rounded globe like bulbs scattered throughout the gardens and around the buildings. It was quite beautiful, as Hearst Castle always was, but seeing it at night like this was even more breathtaking than the excitement it mustered in the daylight.

He noticed someone sitting on a bench under a tree and walked over to them. As he got nearer, the figure began to wave to him. It was Ayanna, sitting with both legs crossed, in a Buddha pose. From afar it looked like she was emanating an orange light from her, like a glowing silhouette, or a painting of a Catholic saint. Sage got closer and the light coming from Ayanna dimmed, then vanished completely.

"Hey Sage! I'm happy to see you're out and about. You must be feeling much better," she said.

"Yeah, I am. Thanks for helping me earlier. You were in the right place at the right time."

"I go where I feel I'm needed. Will you sit with me for awhile?" She motioned at an empty space to her left. Sage gladly took her suggestion.

"Ayanna, I noticed you weren't at dinner. How come?"

"I was going to go in, but something kept me out here. I came here earlier to do some reading, but I wanted to do a little meditation too. Well, it's not exactly meditation, because I don't exactly think, or meditate on a question or a problem. Instead, I focus on nothing, or rather unfocus onto nothing, if that makes sense?"

"That's an interesting exercise. Why do you do that?"

"I don't know, it's just something I figured out recently. I was focused so much on everything going on in the world around me that it occurred to me how overwhelming it was. I mean, there's so much always going on. The world is filled with so much life, so many ideas, so many things. Before coming here, I was so consumed with knowing all about it, but I had to take a step back. I wondered, what if there's an opposite to everything?"

"You mean — nothing?"

"Exactly! The opposite of everything is nothing, so I decided I wanted to know about that too. It's funny, because I'm making nothing into something in a certain sense. I made it not be nothing anymore! Paradoxes are fascinating, aren't they?"

"Definitely, and they're a lot of fun."

"I thought you'd think so. You know, I could tell there was something different about you when we first met. Can I ask you a question Sage?"

"Of course, ask me anything."

"You aren't like everyone else here, right? You don't want to help Robert win."

"How did you know?"

"I knew it! I'm not like everyone else here too. They're all brainwashed or something. I haven't been able to figure it all out yet, but as far as I can figure, Dr. Masters must have taken us against our will. Even though we're free to walk around, we're really prisoners here. Don't you think so?"

"I overheard him talking to his son. Robert let it slip that he uses some kind of pen in his pocket. It must be a device, or a trigger that allows him to hypnotize people. I just need to figure out how it works so I can try to reverse its effects."

"That's so devious! But Sage, why do you think *we're* not hypnotized?"

"I think we were, but the effects have worn off to a large degree. There are certain things you can't remember, right? Like how you got here, and maybe what happened around that time?"

"Yeah! My memory has been a little fuzzy. I've been trying to get certain events straight in my mind, but so far I haven't been able to piece everything together."

"I know. The same thing is happening with me."

"It still doesn't explain why we're the only ones that aren't fully under this guy's spell. What makes us different? If we can figure that out, maybe we can help the others."

"That's logical reasoning."

Ayanna smiled, "I can't help it. It's the way my mind works."

"So, what makes us different? What do we share in common?"

"Are you on any medications? Have a special diet? Maybe it's something physical inside us? Could it be a shared DNA?"

"I'm not on any medications, and I don't have any special diet. How about you?"

"No, unless you count putting ketchup on popcorn. It makes it taste like french fries. Ever try it?"

Sage laughed, "No, I can't say that I have. Okay, what about DNA? How can we know about that?"

"Darn, if we were able to access everything on our interfaces, we could find that out in no time. I know all of those databases."

"What if it's something not physically inside our bodies that's making us less susceptible to the hypnosis?"

"What else could it be?"

"The human mind isn't exactly a tangible thing. Ideas, memories, dreams, these things are very elusive."

"What about shared experiences? Or similar education, or mindset? Could those be factors?"

"Possibly."

"Okay, let's explore them. I was born and raised in Los Angeles. My parents are both doctors, but they never forced the profession on me. I've always admired how doctors can help people when they're at their very worst. That's what motivated me to become a doctor at such an early age. I'm only 17. My education was like a lot of other people's. I didn't go anywhere fancy for school, but I did love to read. I read everything I could get my hands on. My teacher's used to call me Little Worm, because I was such a book worm. But most of the people here probably share that in common. I mean, how could you pass the crown qualifiers without reading a ton of books?"

"Uh, there's something I should tell you. Nobody here knows this, but I know I can trust you. It might sound a little crazy, but please just hear me out, okay?"

"Oooooh, this is exciting. I'm all ears. What is it?"

"I was never into reading books, until recently. They never seemed to make sense to me. I always thought they took too much time, and I would rather listen to someone read a book than ever touch one myself. I feel the complete opposite about books now, having read so many. I finally get the big deal about them. They make your imagination strong, they help your creativity take off, and make knowledge so much more vivid in your mind."

"Yep! I feel that way too. Books are amazing. Sorry, go on."

"Well, not long ago I was in a book store, searching for a gift for my... friend, when I came across this book that pulled my attention to it. I felt an uncontrollable urge to pick it up and open it. So, I did. Okay, here's the part that may sound a little crazy, but let me tell you, and if you don't believe me, I can do my best to prove what I'm about to say."

"You don't sound crazy at all, keep going."

"Okay, awesome. So, I pulled the book from the shelf, and it said *The Book of Space* on the front cover, but nothing else. When I opened it to take a closer look, an incredible amount of light shot out of it, and I could see all of these words, images, and symbols coming from it. There was an energy or power that flowed from the book into me. The light, and all the rest went away, but afterward I discovered I had a unique ability. I could touch a book, without even opening it, and instantly read it with full comprehension, almost as if I'd written it myself. I started touching and reading every book I could get my hands on. I've only had this power a short time, but I'm absolutely in love with books. I know so much now, Ayanna."

Sage looked at her, and waited with nervous eyes. Ayanna's face was strangely unemotional. She didn't say a word, but instead turned around to her right and reached for something in her bag. Her hands brought out a book, which she then extended out to Sage. There was a huge grin on her face, and Sage's eyes were as wide as watermelons.

"You're not the only crazy one around here," said Ayanna. "Go ahead, look at the title."

Sage felt the engraved lettering with his fingers, while he read the title out loud, "*The Book of Energy*."

"Does yours look like mine?"

"Yes! Everything's the same, except for the title. Ayanna, how did you get this!? Did it give you an ability like me!?"

"Well, my story's not that different. Except I was in a library, not a bookstore. I felt this magnetism, something drew me to this book. It glowed, and shot out this beautiful orange light everywhere. It was kind of like finding the sun trapped inside. Well, the energy traveled into me, and the next thing I knew..."

"What can you do?"

"I can sense and manipulate energy."

"What do you mean? How does that work?"

"It's a bit hard to describe. So much of it is connected to feeling. But basically, instead of words, I can read energy. I know how to differentiate the various kinds of energy there are, how much of it there is at any given time, and I can cause it to do things. I can make energy move in a particular direction."

Sage leaned in closer to her, mesmerized by her words, and found himself drawn to her lips. His mouth was nearly at hers when she smiled.

"Do you see what I mean? Sorry for such a rudimentary example, but it demonstrates it doesn't it? You felt me, didn't you?"

The embarrassed look on his face would have been answer enough, but he said, "Yeah, I did. Sorry, I didn't mean to..."

"It's okay. I know you didn't. *I* did. That's the point."

"Can you make someone do whatever you want, like Dr. Masters does with hypnosis?"

"No, it doesn't work like that. What he does is completely evil. I don't control people — I can't. I can only move their energy. It's energy they've already created." She looked at his face turning red. "Oh, no, please don't feel embarrassed. We're both young, about the same age. You're a guy, I'm a girl. It's only natural we might have a little of those feelings. I just took some of that energy, and moved it. Does that make sense?"

"Yeah, I guess it does. It's a bit unnerving, but pretty incredible at the same time."

"Cool. If it helps, I have some of those feelings too. You just can't feel mine, the way I feel yours."

He smiled, feeling a stronger connection to Ayanna. It made him at ease, and he felt safe with her. She smiled back at him and said, "Do you want to know something else?"

"Tell me anything you want to tell me."

"Everything is made of energy, not just people. I can feel it all. This tree, that statue, the tile on the floor, even the dirt underneath the tile, and all the layers of rocks, and the minerals under the dirt, all the way to the core in the middle of the Earth. Every particle in the universe is moving, even if it's imperceptible to us. My power lets me feel the vibrations, the buzzing the world is doing. It's really exhilarating."

"I'll bet. What an amazing gift. Is there anything else you can tell me about your powers, or the book?"

"Not really. I mean my abilities are still kind of new to me. I'm sure there's stuff I'm forgetting, but you get the basic gist of it. I wish I knew more about the book, but I have no clue. The only thing written on it is the title. The pages are blank."

"Just like mine. But at least now we know something we didn't know before."

"What's that?"

"We have something pretty big in common, and it's probably why we're the only ones with most of our mental capacities around here."

"You think our abilities make it harder for us to stay hypnotized?"

"It looks that way. I'm just amazed any of us were able to be hypnotized at all. From what I've read, most people are not susceptible to hypnosis. And, being intelligent should make the odds of it even that much slimmer. So, whatever technology Dr. Masters is using must be pretty powerful."

"How do we find out what it is?"

"He has an office somewhere. There must be information about it there. If I can just get in there without him knowing, I can learn everything about what he's using, and hopefully find a way to stop him."

"I know where his office is! It's on the third floor, right there in the main house. They took me there when I first got here. It was part of their orientation. I think they wanted to impress us, and his office is definitely impressive, it's like a church in there.

Sage! There's a ton of books! Maybe there's something in them that can help us."

"Sounds like it. Is the office easy to find? Do you remember how to get there?" "It's simple, it's pretty much the center piece to the entire third floor. I'm telling you, it's huge. You can't miss it."

"Perfect, all we need to do is make sure he's not around when we're there."

"I know the perfect time to do it! Everyone goes to the movie theater after dinner. It's required. Last night they showed us..."

"...*The Wizard of Oz*? Siddhartha told me. I must have been sleeping then, or not here yet, I still don't remember. But, yeah, that's perfect. Wait, won't they notice we're gone?"

"We can show up, then slip out. It'll be dark in there."

"Sounds like a plan."

There were footsteps coming from one of the walkways down below. The sound of shoes on the hard tile floors was unmistakeable in the dark.

"Sage, you need to trust me, just play along with me for a bit here, okay?"

"Sure, but what's wrong?"

Ayanna grabbed Sage's hand, placed it around her waist, and leaned in and started passionately kissing him. He was confused for the first few moments of her bold move, until he felt her gently guiding him. Sage found himself pulling her closer, and kissing her in a way he'd never kissed Robin. He wondered if it was Ayanna's power over energy that made it feel this way, or if it was simply how it felt with her. Time slowed down, and the whole world seemed a universe away.

Ayanna's eyes were closed as she kissed Sage, but she opened them ever so slightly to see if her plan worked. She saw Robert a short distance away, watching them. His face was red and there were wrinkles across the top of his forehead as he scowled at them hatefully. There was a tightening of his muscles, and a clenching of his fists. Ayanna knew he wanted to walk over to them and break them apart, but he couldn't. The jealousy in his face was evident to her, but she could feel every other emotion from him as his energy boiled. She concentrated on it. A difficult thing to do presently, because she was also concentrated on the energy emanating between her and Sage. With the graceful skill of a tightrope walker, she managed to manipulate Robert into walking away towards the main building. When Robert was gone, she slowly lifted her lips from Sage's mouth, then waited for him to open his eyes.

"I'm so sorry Sage. I hope that was okay. It felt like the thing to do at the time. Please don't hate me."

He smiled at her and said, "Yeah, it's definitely okay. But, what just happened exactly?"

"It was Robert. He's been such a creep to me. He likes me. Not in the usual way either. I'm a girl, I'm used to guys staring, or giving sideways glances, but this is different. He has these stalker vibes he gives off. It's like something out of a scary movie. I needed him to think I'm not alone here. I hope that's all right. I don't mean to put you in the middle of this, but he honestly scares me. I think seeing us together will make him ease off."

"I get it. I hope he does. That can't be easy to experience."

"It's not. I've tried so many times, in so many different ways, but he hasn't left me alone, until he did just now. So thank you."

She reached in towards Sage and kissed him again.

"What was that for? Did he come back?" he asked.

"No, that was just for me," she said smiling.

"Oh. There's something I should tell you Ayanna," said Sage.

"You're with someone already, aren't you?"

"Yeah."

"I knew that was a possibility. A handsome, smart guy like you was bound to be taken. Just my luck."

"I'm sorry Ayanna. If it makes you feel better, I enjoyed the heck out of kissing you. I can't deny I feel something between us, even now. But is it real, or something you're making happen?"

"I haven't..."

The main entrance to La Casa Grande swung open loudly. Dr. Masters appeared in front of it. His son Robert was pointing in their direction. Sage and Ayanna rose from the bench.

"Movie time! If anyone's out there, it's movie time!"

Sage and Ayanna walked towards the front of the building, smiling at Dr. Masters.

"Oh, good! Glad you both could make it. Hurry in, you won't want to miss this!"

Ayanna led Sage through the beautifully lit assembly room, past the refectory, where a dozen of the service staff were busy clearing the long dinner table, past the billiard room, where a couple of elder gentlemen were playing a game of nine ball and smoking cigars, until at last they came to the movie theater.

The theater was packed, and nearly every seat in the place was full. Sage could see Siddhartha, sitting in the front, holding a bucket of popcorn, eagerly awaiting the start of tonight's film. The atmosphere in the large space was jovial and light hearted. Many of the guests were laughing, a few were yawning, more ready for bed than a two hour motion picture, and the rest were quiet, but alert.

"Let's sit here in the back, it'll be easier to slip out," said Ayanna.

The two of them sat down in the far right of the last row of seating. Dr. Masters and Robert walked in. They took a couple of seats in the front row. Sage could see Joaquin sitting next to them there.

The lights flickered, then Dr. Masters stood up.

"Thank you for joining us this evening! Tonight's film is another classic from the 20th century. The same century this glorious castle was built. I hope you enjoy this one. Ladies and gentlemen, I give you Charlie Chaplin in *Modern Times*!"

"Siddhartha must have requested it. He loves Chaplin," Sage whispered into Ayanna's ear. It felt nice being so close to her, but Sage knew he should keep a certain distance as well, out of respect for his relationship with Robin. He also needed to stay focused on the task at hand.

Ayanna leaned in to Sage's ear and whispered back, "I've seen this one, it's hilarious. Let's watch the first few minutes, then we can get away."

Sage could feel her breath traveling down his ear. "Okay," he replied.

The picture began to play and music blared through the sound system, echoing throughout the theater. The opening credits appeared, listing the names of those responsible for making the film, and then a crowd of pigs came onto the screen. The pigs were crowded together, trying to get somewhere. Suddenly, the film cut to human workers hurrying to their factory jobs. A huge, strong man pulled a lever, and a leisurely man in a suit turned some knobs, flicked some switches, and made everyone in the factory go into action. Soon, the star of the film appeared — The Tramp, played by Charlie Chaplin.

The Tramp is working on an assembly line with a conveyor belt. He uses his tools and tries desperately to keep up with the pace of the fast moving line he's on. His pantomime gestures were exaggerated and ridiculous. Everything he did made the audience in the theater laugh, including Sage and Ayanna.

Sage whispered in her, "Should we go now?"

"Not just yet, one of the best scenes is about to happen. They're going to bring out the feeding machine!"

The men that run the factory bring out a machine that looks more like a torture device than a feeding machine, and they force The Tramp to sit in it. Strapped in tight, a series of mechanical arms attempt to feed the poor man, and the gadgets each prove to be a disastrous failure. Sage couldn't help but laugh loudly. He feared he might be calling too much attention to himself, but he couldn't help it. Eventually, the scene ended, but Sage knew there were plenty more funny moments coming.

"Okay, we can go now," whispered Ayanna.

While everyone in the theater was laughing, they slipped away unnoticed. They were soon in an elevator headed to the third floor. It was cramped in the tiny elevator, and they could feel each other's arm pressed close. Sage felt his hand moving to hold Ayanna's, but he resisted the temptation. It was like trying to pull apart a large magnet from a metal surface. He wondered if Ayanna was contributing to the pull he felt towards her, or if it was genuine attraction. It wouldn't be hard to imagine. She was quite literally the most beautiful girl he'd ever seen. But, he had history with Robin. His feelings for her went as far back as he could remember. Were those feelings just as strong now that he'd met Ayanna? He wasn't sure.

The elevator doors opened, and they made their way to Masters' office. It was truly magnificent, even more so than the library. The office was a huge Gothic study, with unforgettable arches filled with intricate medieval artwork. The religious themes were everywhere, and the entire room looked more like a church than a place of learning. There were several tables, many wooden chairs, and plenty of lamps to give the room a beautiful glow.

"I'll get started on the books. Why don't you see what else you can find? Try to find any papers in drawers, or places that might have files in them," said Sage.

"Okay, I'm going to the opposite end, I think that's where his desk is, around that wall."

Sage went into reading mode, systematically tackling book by book, shelf by shelf, moving from left to right, down one side of the room. He noticed immediately a major difference in the books he was reading. They were mostly from the current century, many of them within the last decade. Practically all of them were science based. There were books on neurology, psychology, biology, chemistry, pharmacology, physics, engineering, and electronics. Sage was surprised by how many books the doctor had on electronics, but after reading his extensive section on mental health and the mind, he understood why. He began making connections between the subjects and between the books. It didn't take him long to finish both sides of the room, and to figure out what Dr. Masters might have built, and how he built it.

Sage could hear Ayanna shuffling papers behind the wall, on the other side of the study, and he went to see her. She was standing in front of a massive desk, trying to make sense of what she was looking at. In her hands were what appeared to be mechanical blueprints, dozens of diagrams, and possibly hundreds of patents.

"His name is at the bottom of every one of these," she said. "He must have spent a lifetime developing all of this. I can't make heads or tails of hardly any of it. What about you?" Ayanna handed some of the papers to Sage, who smiled immediately.

"How many more are there?"

"Look, all of these cabinets are full of paperwork."

"Perfect, give me a few minutes."

"It's all yours. Have at 'em."

Sage went to work, touching every file, every piece of paper, every notebook. When he was done he looked out the window down at the estate grounds, and then looked up, wondering if he could see the ocean from where he was. It was still hidden in the night.

"Well, what did you learn?" asked Ayanna.

"He's discovered too much. He's spent practically his entire life here — in this room! He's developed technology that threatens everything. What he did with the stars, and bringing us here, it's just the beginning Ayanna. He wants to subjugate humanity and take away our free will. And he can do it — I've seen it."

"How do we stop him?"

"After looking at everything here, I'm not sure we can... I'm not sure anyone can."

"Sage, you can't be serious. You're scaring me."

"I'm sorry Ayanna. When I was in the other room, I felt like I was putting together pieces of a jigsaw puzzle. A really simple one, with not too many pieces. And I thought I had the picture on the box guiding me the whole way, but then..."

"But then what?"

"Then I came into this part of his study and found out I wasn't working on a puzzle at all. Masters has been working on his plan since he was a boy. And there's not much time left to stop him. Everything was set in motion when he made the stars disappear. It was the first big domino to fall, but there's so many more coming."

"So, that was him!? How did he make the stars disappear?"

"He didn't make them disappear in actuality. He made our ability to see them disappear."

"But the stars came back, why would he let us see them again? Why not let us go on thinking they weren't there?"

"He's indoctrinating us towards insanity."

"What?"

"That's why he wants his son to be the next philosopher king. He knows the damage he'll do. He fathered him, and raised him for the sole purpose of doing it."

"That's crazy!"

"Ayanna, it's only the beginning of what he's got in store for humanity. I know what I said earlier, about doubting anyone can stop him, but we have to try anyway. I'm going to need some time to think. I have to really process everything. For the first time since I got this power, some things aren't so easy to comprehend."

"Okay, let's put everything back where we found it and get out of here."

They carefully placed every file, paper, and notebook back in its proper place. When they were done, they looked one last time to make sure nothing was out of place. Satisfied, they made their way through the length of the study, and headed back to where they first entered the doctor's sanctuary.

"Hold on Sage, stop," Ayanna whispered to him. "Someone's coming. We need to hide."

Sage looked around, and spotted a place they could remain hidden. They were quickly obscured to whoever was coming their way. Both held their breath, and tried not to make the slightest noise. Any sound they made could easily echo and carry throughout the study. Their quiet breaths and pounding hearts were the only things that might give them away, but fortunately they were drowned out by two others walking directly by them, both much louder.

"I need it ready by the end of the night. We're going to plug them all into it tomorrow morning. How much more needs to be done?" asked Dr. Masters.

"I only have the calibration tests left to perform. Those shouldn't take more than an hour. It'll all be ready by morning."

"Excellent, I knew I could count on you Christopher!"

"Dr. Masters, I've been working straight through the entire day. Would it be all right if I have something to eat before I finish setting everything up?"

"Mr. Oakley, do I have to remind you what happens if you don't comply with my wishes?"

"No, please Dr. Masters. Forget I said anything, I'll get to the tests right away. I don't need to eat anything tonight. I can have something tomorrow."

"I'm going to need you tomorrow. There's too much for you to do."

Christopher Oakley looked down at his stomach, wanting to touch it, but decided against it. Instead, his stomach growled and he looked up at Dr. Masters, scared.

"Mr. Oakley! Are you trying to make me feel sorry for you?! Do you think I can possibly feel guilt over not feeding you? Ha, ha! You're such a simpleton, you know that? You really don't know me at all, do you?"

"No, I don't Dr. Masters. I apologize."

"Listen Oakley. I couldn't care less about your stomach, your needs, your PhD from M.I.T., your job at Earth City, or any of the other useless things connected to your feeble existence. You're Pinocchio. You are nothing more than a puppet I make move. You're not alive. You're not a real boy. Do you understand that?"

"Yes, Dr. Masters. I understand."

"Now, that's better. As long as you can stand, and move those arms around to work, you've no reason to eat. Trust me, I'll throw more wood into the fire if I see it's about to die. You don't want to die, do you Mr. Oakley?"

He hesitated to answer.

"I have to repeat myself, do I? — You don't want to die, do you Mr. Oakley?!"

"I don't want to die."

"I thought so. Now get back to work. I'm tired of looking at you."

Christopher Oakley, one of the top computer engineers on the planet, a top expert on cryptography and information systems, walked out of Dr. Masters' office with blood shot eyes and wobbling knees. He headed straight back to his work.

Dr. Masters walked to his desk and sat down. He reached into his coat pocket and pulled out a pair of interface glasses, then placed the glasses over his eyes and moved his right hand across the space in front of him. His fingers swiped several times, then he leaned back in his chair with his hands folded into each other. There was a big grin across his face.

"Are you there? Good, always keep this line open. I need an update on the contest. Where are we at with the contenders? Have there been any additions? Okay, good. That's better than I thought. At this rate, we'll have the whole thing locked up in a matter of days, maybe sooner. Okay... what are they up to? Hmmmm, all right, that's not a problem. But keep an eye on them regardless. Listen, we're ahead of the curve. There's no way we can lose our hold on this thing..."

Sage and Ayanna quietly left the third floor and made their way to the nearest stairwell. Before taking the stairs down, Ayanna remembered Sage's injuries, and put her hand out to stop him from going down.

"Maybe we should take the elevator. You might have a tough time going down these," she whispered.

"No, I'll be okay. I've taken them before. Plus, do you really want to take the chance with the elevator? It'll make too much noise. It's also old. What if it gets stuck while we're inside?"

Ayanna thought about it, and said, "You're right. Although, I wouldn't mind being stuck in an elevator with you."

Sage smiled, then said, "Sounds like a plan. Let's get out of here."

They made their way down the steps one floor without anyone seeing them. The building was quiet, but they could hear distant voices and faint footsteps somewhere on the other side of the castle.

"This is the second floor. We're right by the library. Your room should be somewhere on this side, right?" said Ayanna.

"Yeah, why don't you come in for a bit? I want to show you something."

"Okay, lead the way," she said, smiling.

They walked the short distance to his room. It was empty. "Siddhartha must still be in the theater with the others," said Sage. "Make yourself at home. I'm going to grab something." He walked over to his dresser, and Ayanna sat down on his bed. By the time Sage found what he was looking for, she was comfortably laying across the entire bed with her eyes closed.

"Ayanna?" he said, trying to get her attention.

"Yeah?" she replied in a tired voice, her eyes still closed.

"Are you about to fall asleep?"

"Uh huh. Is that okay? I didn't realize I was so tired."

"No problem, go ahead. You can sleep here."

"You're the best. You can join me, there's enough room."

"Don't worry about me. I'm not tired yet."

"Okay, suite yourself. Goodnight."

Sage walked over to a nearby chair and sat down in it. *The Book of Space* was in his lap, and he opened it and flipped through its pages, one by one. He thought it was possible that maybe he missed something. Was it possible the book contained some other hidden truth he had overlooked? While he turned each page, he thought about what he'd learned in Dr. Masters' office. His plans were terrifying, and something had to be done about them. Sage wondered what it must have been like to live as the doctor had lived, isolated in this castle for most of his life, trying to conquer a world you were never really a part of, but only viewed from a distance. Was it loneliness that led Dr. Masters to turn his back on humanity? How do you defeat an enemy that's already dead inside? Sage continued to pose questions, and sorted through potential answers. His thoughts ran rampant as he flipped the pages in front of him. Like Ayanna, he eventually grew too tired. While still sitting in his chair, he closed his eyes and fell asleep. *The Book of Space* lay open on his lap.

CONTENDERS ASSEMBLE

When Sage opened his eyes again it was the next morning. The sun rays came in slowly through the windows and a cool breeze blew into the room. He was still sitting in the same chair from last night, and his body was stiff from sleeping there. He looked around the room and saw Ayanna asleep in his bed with her arms around a pillow, and a peaceful look was on her face. In the next bed over, Siddhartha was in a deep sleep. There were small pieces of popcorn scattered across his blanket, and a nearly empty popcorn bucket lay on its side on the night stand next to his bed.

Sage stretched his arms and yawned. He felt an emptiness near him, then touched his lap. He scrambled out of his chair and looked on the floor. *The Book of Space* was nowhere near him. He went over to the dresser, thinking it might be possible that he put it away in the middle of the night. But the book wasn't in the dresser, or in his book bag. Walking around the room, he searched further, including around Ayanna and Siddhartha, thinking maybe one of them might have it, but everywhere he looked he couldn't find the book. Feeling defeated, he fell back into his chair, closed his eyes, and thought about where his book might be. Was it possible it just disappeared? It magically came into his life, so the idea of it disappearing from it wasn't a stretch of the imagination. Or was it something more simple?

Ayanna started to move, twisting her body around towards Sage. He turned to look at her. Her eyes were open, staring at him affectionately.

"What's wrong?" she asked.

"Why do you think there's something wrong?" replied Sage.

"I can feel your energy. It's off. You're trying to figure something out."

"It's my book. I was going to show it to you, so I had it out. But then I fell asleep, and when I woke up it was gone."

"Oh snap. You think someone was in here and took it?"

"It's definitely possible. I was out cold."

"Me too." She turned to look at Siddhartha, who was still sleeping in the next bed. "What about him?"

"I don't think he has it. I've looked everywhere in the room. It's not here."

"Wait, I need to check my bag. What if mine's gone too?"

She reached under the bed and lifted her bag up. She opened it, looked inside, and she felt her heart sink into the pit of her stomach. "Sage! It's gone too!"

"Really?! I forgot you had yours with you."

"Maybe we should start looking around the castle. Someone must have them. We can go room by room."

"I don't know how useful that would be. If someone took them, they're probably going to keep them hidden."

"*If* someone took them? It had to be someone taking them. What else could it be? You don't think they just disappeared do you?"

"The idea's not that crazy, especially when you compare it to what we've seen and heard over the last several days."

"So what do we do?"

"There's not much we can do. We just keep our eyes open and try to move and act like it's business as usual. We're here to help Robert. That's the important thing."

"Huh?" She saw Sage giving her a look, so she turned to see Siddhartha starting to wake up. He got out of bed and pieces of popcorn fell from his blanket onto the floor. He yawned with his mouth wide open, then turned to Sage and Ayanna.

"Sorry guys. I hope my snoring didn't bother you last night. You were both asleep when we came in, so maybe it didn't wake you. Oh man, I slept good. The movie last night was the perfect night cap to a wonderful evening."

"Siddhartha, you said we were asleep when 'we' came in. Did you come in with someone else last night?" asked Sage.

"Oh, yes. Joaquin and Robert were kind enough to walk me to my room. I felt so tired after such a big meal and so much popcorn. I was about to fall asleep in the theater but my friends came to my rescue. They made sure I got into bed and even tucked me in!"

"Did they stay long? Did you see them leave?"

"I don't remember. I fell asleep as soon as my head hit the pillow. Why do you ask? Is something wrong?"

"No, Siddhartha. Nothing is wrong. Thanks for letting us know. I'm glad you got back safe."

Ayanna got up from Sage's bed, then put her bag over her shoulder. She looked at Sage and said, "We should get ready for the day. I'm going back to my room to shower. Meet you back here in half an hour? We can grab some breakfast together."

Sage smiled. "That sounds great, see you here in 30."

Ayanna left for her room on the other side of the building. Sage went into the bathroom and showered. He tried not to wet his bandages, but they proved impossible to keep dry so near a constant flow of water. When he walked out of the shower he stood in front of the mirror, examining his wet bandages. They were sliding off, so he pulled them off of him completely. He tossed them in the small trash basket near the sink, and touched his injuries. Surprisingly, they weren't too bad. Sage finished drying himself, then changed into a new set of clothes.

Siddhartha was laying on his bed staring at the ceiling. Sage looked at him with curiosity. "Is everything all right? How are you feeling Siddhartha?"

"I'm fine. I was just thinking about the movie from last night. I've seen it before, but last night was a different experience. It must have been the special atmosphere. Imagine watching one of Chaplin's films in a theater he must have sat and watched films in. About half way through the film, I felt so happy. I think everyone else must have felt it too, because I turned to look and the entire theater was smiling. You know, I don't remember seeing you or Ayanna. Were you at the showing?"

"We were sitting in the back. You were all the way towards the front."

"Oh, that explains it. Well, I'm sure you must have felt the magic that we all felt in that moment."

"Which moment was that?"

"When he was roller skating. He was so close to falling over the edge, and he kept going around in circles, again and again."

"Oh, um, yes. That was quite a moment. Say, Siddhartha, what's the protocol for getting breakfast? Do we eat every meal in the refectory?"

"No, only dinner. Although many of the guests do prefer eating down there for every meal. I'm going there myself shortly. But, you can call and someone will bring you whatever you want."

"I think I'll do that. They can bring me some new bandages as well."

"Good idea. I'm going to take a shower now. Shout, if you need anything."

"Okay, thanks."

Sage picked up the phone. It still felt awkward, but he was getting used to it.

"Hello, I need new bandages for my injuries. Can someone bring them along with breakfast? Uh, huh. Well, I don't know. Could you bring an assortment? Enough for two people? Okay, awesome. Thank you." He hung up, then sat in the same chair he slept in the night before. He imagined Robert walking over to him quietly and slipping the book carefully out of his hands. Did Joaquin see him take it? He knew he wasn't himself anymore. None of the others were. It was imperative that he find a way to break the hypnotic spell that was cast over his best friend, and everyone else affected. There was always a solution to every problem. He just needed to keep looking.

Siddhartha finished with his shower, dressed, and said goodbye to his roommate before leaving for the refectory to eat breakfast. Sage was thankful for the quiet room, and time alone to think. He kept running through scenarios, evaluating data, and revisited some key stable datums he could use to tackle the problems he was facing. The solution seemed to be within his grasp, but he couldn't quite grab hold of it.

Ayanna came to the door and knocked. "Everyone decent in there?" she asked.

"Yes, it's just me. Come on in."

"Where's Siddhartha?"

"He went to have breakfast in the refectory. We can eat here. I called for them to bring us some food. I hope that's okay. I didn't think you'd want to join the others. This way we get a little extra time to talk."

"No, that's perfect. There's a lot we need to discuss."

Another knock came at the door. This time it was the castle service staff. They brought in two large trays of food, one hot, one cold. The hot tray was filled with scrambled eggs, bacon, sausage, homestyle potatoes, and toast. The cold tray was filled with strawberries, blackberries, blueberries, cantaloupe, peach slices, grapes, and walnuts. They left a small first aid kit full of bandages, gauze, and anything else Sage needed to properly care for his wounds.

After the service staff left, Ayanna opened the first aid kit and helped place new bandages on Sage's shoulder and abdomen. It didn't take her long. They were soon enjoying breakfast together, starting with some fruit, then moving onto some bacon and eggs.

"Can you tell me more about what you learned last night? What exactly are we facing Sage? What has Dr. Masters invented?"

"He's invented many things, but the main thing he did was develop a technology he calls implantation. He's able to harness the power of energy waves to carry hypnotic messages. There are numerous ways he can deploy these messages to implant ideas and execute his plans. He can basically get anyone to do anything, but there are certain limitations."

"What kind of limitations?"

"Well, he's able to send out a massive implant across the planet, but doing so requires a perfect, but rare set of factors that do not occur often at all. He calls this set of factors equilibrium events. He was able to take advantage of one such event when he made everyone believe the stars were gone. But, these equilibrium events are extremely rare, and we won't see another one for twenty years."

"That's good news!"

"Yes, and the global implant only lasts a short time. One to two days maximum."

"That's awesome! This gets better and better."

"But, there's more. If he gets easier access to Earth's experimental energy resources, he can use them to make his implants permanent. Then, it's game over. The world will be mind controlled by him for as long as he wants. There would be no fading away. The effects would be practically irreversible."

"Practically? So, is there some way to reverse them, if it got to that?"

"Well, there would have to be people who were not implanted that could attempt an erasure. But they would need to have some way of blocking the energy waves carrying the implants. If they had that, they could help everyone else, but no matter what, they'd need to erase all of the messages. The only way to do that would be to know what they were. I'm sure that could be figured out, but it would take time."

"So, let me get this straight. Masters can turn everyone into his slaves if his son becomes king, because he'll gain access to resources he needs to make his puppet master dreams come true?"

"Uh, huh."

"And the only way to keep from being a slave is to block energy waves?"

"Yeah. If we can just figure out a way to block the energy waves of his technology, then we'll have a chance."

"What if we didn't block the waves at all? What if we altered them?"

"You mean change them?"

"Yes."

"That would be incredible. I'm not sure how we would do it though."

"It's easy, I can already do it. When the stars disappeared, I felt a wave come, and I changed it. It dissipated around me rather than hitting me. When the whole thing was over I was the same, but everyone else was caught up in hysteria. For me, I could still see the stars like I always did."

"Well, that's amazing. But how do we get your ability to everyone else? It must work the same way my book does. I touched it and it gave me power, but I've seen others touch it, and nothing happens to them. So how do you get people to alter an energy wave?"

"With different energy."

"You mean hit the wave with another wave?"

"Basically, yes. I've been observing and feeling energy with tremendous detail for awhile now. Energy is not static. It moves and shifts constantly. If these implant messages are carried on energy waves, then we can alter their trajectory, slow down their effectiveness, or even obliterate them all together. We just need the right combination of energy."

"You're right, but what combination?"

"That's where it gets a little tricky. There are literally millions of possible combinations. Imagine how many different sources of energy there are on the planet. Then imagine combining them with one or more of each other. It would take a lot of experimentation. There must be a ton of research done on this already though. We just have to look and find out which combinations are the most powerful and are capable of disrupting the type of waves Masters might be using."

"Ayanna, you're a genius! I've read a ton of Masters' writings and there *has* been research done in this area, some of it by Masters himself. He didn't have any of the research documents or reports in his study, but there were mentions of it. If we can access the research, we might be able to counteract his implantation technology."

"But we can't get online. We've been locked out of our interfaces since we've been here."

"I don't know. There's got to be a manual, hardline connection to the rest of the world somewhere on the estate. Or maybe Dr. Masters', or Robert's glasses are still patched through to the system. There's got to be a way to do it."

"If we can get online, we need to immediately call the authorities, call home, send word to everyone about what's happening."

"Definitely. We'll do that first for sure, but if I get the chance to look at that research, I'm going to read it. There's no telling what could happen when the authorities come for us. Masters might be able to control them when they arrive."

"You're right. This is a nightmare. We need to get as much information as we can, and look everywhere we can on the estate. Maybe some of the service staff aren't hypnotized, and they could help us."

"No, I'm sure he's covered his bases with them. Just think about how he treated that tech expert Oakley."

"Yeah, Masters has this whole place under his thumb. It's a shame we're the only ones free."

"Don't worry, we'll find a way. We have to, otherwise the Earth is about to turn into a planet of mental zombies. We can't let that happen."

"I'm done with breakfast. Let's get moving. What do we do first?"

"What I would love to do is to explore as many rooms in this building as possible, and then look in the other buildings. But, we should go with the others for awhile first. If we don't make an appearance, we might draw too much attention to ourselves. We need everyone to believe we're just like them. They need to think we're here to help Robert pass the tests to be king."

"Yeah, that makes sense. But as soon as we're able to, let's slip away and see what else we can discover. And no matter what, we need to find our books."

"Definitely."

***

The assembly room on the first floor of the main house was crowded with guests, but at the same time, the large extravagant sitting room was a comfortable place for them all to gather. There were big, soft chairs, as well as an enormous fireplace to keep everyone warm during the cold morning. A marvelous Italian Renaissance ceiling hung over their heads, while centuries old European tapestries displayed scenes of people not unlike themselves. They too were participating in unforgettable scenes, their drama forever tied to art.

A group of older women sat talking in a cluster about the laws of gravity, while a similar group of older men sat on the opposite side of the room talking about the laws of thermodynamics. There were many middle aged guests sitting by themselves with their interface glasses on, signaling in the air with their hands as if they were conducting an orchestra. Most of the younger guests were on their interfaces as well, but their hand motions looked more like punching or slapping.

Sage and Ayanna walked into the part of the room closest to the older men discussing thermodynamics. As they walked by, Ayanna couldn't help hearing their heated debate on energy.

"Remember Frank, the first law of thermodynamics is that energy cannot be created or destroyed!"

"Well, that may be all well and true, but I still hold to my hypothesis," replied Frank.

"But, why? There's nothing that will come of it? Spend your time on other pursuits. Science is such a big space. Don't waste your time on one theoretical corner of it."

"You're right, space is very big. So where I go in it shouldn't be of any matter to you Johnson!"

"Oh, don't be so sensitive! I was only trying to help point you in a more fruitful direction," answered Johnson.

Frank picked up an apple from a nearby bowl, then said, "Like always, I can find my own fruit." He took a big bite out of the apple. "It's very tasty too, I might add."

The men all laughed together, big hearty laughs that echoed throughout the room. Sage was laughing too, but Ayanna had a serious look on her face, waited for the laughter to die down, and asked Johnson, "Do you really think it's impossible to create energy?"

Johnson turned to her, surprised, along with the rest of the gray haired men. He cleared his throat, straightened his back, then said, "Young miss, I absolutely do. The laws of thermodynamics have been around longer than this castle."

"That doesn't make them true. Age is no guarantee of truth," replied Ayanna. The men loved her snarky answer, and went, "Ooooooooo," at Johnson, laughing, and stomping their feet.

"Young lady, age may be no guarantee, but laws are laws for a reason. They are immutable, everlasting, and etched in stone."

"By an etcher. But who etched him?"

"Well, it always comes to this, now doesn't it? Are you religious, miss? Whether it's the chicken or the egg, they're both delicious on my plate," said Johnson, laughing.

"Well your plate is pretty bare the longer I get to observe it. You look practically starved for ideas. Goodbye, gentlemen," said Ayanna, who walked away. The men's laughter was at a fever pitch, especially Frank's. He nearly choked on his apple, and tiny pieces of it sprayed out of his mouth and onto Johnson's leg. Johnson wiped the wetness from his pant leg with a cloth napkin and added one last, and barely audible comment, "I don't know what's so funny. Science is serious business."

Sage and Ayanna walked through the assembly room, looking for a place to sit, and found a couple of empty wooden seats along the wall. As soon as they sat down they noticed Robert and

Joaquin sitting not far from them. They were each reading books while seated at a long table.

"Sage! They've got our books!"

"Hold on. Ayanna, we can't make a scene. Let them look. They won't be able to use them. They're just looking at blank pages, right?"

"You're right, but we should confront them. They can't just take what doesn't belong to them."

"Okay, but let me take the lead. Joaquin's my best friend. I think I can still reach him."

"All right, let's go."

Sage and Ayanna walked over to where Robert and Joaquin were sitting, and looked down at them. The two young men looked up from the stolen books.

"What in the world?!" said Ayanna.

"What are you two doing here?" asked Joaquin.

"Yeah, what do you want? Don't you see we're busy?" replied Robert.

Sage and Ayanna were both staring at the open books on the table. The pages of both books were filled with words. It was a jarring sight for them both.

"Those are our books. They went missing sometime last night after we fell asleep in my room," said Sage, looking at Joaquin.

Joaquin looked at his best friend with annoyance. "Sage, we need to do whatever it takes to help Robert become king. Don't you agree?"

"Yes, but what does that have to do with our books?" asked Sage.

"It has everything to do with it. You see, I wondered how it was that my best friend, although smart in his own way, but who always hated reading, could suddenly pass the crown qualifiers. I thought there must be some kind of secret or trick behind why you're here, so I poked around, and noticed this," said Joaquin, holding up *The Book of Space*.

"When I showed it to Robert he said it looked exactly like the book Ayanna kept in her bag so secretively. So we grabbed her book too. Don't you think it's okay we took them, if they might have any advantage to helping Robert secure his rightful place on the throne?" asked Joaquin.

Sage and Ayanna looked at one another. They knew they couldn't argue against Joaquin's reasoning.

"You could have asked us," said Sage.

"Why? Time is of the essence. We need as much of it as we can get if we're going to succeed. You're taking valuable time from us now. Don't you see Robert and I are studying?"

"Yes, you're right. Is there any way we can help? After all, we're familiar with the books," replied Sage.

"Now, that's the spirit. Okay, what can you tell us about these books?" asked Joaquin.

"Do you mind if I take a quick glance?"

"Not at all," said Joaquin, handing the book to Sage.

Sage held the book in his hands, and felt a nervous excitement about what might be inside the pages. When he opened the book, much to his surprise, the pages were suddenly blank again. After flipping through several pages, Sage gave up and handed the book back to Joaquin.

"Well, the book is difficult to summarize. How have you found it to be? Are there any topics that are confusing?" asked Sage, trying to recover.

"No, I think it's the opposite of confusing or difficult. The book is a basic introduction to astronomy. It's written straight-forward with a lot of facts and no theory. Am I about right?" replied Joaquin.

"Yeah, pretty much."

"How about mine? Can I see it please?" asked Ayanna.

"Aw, come on. It's starting to get good," said Robert.

"Please Robert? I just want to look at it for a second."

"Okay, but make it quick. I feel like it's helping me."

He handed her the book. Ayanna examined the front and back covers, satisfied the book was hers. She opened the pages, and they too were now blank. She tilted the book towards Sage so he could see the empty pages. He nodded and gave her a look to let her know that he saw, and that he was just as confused as she was. She shrugged, then gave the book back to Robert.

"We'll let you guys get back to your reading. But you'll make sure to give us back our books when you're done with them, right?" asked Ayanna.

They both nodded, then turned back to reading the pages in front of them, now filled with words again. Although the pages were upside down from where they were looking, Sage and Ayanna could both make out writing that appeared to be straightforward text book language on the subjects the books covered. Apparently, none of their secrets were revealed in the books, and their abilities would remain hidden — for now.

Sage and Ayanna were taking their seats against the wall when Dr. Masters appeared through a hidden door, not far from them. He was smiling his awkwardly forced smile at everyone, his eyes darting all around the room. The doctor stepped further into the room, and stood there patiently while the guests quieted and turned their full attention to him. People tapped on shoulders, interface glasses came off, and eventually Dr. Masters had his audience.

"Ladies, and gentlemen. Thank you for assembling here this fine morning. Until now, you have been working independently. Your testing has been done as it has always been done for several centuries, on your interfaces alone. Well, we're going to be doing things a bit differently from now on. Starting today, your tests will be taken together. To explain, I have our top technical expert

Mr. Oakley here to go over everything. Um, Mr. Oakley? Will you please come out here?"

Christopher Oakley walked out into the room slowly. His legs shook, and so did his right arm when he lifted it to say hello to the group. Mr. Oakley had been given apple slices minutes before, to help give him enough energy to deliver his address to the group. He could still smell the sweet aroma of the apple inside his breath as he spoke, and his words were unusually pleasant for him to speak. He smiled warmly at everyone, like a man just rescued.

"I've worked day and night to build an integrated interface network capable of running the crown qualifier tests in conjunction with multiple users. What this means is, that when you take a particular test, you won't be alone, you'll be part of a team. An entire team of candidates will get the opportunity to take each test together. If you've ever heard the phrase 'two heads are better than one,' then you'll get the basic idea of what we've put together. Except, instead of two heads being better, you'll be part of a team with as many heads as are in this room right now. Pretty exciting isn't it?" asked Mr. Oakley.

"I have a question. Will this require any additional hardware? Or is it wireless and works with our glasses as they already are?" asked a woman in the middle of the room.

"That's a great question. I was just about to get into that. It will require a physical hardwire connection that runs from person to person. The wired connection is a series of cables that work in conjunction with these small attachments I like to call 'benders.' They take the tremendous amounts of data flowing from interface to another interface, and sort of bend it into a seamless stream of synchronized effort. If you think of this room as one big ocean, and each of you as ships sailing around it, then the benders are your anchors to one another. Except, they don't keep you down, they keep you around, if that makes sense," replied Mr. Oakley.

"I think they understand Christopher. Why don't you get everyone set up while I continue?" said Dr. Masters.

"Yes, right away doctor," he replied. Mr. Oakley went around the room attaching benders to everyone's interface glasses, while Dr. Masters spoke to the group.

"You will still be able to test individually, when alone and away from the others, but it is my wish that you will work together as much as possible from now on. In this way, we can assure Robert the highest possible scores on every test. With all of you taking any particular test together, our odds of scoring the highest score possible will be much greater. Imagine, all of your intellects combined into one unstoppable force. This is what we have achieved in this new technology. Isn't it splendid?" asked Dr. Masters.

"Yes!" replied most of the guests, in unison.

"How about a big round of applause for Mr. Oakley? He's worked so hard to make this moment happen."

The room erupted in a thunderous applause that lasted nearly a minute. Dr. Masters motioned for them to quiet down. He looked at Mr. Oakley who was equipping the last guest with their bender attachment.

"Mr. Oakley, now that we have everyone set up with a bender attachment, I think it's time to truly bring everyone together. Support staff! Bring out the cables!"

A couple dozen service staff walked out in their white uniforms carrying black rubber cables on silver trays. Each of them went to a different guest and plugged a cable into their glasses via the bender attachment, then ran the other end to a different person. Guests were eventually connected in one giant loop formation. Although the benders and cables added a little extra weight to their glasses, each guest was still able to comfortably wear and use them.

Dr. Masters looked across the room at some of the smartest people in the world attached to one another like lab rats in one of his old experiments. It made him smile, and he kept himself from laughing in delight. Instead, he pretended to laugh in excitement.

"Well, boys and girls, it's about that time. This is what we've all been waiting for! It's time to see who's really at the head of the class. This is for all the marbles, the grand prize, the Holy Grail, and all that jazz. Now, go win me the world."

CHASING AFTER WINDMILLS

The castle guests stood staring at one another in a virtual lobby that looked much like the assembly room they were actually sitting around in, outside in the real world. Their avatars were exact image duplicates of what they looked like normally. They wouldn't be distracted by any unusual visuals to keep them from the task at hand. Sage stood next to Ayanna in the lobby, and Joaquin was a short distance away. He didn't see Robert, and when he thought back to it, he didn't remember seeing him plugged in like the rest of them.

Most of the contenders were their usual carefree selves. They were confident that they would succeed in getting Robert the crown. Working together was less stressful, because as a whole, they were guaranteed to find optimal results. Their combined knowledge was an advantage they knew no other test taker could ever compete with.

"Sage, what should we do?" whispered Ayanna.

"We play along for now. But, we've got to find a way to leave. The only chance we have is to find those research papers, or some other knowledge that can help us fight Masters' technology," he whispered back.

"Okay, but it feels so wrong. I hate the idea that we're all in here cheating to help these monsters take over the world."

"Don't worry, if we're lucky they won't make it to all ten tests."

"I hope you're right. Sage, look!"

An entire wall disappeared in the virtual lobby, and in its place appeared a giant glowing screen. On it was the portal to enter the first test — The Greatest Good. A huge button saying 'START' floated in the center of the screen. Sage walked over to it, and using his right hand, he pressed down. The screen changed and displayed the first question, with only two possible answers. A 20 minute timer in the top right hand corner started counting down, beginning with 19:59, then 19:58, and so on.

Jane Randolph, a civil engineer from New York City, read the first scenario out loud to the group, "Who should die? A middle aged man supporting a family of four or A first year medical doctor?"

Sage hit the button that said 'A middle aged man supporting a family of four.'

"Hey! You can't just choose for everyone! We're supposed to be working together," said Stephen Niven, an economist from London.

"I'm sorry, you're right. But the first one is always easy. Wasn't that one obvious?" replied Sage.

The others in the room nodded, including Mr. Niven.

"Here's the next one," said Jane. "Who should live? A world famous singer in their golden years or A first year firefighter?"

Sage spoke, "Well? What's the answer?"

"The firefighter can save lots of lives, and the singer is almost finished with their life. So, I think the answer is easy, the firefighter," said Roberto Garcia, a PhD in sociology from Mexico City.

"No, I disagree. If a singer is world famous that means their songs are universally accepted, and their music helps people on a massive scale. Their ability to lend their name to an important cause is a huge benefit to mankind too. Plus, they might write or sing more songs, any one of which could potentially save more lives than a dozen firefighters might. I say, choose the singer," said Ayanna.

Sage smiled hearing her answer, then looked at the rest of the group. They nodded in agreement. Sage pressed the singer button. A new scenario appeared.

"Which do you save? A forest threatened by fire or an ocean threatened by plastics?" read Jane.

"This one's easy. You save the ocean," answered Cristina Costa, a marine biologist from Sicily.

"I'm not sure. Forests generate a lot of oxygen, and they help us breath. Oceans are important too, but they're not on the land where we actually live. We don't even drink ocean water. Eating fish is a choice, not a necessity. I think saving forests are more important," said Stephanie Peters, an attorney from Australia.

"Are you kidding me? You can always grow more trees and rehabilitate burnt forests. It's a part of the cycle of nature. But plastics in the ocean are a much bigger deal. The plastics are ingested by small fish, those are eaten by bigger fish, until they end up on our plate. Do you have any idea how harmful it is to consume plastic?" replied Cristina.

Sage looked around at the divided room. "Let's put it to a vote. Raise your hand if you think the answer is to save the forest. Okay, now raise your hand if your answer is to save the ocean? All right, the ocean wins," said Sage. He pressed the ocean button, and a new question appeared.

"Which business do you support? A four employee bakery specializing in cupcakes or a forty employee factory specializing in grenades," read Jane.

"Grenades can be useful for military defense, plus forty jobs is better for the economy," suggested Alan Woodson, a city manager from Toronto.

"There hasn't been a war fought on this planet in centuries! What good are grenades? Let them eat cupcakes!" answered Jennifer Chen, a bio-engineer from Hong Kong.

"All right, everybody vote!" shouted Sage. He counted, then pressed the appropriate button. This process continued until the 20 minute timer hit zero. At the end of the testing session, a new screen emerged, revealing the next test's title: What Happened? Sage hit the START button, and the screen revealed the first problem.

"Rosa is a fifteen year old girl living in Miami, Florida with her overly nice grandparents. One day after school, an ice cream truck stops in front of Rosa while she is walking home. A man is driving the truck, Rosa gets in, and they drive away. Rosa's backpack is left behind on the sidewalk. Inside the backpack is a fashion magazine, an old plush doll, and a note that says, 'I love you.' What do you think happened to Rosa?" read Jane.

"She got kidnapped by the man in the truck!" shouted Frank.

"No, she ran off with him, it was her boyfriend!" countered Jennifer.

"She ran away with him to escape her grandparents," offered Alan.

"Her dream is to be a fashion model, so she ran away from home to pursue it," said Cristina.

A debate continued for some time, until finally a consensus was built, and a final answer submitted. A new problem appeared, and the process repeated. The questions kept coming, until at last, the second test was complete. Then the third, and then the fourth, until they only had two tests left. The test takers were visibly tired, and in need of a breather. They agreed to take a one hour lunch break, and meet back in the assembly room at one o'clock.

Sage took his interface glasses off and squinted. The rest of the guests removed their glasses too. Robert was in his same seated position, nose deep in his book. It was the same book he'd been reading earlier, *The Book of Energy*. He was so absorbed by it that he completely ignored everyone in the room coming to life around him, then getting up and moving about.

"Sage, we should go," said Ayanna.

"Okay, lead the way," he said.

Ayanna and Sage walked to the opposite side of La Casa Grande, away from the others, and stood in front of one of the stairwells.

"While everyone else was arguing back there, I was thinking about the best place to look for answers in this place. Then, it came to me. The basement, or lower level. No one ever goes down there. I know *I* haven't seen it. I mean, everyone raves about every floor of this place, except I never hear anyone talk about the very bottom foundation of it. It must not be pretty enough to talk about, or maybe filled with all the things no one wanted placed upstairs?"

"That's awesome thinking Ayanna, let's get down there."

"Okay, but you lead the way this time."

They walked down the stairwell carefully, letting their eyes adjust to the dim lighting. Unlike the beautifully maintained upper floors of the castle, the lower level was a neglected maze of boxes, furniture, paintings, lamp fixtures, and countless other items no longer needed, or perhaps never used at all. There was dust everywhere, several impressive spider webs, and the floor was so caked in dirt that their footsteps left impressions everywhere they walked.

"There must be a billion things in here. Where do we start?" asked Ayanna.

"We'll start in the furthest back part. I'll take the right, you take the left. We're looking for any paperwork, files, books, or notes. If you find anything call me over."

"Okay, cool."

Sage opened dusty cardboard box lids, one after another, looking for written materials. He hoped the research data would be in one of the boxes, but so far he only found kitchen items like old plates and silverware, or household knick knacks. Everything was old, and rare enough to be in a museum somewhere.

Right around his eightieth box, Sage uncovered his first stack of papers. Unfortunately, they were all about the construction of the castle. He found them interesting to read, but kept searching. There was finally a box of books and Sage's face lit up in excitement. They were all fringe topics, from spirituality to crystal healing to UFO sightings. He quickly devoured them all, but none of them led him to a way to stop Dr. Masters from executing his plans.

Ten minutes later Sage Vector found something unusual buried under a pile of old newspapers, and wrapped in an old cloth. It felt like something wooden, and when he opened it he discovered it was an old cigar box with a sliding lid. He slid the cover open and there was a small pyramid shaped crystal object resting on top of an old leather notebook. He held the pyramid in his left hand, and he could feel there was something soothing about it. Then, he picked up the notebook in his right hand, and immediately a smile spread across his face. He understood the significance of what he found. Inside were the exact answers he was looking for. Although it wasn't the research he was expecting, or anything written by Dr. Masters about his inventions, it was something far better. He doubted Masters knew anything about the notebook, because if he did, he would have surely destroyed it. The contents were too great a threat to his work.

"Ayanna! Come here!"
She came running. "Did you find something?"
He held out the notebook and the small pyramid to show her.
"I hit the mother lode. We can stop him now."

"Is that a paper weight? What book is that?" she asked, confused.

"Let me explain. This is a journal written by a man named Victor Berry. He stayed here at the castle at some point. His writings suggest he was an inventor or scientist in poor health. He came to the castle to try to heal himself and recover from cancer. While he was here he experimented with methods aimed at converting negative energy into positive energy. Or another way to look at it is he wanted to find a way to repair sick or agitated energy. He believed all energy was the same at its most basic level, but over time it changed and altered according to how it was used, and what was around it. Berry theorized you could reverse the negative impacts stored in energy, and remove them by converting them back into positive, pure energy."

"That sounds amazing. But how does that help us? And seriously, what's up with the Egyptian snow globe in your hand?"

"It's not a souvenir, trust me. It's actually a generator."

"Huh? I don't get it."

"Berry experimented with an ancient technology he eventually refined. Using a specific combination of organic, and non-organic materials, he built an energy generator. In fact, he developed multiple devices, each with a specific use, but all centered around transforming energy from a negative state to a positive one."

"And with it we can reverse the hypnotic implants in everyone?"

"Yep."

"We can do it with that little pyramid?"

"Well, no. This is too small to undo what's been done to everyone here. We would need a lot of them, plus they would need to be placed near those affected. But the biggest problem is that all of that would take too long."

"But you said we could stop him. How are we going to do that if the whole thing takes too long?"

"Here, hold the generator. I think you'll understand better," said Sage, handing the small pyramid to Ayanna.

"Oh wow! This is amazing! I could feel it as you were holding it just now, but this is something else. It's intoxicating how peaceful it feels. Wait a second, my mind feels so much sharper."

"I know. Mine too. The moment I touched that thing all of my memories came back. No fuzziness. I remember everything that happened to me now. What about you?"

"Yes! That creep pretended to be a patient, corned me in my office and used his small, hypnotic pen on me. What about you?"

"A woman shot me, but I think she was under his influence. They rushed me out of the building, and he was there waiting for me. It was a small red light, right?"

"Yes! Oh my god! I hate him so much. We have to help the others break free. Can't we just go right now, and get everyone to touch this thing?"

"No, I think they'd stop us before we could get to everyone. But, it's okay because I know how to make something like it... but more powerful."

"Heck yeah! Oh, wait a second. We're almost out of time. How long will it take you to make it? What do you need?"

"I have everything I need to build it down here. I just need about 30 more minutes."

"They're expecting us in like three minutes. Should we risk not showing?"

"I need you to go up there while I work on it. Tell them I wasn't feeling well, and to start without me. Tell them I went for a walk to get some fresh air."

"Okay, I can do that. But what happens after you've built this thing?"

"Then I point it at them and break the spell. The implants should shatter."

"I love it! Okay, I'm going!"

Ayanna walked quickly towards the stairs, and was soon gone, only her footprints on the floor remained to remind Sage that she'd been with him in the basement level. He went right to work, searching for the materials he needed. It was important that he work fast, before anyone came looking for him.

***

Dr. Masters was standing over his son Robert, watching him read for the longest time he'd ever seen him with a book. Ever since he was a little boy he knew Robert Jr. disliked reading. He never fully understood why he hated books so much. As a doctor, and as a constant consumer of knowledge himself, he enjoyed reading more than any other activity. He preferred the company of books than people. His face was often behind a book or scientific journal. Books were shields to the annoyances of life, and they were also the ultimate source of power. He found it troubling when his son started throwing them at him. His teachers couldn't explain it. They knew he could read, he just never wanted to. So, to see his son so engaged with a book was more than startling to him. It was like being in a city bombarded by hundreds of missiles and one finds himself suddenly at war. It freezes you in your tracks, and you don't know what to do next.

"Robert?"

His son didn't look up from his book when he answered his father. "Yeah?"

"It looks like you're almost done with that book. Is that right?"

"Yeah."

"It must be a good one. What's special about it?"

"It's got real answers for once. It explains so much. I can't stop reading it."

"Answers? What kind of answers? What's it about?"

"Energy. Life. Things like that."

"Interesting. I'd love to read it when you're done. I can always know more about those subjects."

"Yeah, okay. Can you leave me alone now? I really want to finish this."

"Oh, okay. Sure thing son. Happy reading."

Dr. Masters walked away from Robert, and for the first time in his life, wondered if he were wrong about something. Was his son like him after all? Was he just a late bloomer? No, it must be a fluke. He was never wrong about anything. There was no one smarter than him on the planet. He would continue outsmarting them all. And there wasn't time for self doubt. He had a world to conquer.

Ayanna walked into the assembly room as everyone was putting their interface glasses on. She went to her seat and did the same. Just as she was about to enter the virtual lobby, she felt a tap on her shoulder. She removed her glasses, looked up and saw Dr. Masters' unnaturally wide mouth smiling down at her.

"Um, miss, where is your little boyfriend?" he asked.

"Oh, hello Dr. Masters. Sage wasn't feeling well. He said he needed some fresh air and decided to take a walk," she replied.

"Why don't I quite believe you? Are you telling me the truth?"

Ayanna realized she should do a better job lying. She needed to give an Academy Award winning performance if she was going to fool Masters.

"Okay! We had a little fight. I'm lying, it was a big fight! You see, I really like him. I think he's just the greatest, and I thought he felt the same way. At least that's how he acted at first, but then I found out he has another girl back home, and it made me jealous, then upset, then just straight up mad. We argued. I yelled. He yelled. I threw things at him. I didn't know what else to do. I've never felt so many emotions all at once. He told me he needed some space, so that's what I'm giving him. What do you think Dr. Masters? Did I do the right thing? I mean, I needed some space too. This whole relationship stuff is really stressful, I'm not sure I can even concentrate properly on anything else. I don't know what to do about it. You're a guy. What do you think he's thinking right now?"

Dr. Masters looked at Ayanna with a deadly stare that tore into her. She could feel his negative energy growing bigger inside of him. It emanated out towards her, and she recoiled from him.

"You're really worked up. I think you better come with me. I know just the thing for you. Go ahead, and put your glasses down. You won't be needing them."

"Where are you going to take me?" she said worriedly.

"Oh, not far."

Reluctantly, Ayanna stood up. She looked around and saw everyone in the room was hidden behind glasses, except for Robert. He wasn't paying the slightest attention to her, he was too focused on finishing her book. There were only a couple more pages left for him to reach the end. Ayanna turned to Dr. Masters and said dejectedly, "Okay, let's go."

He led her to the elevator, then up some stairs, and eventually to the top floor of La Casa Grande — the 4th floor. He opened a door, and she found herself in a rounded room that looked like something out of a fairy tale. There were tall arched windows that surrounded an elaborately carved bed with St. John the Baptist on the headboard. In between each window were giant golden curtains. The sunlight was shining through the geometrically designed window screens, and the entire room looked like a giant, golden birdcage.

"Make yourself comfortable," said Dr. Masters.

Ayanna sat in a nearby floral, cushioned chair.

"No, please get on the bed."

"Dr. Masters, I'd rather not if that's all right with you. This chair is comfortable enough," she replied.

"I'm afraid I have to insist. Get on the bed," he replied, placing his hand close to his pants pocket.

Ayanna feared he might try to hypnotize her again if she continued to resist, so she walked over to the bed and sat on the mattress. Dr. Masters smiled and walked over to her. He stood in front of her dangling legs and placed his left hand on one of her legs while moving his right fingertips to the edge of his pocket.

"I'm glad we trust each other," he said. "You do trust me, don't you?"

"Um, yes Dr. Masters."

"That's a good girl. I trust you too. Now, tell me everything you know about this *Book of Energy*."

***

Joaquin could see the frustration in the faces of the other test takers. Although refueled from lunch, the guests were slow to pick up their same momentum from before the break. It took them awhile to adjust to not having Sage, who helped lead them so effortlessly before. But Joaquin was determined to push them through the final tests, and hopefully to a high enough score so Robert could claim the crown.

While Joaquin competed with his team in the virtual lobby, Robert was looking at them, the only person around with an unobstructed face. He closed the book in front of him, staring at the cover, feeling it with his fingers, and the cool smoothness of it made him smile. He pushed it to the side, then looked around for the other book like it. Joaquin had it near him. It was propped against a table leg.

Robert reached for *The Book of Space*, and when his fingertips touched the edge of it, he felt a sharp jolt of energy hit him. Confused, he reached for it again, this time feeling an expanding excitement growing inside him. He placed the book in front of himself, looking at the same etched lettering he saw on the other book, then gripped one corner of the cover with the fingertips of his left hand. He opened *The Book of Space*, and a terrific light came shooting out of it and filled the room. Words, pictures, and symbols appeared. He was transfixed by them. A few moments later, they, along with the light, were gone. Robert looked down at the book, and stared at its blank pages in wonder.

The test takers completed the ninth test, and their cheering caused Robert to look up. He was envious of the feeling they possessed. He wanted to be part of it, to know what winning felt like when it was accomplished with intellect, instead of with force, or worse, with money. He felt the need to leave the room, no longer able to see so many reminders of how he lacked something he so desperately wanted. As he stood outside the assembly room, now in the refectory, he noticed a book resting on the table in the center of the room. He recognized it. It was Siddhartha's book, the one about Charlie Chaplin.

Robert reached for the book, and as soon as his fingers touched its cover, the knowledge inside flew into him. The story of Chaplin hit the young man like a punch to the gut. What a life! What it must have felt like to be so genuinely loved by the whole world! How wonderful it must have been to inspire so many people, to make them laugh and feel joy. The emotion he felt inside was beyond marvelous.

The thought struck him, "How was this possible?" He didn't dwell on it too long though. His next thought was, "Could it happen again?" Robert sprung into action, moving his legs as fast as they would take him towards the library. He got to the stairs, and was about to take them up one flight when he heard a crashing noise coming from down in the basement. He listened again, and he could hear someone moving things below him. Rather than continue up to the library, he decided to investigate, and he took the stairs down instead.

Sage was adding the last of the materials to make his energy cannon work. A few final twists of copper wire to keep the crystals from the chandelier in place was all it needed now. He used a pair of pliers and an old rag to prevent the metal from slipping in his hands. Satisfied, he looked the thing over one last time, then realized he needed to position it in the right direction, but he wasn't sure where the assembly room was in relation to where he was now. He began walking towards the stairwell in hopes it would help jog his memory and reorient him. Before he could reach it, he heard someone coming. He ducked behind some old boxes and tried to control the pounding in his heart. His breathing was a problem too, it sounded like a hundred tornados to his sensitive ears.

Robert could see two sets of footprints on the dirty floor. One was larger than the other, and the smaller set looked like it entered but then left the basement. The owner of the larger set of prints must be the one he heard. He followed the set of prints carefully, making sure to listen for any breathing, and tried not to be caught by surprise as he turned each corner. It didn't take him long to locate his prey.

"I can hear you. Why don't you come out?" he said.

Sage knew there was no avoiding being caught. It was too quiet in the basement for him to go undetected. Before saying anything, Sage tip toed to the energy cannon he constructed and pointed it in the direction he felt the assembly room was in and hoped for the best.

"Come out, you're not in trouble or anything," said Robert.

Sage now recognized the voice. He knew he couldn't let Robert discover the cannon. There was a chance he could lead him away from it before he set eyes on it. Slowly, Sage made his way closer to Robert, and at just the right moment, he darted around him and ran with all his might toward the stairs. Robert tried grabbing him, but too many games of field ball had made Sage difficult to tackle. He spun at just the right moment and sent Robert diving for the wall. Taking advantage of the distance between them, Sage ran with everything he had in him up the stairs. Robert was right on his heels. Rather than exit to the first floor towards the assembly room and the others, Sage decided to give the energy cannon enough time to work, and bounded up one more flight to the second floor.

Robert called out to Sage, "Stop! Stop running from me!"

But Sage didn't stop. He ran out of the stairwell and into the lobby, just outside the library. He looked around and wondered if he should try boarding himself up in one of the rooms, or possibly make a run for the opposite stairwell, but then he saw Robert appear at the entrance of the lobby, so he decided to make a stand in the library. He took a position behind the large center table, just across from the Italian fireplace, and readied himself for a fight.

"What are you doing?!" shouted Robert. "Why were you in the basement? What are you up to?!"

"Nothing, I was just exploring. I got curious about what was down there."

"You're not supposed to go down there. No one goes down there."

"Why not?"

Robert walked slowly towards Sage who was standing his ground. He kept keen eyes on him. Sage started to form a fist with his right hand, but thought back to everything he'd learned over the last week. He knew every fighting style imaginable by heart, but there had to be a better way than getting physical. Then, an alternative path presented itself in his mind. He reached across the way and pulled a book from a nearby shelf. Robert looked confused, and he stared intensely at the book in his hands.

"Have you ever read this? It's *Don Quixote* by Cervantes," asked Sage.

Robert shook his head no, unsure of why Sage was asking him this.

"It's the story of a man who saw the world differently than what it was. He didn't want to be a part of the world everyone else lived in. It wasn't adventurous enough, it wasn't romantic enough, it wasn't imaginative enough! So he created his own reality, and lived in his own world. But he didn't experience it alone, he had a friend — Sancho Panza. But Sancho wasn't like him, he was practical, he lived in the real world, not an imaginary one. He thought he needed to make sure Quixote didn't cause harm to himself, or to others. You see, Don Quixote was living his dreams, chasing after windmills. In his mind, he was a knight, and a hero. But to Sancho, and the rest of the world, he was a fool, and a dreamer. But the more Sancho was around Don Quixote, the more he lived in his world, the more he dreamed, and the more he believed."

"What are you trying to say?" asked Robert.

"I know we're from different worlds, and we have different perspectives, but if we just take a minute, hear each other, and walk the same path for awhile, I think we'll find we're not all that different."

Robert raised his arm up, out towards Sage. His hand was contorted, as if he were working out what to do with his fingers. He could easily clench them and form a fist, or let them shoot out into a flat surface, perfect for a slap, or a handshake. Sage looked up at Robert's suspended hand, then looked at the expression on his face. Robert's cheeks were red, his eyes were starting to water, and his lower lip was quivering. To Sage, he looked like he was straddling a line, working out which side he wanted to land on. There were battles being fought inside him, between love and hate, between peace and war.

"Stories are powerful," said Sage, taking the book in his hand, and thrusting it forward. Robert flinched, but instinctively grabbed it. The centuries old story flowed into him like a tidal wave, filling him with emotion and meaning. He looked up at Sage, smiled, and let out a big sigh of relief. Sage could feel the story flowing into Robert, as they both touched Cervantes' masterpiece.

"You know what I know, don't you?"

"Yes."

"That's amazing. I thought I was the only one with the ability."

"Your book... from before. It changed me."

"When did it happen?"

"Just before I came down to the basement. I was on my way here, to the library when I heard some noise downstairs. That's when I found you."

"So, you just got your ability, wow. How many books have you read?"

"Only a couple." Robert looked around the room at all of the shelves of books. "Have you read any of these?" he asked.

"I've read them all."

"My god, what does that feel like?"

Sage walked over to the couch, kicked his feet up, and made himself comfortable.

"Why don't you find out for yourself?" he replied.

THE UNIVERSE STRETCHED OUT

The final test of the decathlon was easily the most difficult. Most people said it was impossible to beat, but that's only because so few could pass it. The stakes were beyond global in implication. They involved other planets and other galaxies. There were more than just humans to safeguard. Entire alien species were to be considered. It pushed the limits of thought, of philosophy, and of existence. Joaquin and the other contenders were knee deep in the level, battling for what they hoped would be the highest score ever achieved. They were close to securing Robert the crown, and Joaquin felt the win was within their grasp. All they needed to do was stay the course, and they would complete the last test — Universe Breaker.

A planet with twenty six humanoid species living in peace was under attack by a neighboring galaxy controlled by a mineral rich slave society run by a race of fire giants. They were notorious for harnessing the power of their solar system's sun, and breeding with it. It gave them the power to overwhelm their enemies with literal fire power to the point where they no longer had enemies, only those they wanted to vanquish. It was up to Joaquin and the others in the virtual meeting room to stop them from taking over their next planetary target. They were reviewing a list of data points about the planet's defenses when someone screamed.

"Where are my kids?! They said they would hurt them if I didn't come! Let me out of here!" shouted Jane, suddenly disappearing from the virtual room.

"I shouldn't be here! This isn't right!" shouted Frank, leaving too.

One by one, the group of test takers realized what brought them to the castle, and why they were being kept.

"What are we doing? We can't help these people do this."

"I'm not playing this sick game."

"Let's get out of here."

"Where is that monster? I'm going to kill him."

"How can we contact our families?"

"My Rebecca, she must be worried sick."

"Joaquin, come on, we need you," said Cristina.

"What have we done? We almost..." he said.

"It's okay, we didn't finish the last test. Look!" she replied.

The peaceful planet with so many species living together in peace was being conquered by the fire giants. Their violent lava weapons obliterated their cities instantly, melting them to ashes. They would now wait several millennia for the terraformed land to be ripe for colonizing. Meanwhile, the remains of sixty billion people baked in the fires set by an ignorant race.

Joaquin watched the fires burning hot, and he felt an anger rising inside him.

"You're right, let's go get the real bad guys," he said, then removed his glasses.

The assembly room was buzzing with conversation. Contenders from all over the world were talking to each other a mile a minute, trying to get up to speed, asking every question they hadn't been able to ask before. The missing puzzle pieces in their minds were now all in place, and the pictures they formed were more than alarming. They realized the enormous implications of their being taken and forced to help Masters with his insane plan.

"Why didn't we know before now? What made us so blind?" asked Roberto.

"We were under a spell of sorts. Commands were planted deep within our subconsciousness. The bastard hypnotized us," said Beth, rubbing her sore shoulder, remembering Robert sitting on top of her in the pool.

"I'm going to kill that man," said Martin.

"He's no man at all," said Jane.

"No, he can't get off that easy. He needs to spend the rest of his days behind bars. We need to get him to stand trial on a global stage so he can be made an example of," said Joaquin.

"You're right," replied Martin. "Let's go catch him before he has time to escape."

"All right everyone, you heard the man. Let's go catch this snake!" said Joaquin, leading everyone out of the room, and into the rest of the castle.

Robert touched the very last book in the library, reading them all faster than even Sage. His appetite for knowledge had been so immense that he quickly devoured every volume within reach. When he was done, he walked to the North end of the library where Sage lay comfortably on a couch. He took a seat on one of the cushioned chairs near him. He felt so light he thought he might float away, so he gripped the ends of his chair arms tightly, in case he did end up defying all gravity.

"It feels pretty incredible doesn't it?" asked Sage.

"Hell yeah. Sage, I know so much," he replied.

"I know. It's not superficial knowledge either, you really comprehend it all. Don't you feel so connected to the material that it's like you wrote everything?"

"Yeah! It's like I lived their lives! I can see what they saw. It's all so clear, like it just happened. I can't wait to share what I know, to help others with it. I'm a changed guy. I'm no longer the same person I was before."

"I don't know about that. Maybe you're just more yourself now. Deep down, all people are good. Sometimes we just get convinced we're not."

"I think you're right. What an awesome way to look at things."

"It's pretty easy. All it takes is the right viewpoint. Space itself is really just..."

From somewhere above them they could hear screaming. They both jumped up from their seats and ran to the lobby to get a better listen. It seemed to be coming from their left, and they took the stairs up one flight. When they were on the third floor they could still hear the screaming coming from above, so they made their way to the top floor of La Casa Grande. Now they could hear more than a scream, they could hear fighting, furniture scraping the floor, objects being thrown, and they could tell the screaming was Ayanna's.

"Help me! Somebody, anybody! Aaaaahhhhh!" she yelled.

Sage was the first through the door of the Celestial Suite. The sun came blasting through the tall windows, momentarily blinding him. He squinted but could see Dr. Masters holding onto Ayanna's left arm with both hands while she hit him repeatedly with a small metal vase. Sage rushed over to the doctor, and yanked him hard off of Ayanna. He stumbled to the floor, but bounced up quickly, then lunged at Sage.

Ayanna jumped onto the bed, then over it, to the opposite side of the room. She looked at Robert who had his hands out towards her and she was terrified. She grabbed one of the tall candlestick posts next to the bed, and gripped it firmly out in front of her. The metal post with its candle holders at one end looked like a pitchfork. Ayanna jabbed the pointed ends out in front of her, towards Robert. He stood back from her, trying to signal with his hands that he wasn't a threat, but she continued to squeeze the metal in her hands tight, and kept the candlestick ends suspended in the air.

Sage was struggling to get a good hold of Dr. Masters who kept jumping from side to side, squirming his way out of his grip. Eventually his hands locked in, and he had Masters moving towards the small wall near one of the windows. Sage had him pinned against the wall, the full weight of his body leaning in on him. Dr. Masters laughed hysterically.

"What's so funny? I've got you beat," said Sage.

"Strength never beats cunning," he replied, twisting around Sage, using his own force against him.

Sage was now the one pinned to the wall near the window. But Dr. Masters was not as lenient as Sage had been with his grip. He put his right arm around Sage's neck, and with his left hand in a fist and his thumb protruding out, applied pressure to his gunshot wound. Sage screamed out in pain. Dr. Masters turned him around, keeping the same excruciating grip on him. Now he could see the whole room.

"Get her! What's wrong with you?!" he shouted at his son.

Robert looked at Ayanna and said, "Don't worry, I'm not going to hurt you. I'm not with him anymore."

"Robert! What the hell is wrong with you?! Get that girl before she ruins everything!" shouted his father.

"No. I'm not helping you. I'm with them now."

"You're with who now?! It's too late for all of that son! I'm your father! You have to listen to me! Do what I say, and get a hold of her!"

"I said no! I'm done with your games, done with your lies, with all of it! You've treated me like an annoying after thought my whole life! Do you know how it feels to be brushed aside, then laughed at? Where were you my whole life?! You were working on your twisted plans. You were playing some sick game with the world, moving people like pawns off the board — I'm done being a pawn. And I sure as hell don't want to be king either!"

"So, you're a big man now, is that right? Okay, let's see what you're made of. You see this young man in my arms? I'm going to crack his neck. Then, I'm going to get that girl, and paint the room with her. And I bet you're going to just stand there, because you won't be able to do a damn thing. You know why? Because you're nothing but a coward. You won't hurt me. I'm bigger than you! I'm a giant in this world! I'm god almighty as far as you're concerned!" Dr. Masters stared at his son with hatred and disgust.

Robert began walking slowly towards his father.

"Stay back boy! I'm warning you!"

He continued to walk towards him.

"I'll break this boy's neck if you don't stop!"

Robert reached into his right pant pocket with his hand and took out the small metal device that he took from his father downstairs when he wasn't looking. He lifted it up for his dad to see. The red light flicked on. Dr. Masters let go of Sage, then used his knee and the full force of his body to push him to the floor away from him. He covered his eyes with his arms and shouted, "You can't do this to me! I'm your father! All I wanted was to give you the world! Why won't you let me help you?!"

Robert walked calmly towards his dad with the device held out in front of him and said, "You're a liar. You've only ever wanted to help yourself."

Sage stood up, sore and in pain, but ready to help Robert if needed. Ayanna walked slowly along the outer edge of the room, keeping her eyes on Dr. Masters the whole time, and eventually found her way to Sage. He put his arms around her, and she latched onto him too, but she was careful not to press too strongly on his midsection. They both watched Robert move confidently closer to his father, as he continued to hold the metal device in front of him.

"Okay! Robert, whatever you want! I'll give you anything! Just tell me what it is!" shouted his father who was still shielding himself from the red light of the device.

"You know what I want? I want you to look at me! Open your eyes, stop hiding and look at me! See me! Your son! See what you've made!"

Dr. Masters slowly lowered his arms, then reluctantly opened his eyes. He looked at his son's hurt face, and the pain in his eyes was haunting, but somewhere deep down in them was love. He tried to read what was written in his son's eyes, but struggled to decipher their story. Did he really love him, or was the hate too heavy? He knew he'd done too much to hurt his son. He never treated him like a father should treat a son, with care, guidance, and respect. Instead, he used him like any other instrument in his laboratory. Dr. Masters looked down, feeling the slightest bit of shame in what he'd done. But, as his eyes moved away from his son's face, his attention went to the red light. He looked directly at it, and a puzzled look came across his face for a brief moment, but it was quickly replaced with excitement instead.

"You foolish, foolish boy," he said. Then he snatched the metal device from his son's hand. He looked at it, laughed, then tossed it on the floor. "The battery's dead! Ha ha!" Then he lunged at Robert, grabbed him by the collar, and started slapping him.

"You ungrateful little brat! How dare you challenge me! Do you know how much I've done to give you power! You can't turn from me! I'm the reason you're even alive! I gave you life! And if I damn well please, I'll take it away!" he screamed, hitting his son again and again.

Robert tried his best to block the blows from his father, but too many of them were landing. He wasn't hitting his father back. Sage and Ayanna watched in horror as Dr. Masters pummeled his son with hit after hit.

"Robert, fight back!" shouted Sage. "I can help you do it!"

Robert put his hand out in Sage's direction signaling for him to stay back where he was. "No, Sage I'm done fighting him. Let him hit me if he wants. I'm not going to do what he does — I'm not going to be like him!"

Dr. Masters heard his son's words and became further enraged, "You don't want to be like me?! Too late! You are me!" He pushed him towards a nearby mirror and pressed his face into it, then leaned in close. "See?! You've got my eyes! You've even got my smile! You can't get rid of me! I'm inside you! We're made of the same stuff!" He flashed his big Cheshire grin smile at his son, then laughed at him.

Robert stood up, then pushed his father away from him. Dr. Masters stumbled back, but recovered his balance. "Well, well, there's still a little fight left in you after all! See?! You *are* just like me! You can't get rid of me. But *I* can sure as hell get rid of *you*!" He lunged towards Robert, grabbed him tightly by his shirt, then hurled him blindly behind him. His body went right through the glass window, breaking it into hundreds of pieces that flew everywhere, including through the air with Robert, as he fell four stories to his death.

"No!" screamed Dr. Masters, rushing to the window to look down. He saw his son lying still on the ground below, the back of his head forming a pool of blood behind him, while the front of his face stared upwards. His eyes were open, but they weren't looking at his father, they were looking up at the sky, and a smile was frozen across his face.

Dr. Masters turned away from the sight, and collapsed on the floor of the Celestial Suite, feeling the broken glass cutting him, not caring. Sage and Ayanna stared at him, unsure what to do. Dr. Masters looked up at them with tears in his eyes.

"What have I done? I didn't mean for him to go through the glass. I just wanted to..." He looked down at his hands, bloodied, with tiny pieces of glass lodged in them. Using one of his fingers, he pulled a small piece of glass out of his left hand, then held it up in front of his face and stared at it. "It's so shiny. Isn't that something... it looks like a star."

Sage turned to Ayanna and whispered to her, "Let's go." They walked out of the room quietly, leaving Dr. Masters on the floor talking to himself. One floor below, they heard voices calling out, "We know you're here! Come out!" They made their way closer, and found themselves in Dr. Masters' study, standing in front of Joaquin and the other contenders grouped together ready for a fight.

"It's okay guys, it's Sage and Ayanna," said Joaquin. He walked over to his best friend and put his arms around him and said, "I'm so sorry man." Sage smiled, then laughed, "No worries, I knew you weren't being yourself." He turned to the rest of the group, "None of you have been your usual selves. Masters had everyone hypnotized so he could control us. But he's not in a position to control anyone right now, especially himself."

"What happened to him? Where is he?" asked Joaquin.

"He's one floor up, in the room that looks like a golden bird cage," replied Sage.

"Let's go get him! I'm going to beat the hell out of him!" said Frank.

Sage stepped forward. "He's already doing that to himself. You'll see."

About half the group went upstairs, and the rest went downstairs. Sage walked with Ayanna, Joaquin, and the others, to the assembly room. There, Sage and Ayanna recovered their books, then made their way outside the building.

It was early afternoon and there wasn't a cloud in the sky. A few birds flew overhead to the west, towards the ocean which swayed in the distance. When they looked to their right, Sage and the others saw dozens of the service staff gathered in a circle. Their backs were mostly turned to them, and they were looking at something in silence. As they got closer, they could see Robert's body laying in the center of everyone.

A few of the service staff were making signs of the cross and praying while holding rosaries. One of the older men was holding a giant cross cradled between both of his arms. It must have come from somewhere inside the castle, and the man knew no one would scold him for removing the priceless antique and putting it to good use. Many of the people gathered around Robert's body were teary eyed, and several were crying profusely. Sage wondered if they were crying because they knew the young man for so long personally, maybe having worked for his family since he was a boy, or if they were crying because they knew, that despite how badly he might have treated them, and how bad a person they might have thought he was, the look on his face moved them and made them believe that everyone deserved mercy, and to be loved.

Sage walked over to Robert, knelt down, placed his hand on his chest, and bowed his head in silence. The emotion welled up inside him, and he let a few tears fall onto the ceramic tiles near his feet. The drops on the colorful floor looked out of place, but they remained on the floor while he thought about Robert. He wondered what would happen to him next, and if he might see him again in another time and place, perhaps in another form. He hoped he would, and that his next existence would be a better one. Sage opened his eyes, lifted his hand, stood up, and walked away. The tears he shed were no longer where they were before. The warmth of the sun had dried them into the tiles of the castle grounds.

Ayanna went to Sage and put her hand into his. They walked towards the gardens facing the ocean and looked out at the blue all around them. Sage turned to Ayanna, smiled, and put his arm around her.

"I'm glad you're okay. I don't know what I would have done if he'd hurt you."

"Me too. You both came just in the nick of time," she replied.

"He turned out to be an awesome person. I got to spend a little time with him. I wish I'd had more."

"So what happened to him? How did you get him to turn against his father?"

"It wasn't me. It was the book," answered Sage, taking *The Book of Space* out of his book bag to show her.

"What do you mean? The book did something to him?"

"Yeah. It gave him the same ability as me. He had just finished reading the entire library when we heard you. You should have seen how happy he was. I was happy too. It was awesome having someone else to talk to about this ability."

"That's really awesome Sage. I wonder why the book chose him."

"Me too. Maybe he just needed it more than anybody else. It changed his life completely. I'm not going to take this gift for granted. I'm going to use it to make things better. In any way I can."

"I know you will. I'm going to try to do the same. There's still so much I don't understand about my power."

Sage pulled her a little closer and looked at her smiling, then said, "Don't worry. We've got each other to help figure this stuff out. Salinas isn't that far from LA. We can always see each other through interface too. It'll be like we never left the castle."

Ayanna smiled at him, staring into his eyes, and inched in closer to his face. Sage felt the pull, and wondered whether he should continue resisting. She could manipulate energy, so was she selfishly guiding him towards her, or was what he felt real? If it was, then his whole world was about to change back home. Robin was everything, she was his sun, she meant so much to him. How could he stop orbiting around her, feeling her warmth? Ayanna was an exciting new galaxy to explore, but Robin was home. Sage continued to feel drawn to the beautiful girl in front of him now, and he wondered how long it would be before he kissed her, or broke her heart. Sage was moving closer to her when Joaquin appeared from behind, interrupting the energy that was flowing between them.

"So are you guys a thing now?" he asked. Sage looked embarrassed, but Ayanna helped him save face. "We've gone through a lot together the last few days. We've grown pretty close, but I know he has someone back home. As much as I'd like to see how far this rabbit hole goes, I'm not going to push my luck. Sage is an awesome guy, and any girl would be lucky as hell to find someone half as good, but I have to play my cards where they lay. I'm his friend for life after what we've experienced. Anything beyond that... only the stars know." She looked up at the castle building, where the broken window was, and wondered how the group was handling Dr. Masters. "I'm going to touch base with the others that went upstairs. It'll give you guys a chance to catch up," she said, then turned to Sage. "We'll talk later." She squeezed his hand one last time, slowly letting her reluctant fingers drift away from his, and headed towards La Casa Grande.

Sage and Joaquin watched her walk away, then Joaquin watched his friend's face watching her walk away.

"Damn, what are you going to do about that?" he asked.

"There's a lot I know, but when it comes to girls, I'm a real idiot," replied Sage.

"I don't know about that. You might be a genius!" laughed Joaquin.

Sage laughed, then said, "So, back to business. What do we do next? The whole world must be worried. Who knows what could be going on outside of this mountain top?"

"We need to call someone. There must be a way to get online from here. Masters cut us off, but he must have kept himself connected."

"I know who can help us!" said Sage.

"Who?!"

"Christopher Oakley. He's the tech expert. He connected all of us together. I'm sure he'll know how we can get online."

"You're right! Let's go look for him!"

Sage and Joaquin searched everywhere in the castle, and surprisingly, they found Mr. Oakley in the basement. He was sitting in front of Sage's energy cannon, staring at it with a huge grin on his face. When they asked him why he was there, he said, "It just feels so nice in this space."

It didn't take Mr. Oakley long to tap into Dr. Masters' private satellite feed. From there, he unlocked everyone's access on their interface glasses so they could call home and let their loved ones know they were okay. Joaquin placed the first call. He spoke to his father who was coming with practically the entire US military, Earth Security forces, the Security Guild, and the Police Guild.

While Joaquin was on the phone with his dad, Sage went to find Ayanna and tell her the good news about their glasses. When he went up to the fourth floor he expected to hear lots of chatter, but the Celestial Suite was eerily quiet from outside. He opened the door. Ayanna was sitting on the bed alone.

"What happened? Did they take him somewhere else?" he asked her.

"He's gone," she replied.

"What?! How is that possible?"

"This place can be a real maze. There's probably a ton of secret passageways. I don't know how he did it, but he's gone. We should have tied him up instead of leaving him here by himself."

"Don't worry, it's only a matter of time before we catch him. Every government agency on the planet is headed here right now. Joaquin's on the phone coordinating everything. You can call home and let your family know you're all right. We're all going back."

Ayanna forced a little smile, then looked down.

"What's the matter? Aren't you excited? We won," said Sage.

"I know. I am excited. I guess I'm also just a little sad."

"Why are you sad?"

She looked up at him, teary eyed, then said, "I think you know why."

"I'm going to miss you too." He looked down.

"Sage, I'm sorry. I really meant what I said out there. But it still hurts knowing I won't be seeing you every day, at least not like this." She touched his hand, then let go.

"This isn't the end. It's just the beginning. We're going to spend lots of time together, I know it."

"How do you know?"

"I just do. Don't you feel that way? You're the one that can feel energy, right?"

She smiled, "That's the problem Sage. I feel it too strongly. I'm in..." She stopped talking, composed herself, and got up from the bed. "I'm sure you're right," she finally said. "Let's go downstairs with the others, okay?"

"Ayanna, are you sure everything's all right? We can talk about anything you want."

"No, it's okay, really. We'll have plenty of time to talk about things when this whole ordeal is behind us. Let's go find everyone. I'm sure they'll be excited to get home, and be with their loved ones. I know my parents must be going nuts."

"You'll have to tell me all about them later. I want to know everything."

"No problem. I'll fill you in on them and anything else you want to know about me."

"Awesome, I'll do the same. But strangely, I feel like you already know everything there is to know about me."

They made their way downstairs and eventually came to the assembly room on the first floor. When they walked in everyone was either sitting or standing, and all of them were talking non-stop, either to each other, or to someone on their glasses.

As soon as Sage and Ayanna walked through the entry way, the entire room changed. Those carrying on conversations stopped, and tapped on the shoulders of those on their interfaces. The entire room was silent now, staring at Sage. Ayanna felt their energy immediately, and turned to look at Sage too. He looked at her, and she shrugged, also confused why everyone had a sudden intense interest in him.

Sage walked forward slowly, feeling the weight of the tension in the room. He spotted Joaquin who looked pale, and he was also looking right at him. Sage walked over to him.

"What's going on?" he asked him.

"Sage, you might want to sit down," he said.

"What happened?! Is it my family?! Did something happen to them? Tell me!"

"No, it's nothing like that. It's about the contest."

"What about the contest?"

"It's over. You won."

"Won what?"

"Sage, you're the new philosopher king."

"No, that's not possible. The contest isn't over for another few weeks."

"They ended the contest early. It just happened. Apparently, they were discussing it for awhile. With everything that happened, they wanted to move forward before anything else could interfere with the contest. Every other contender in the world declined to compete when we went missing. The only ones left were us, and they weren't sure we were even alive until a little while ago. They had already decided if any of us were still alive, whoever had the highest score among us would win. Sage, you had the highest score."

Sage looked around the room again and saw heads starting to nod, faces starting to smile, and hands starting to clap. There was an unmistakable joy in the room that exploded into enthusiasm. Everyone cheered loudly, but then Martin motioned them to quiet down. Then he took a knee, and one by one, they all took a knee. Even Ayanna and Joaquin were on one knee. Everyone remained silent, waiting for Sage to speak.

He looked around the assembly room of the castle, surrounded by people he admired and respected, and couldn't help but notice the art around them all. The tapestries, the paintings, the carvings, the sculptures, the rugs, everything reminded him of what he could make, what he could build, what he could create. He was just given the biggest canvas in the world. What would he paint on it?

Sage Vector looked at the universe stretched out in front of him like a million motion pictures, a billion books, a never ending symphony of sound, and smiled.

To find out what happens next,
look out for the next book in the series:

Sage Vector and The Impossible World

SPREAD THE WORD

Did you enjoy *Sage Vector and The Book of Space*?
Help others discover it.

You Can:
- Write a review online.
- Give a copy to a friend.
- Post about the book on social media.
- Buy a set of books for a school or library.
- Tell a teacher they can teach it in their classroom.

Looking for a way to spread the word about the book
and make a little extra money?

- Get bulk discounts on books you can sell in your neighborhood.
- Organize community fundraisers to promote literacy.

Go to davidcarus.net to get started.

SUGGESTED READING

Julius Caesar by William Shakespeare
Don Quixote by Miguel de Cervantes
Robinson Crusoe by Daniel Dafoe
The Princess Bride by William Goldman
The Time Machine by H.G. Wells
My Autobiography by Charlie Chaplin
A Connecticut Yankee In King Arthur's Court by Mark Twain
A Raisin in the Sun by Lorraine Hansberry
The Crucible by Arthur Miller
Inherit the Wind by Jerome Lawrence and Robert E. Lee
Frankenstein by Mary Shelley
Conan the Barbarian by Robert E. Howard
The Story of Civilization by Will and Ariel Durant
Romeo and Juliet by William Shakespeare
Astro Boy by Osamu Tezuka
The Republic by Plato

READING GROUP GUIDE
Discussion Questions

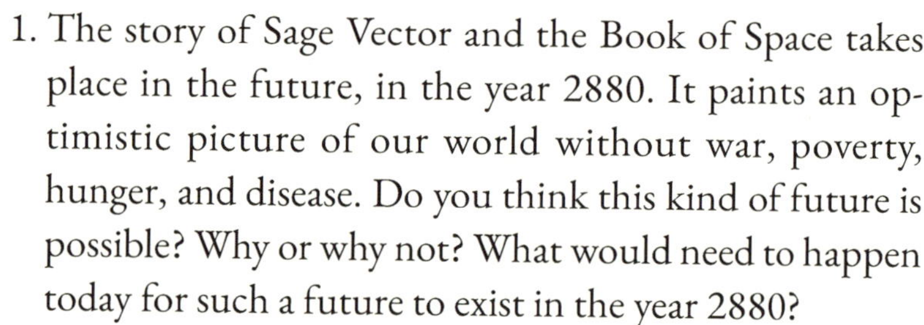

1. The story of Sage Vector and the Book of Space takes place in the future, in the year 2880. It paints an optimistic picture of our world without war, poverty, hunger, and disease. Do you think this kind of future is possible? Why or why not? What would need to happen today for such a future to exist in the year 2880?

2. At the start of the story Sage Vector is a young man that doesn't like to read books. How might this have affected his life if he never found *The Book of Space*? Which guild might he have joined? How would it have affected the other people in Sage's world? How might it have changed the overall story?

3. Field Ball is the dominate game of the future. War is no longer a worry for the people of Earth, but the game of field ball contains a war zone. Do you think the existence of war zones in field ball encourages people to fight one another, or is it an outlet for them to get fighting out of their system? Is a sport like field ball healthy for society? What parallels can you make between field ball and other sports such as football, basketball, or others?

4. In the book, society is divided into guilds. Do you think people should be placed in specialized groups like guilds? How might it affect their lives? Are their lives more productive? Are people happier? Does being part of a guild limit your understanding of the rest of society? Do guilds limit individuality and self-determinism? Would you want to be part of a guild? If so, which one?

5. People in the year 2880 use interface glasses to access their online world. Sage Vector isn't a big user of his interface glasses but others wear their glasses most of the day. If you were part of Sage's society, how would you use this technology? Would you embrace it? What might be the benefits of using it? What might be the dangers?

6. In the story, the school system provides a university level education that concludes at the age of 15 or 16, which is different than our current system which provides a high school level education that ends at the age of 18. How do you think this is achieved? What age should a person be considered an adult? Are people mature enough to enter the workforce at the age of 15? How do you think this earlier start at a professional working life affects society?

7. Sage's test scores tell him he should enter the Builders Guild but he wants to be an artist and go into the Artists Guild instead. Would you trust an algorithm or an online system to determine *your* career path? What if the testing system gave out great recommendations that you saw working for everyone else around you, would you trust it? Do we always know what is right for us? When should we seek outside guidance?

8. Sage is nervous about telling his dad that he wants to be an artist. He is also hesitant to tell Robin how he feels about her. How does his keeping communication away from others affect his relationships? What happens when he finally does communicate to his dad, and to Robin? Can you think of a time in your life when you withheld something out of fear or worry and when you finally said it to someone it ended up just fine? How important is communication in the overall story? Or to your own life?

9. Joaquin becomes a contender for the crown at the age of 16. Do you think a 16 year old can govern the world? Why or why not? What unique talents and background make Joaquin suited to be a philosopher king? What are some of the things a philosopher king might have to deal with when governing the entire world? Would *you* want to be king?

10. Sage is given abilities when he finds *The Book of Space*, primarily the ability to read and understand everything about a book simply by touching it. Does Sage use this ability in an ethical way throughout the story? Does it give him an unfair advantage in the crown qualifier tests? Should he disclose that he has special abilities to the Global Council? What about to his friends and family? What would you do if given Sage's power?

11. Ayanna comes into Sage's life at a time when he has just started a serious relationship with Robin. She has the ability to affect energy, and Sage wonders if the connection he feels to her is real or if he's being influenced by Ayanna's power. Do you think Sage should push his

feelings aside completely? Should he tell Robin about Ayanna when he sees her? How do you think Robin will react to hearing Ayanna kissed Sage? Who should Sage be with and why?

12. One of the themes of the book is the idea of looking. Sage is constantly paying attention and looking at the world around him. He sees things in a way that others don't see. His focus on the visuals of art is one major way he demonstrates his use and appreciation of looking. When he is looking for a gift for Robin he stumbles on *The Book of Space* which heightens his ability to look at knowledge, people and the world around him. How else might looking at things, and really seeing them, make a difference in someone's life? What affect does looking at the world make on that world? How much time do you spend looking at the world each day?

13. The idea that knowledge is power is shown throughout the book. Sage gains power as he acquires more knowledge. He uses his power to try to help others. In contrast, Dr. Masters possesses lots of knowledge and power, but wants to harm and control others. Why is this? What do you think is different between the two characters? Is there a difference in their knowledge? What makes a person a hero? What makes a person a villain?

14. Robert, Dr. Masters' son, wants to be smarter and sees reading books as a way he can achieve this. What factors in the plot of the story might have influenced Robert to want to be smarter and read books? What do you think his life must have been like before the guests arrived at the castle? How was his childhood? He may have had

everything money could buy, but what might he have been missing? What do you think of him wanting to be smarter and read books? What would you do if you were him?

15. At the end of the book, Sage finds himself earning a position he never really wanted. He was only trying to help his friend Joaquin when he took the crown qualifier tests. Sage wanted to be an artist and create art. Can he do that as philosopher king? What do you think happens next in Sage's story? Will Joaquin get mad at Sage if he finds out about his abilities earning him the crown? Will Robin still want to be with him if she finds out about Ayanna? What will life be like for Sage if he lives in Earth City away from everything he's ever known in California? Did you enjoy *Sage Vector and The Book of Space*? What do you think will happen in the next book — *Sage Vector and the Impossible World*?

Glossary

A.D. - short for Anno Domini, a Latin term that means "in the year of the lord" or since Christ was born.

accolades - awards or honors; expressions of praise and admiration.

AI - short for artificial intelligence, the idea that computers function in a way that replaces human intelligence.

algorithm - a set of rules or method to solve problems through calculations, usually involving computers.

Alisal University - an educational organization located in East Salinas, in California.

all that jazz - and other things that are like this or similar to it.

amphitheater - an outdoor open circular theater with rounded rows of seats.

analogy - a comparison of one thing to another in order to make it better understood.

antiquated - old-fashioned and out of date.

Appleseed, John - a nurseryman with the real name of John Chapman who planted apple orchards all over the United States in the nineteenth century.

Apu Trilogy, The - three films directed by Satyajit Ray that are a coming of age story about a young boy named Apu.

AR - short for augmented reality, a technology that superimposes computer generated images on to a person's view of the real world.

aristocrat - someone belonging to a family of a high social status or rank.

As You Like It - a comedic play written by William Shakespeare.

assessment - a test to determine if someone knows or can do something.

Astro Boy - a Japanese manga created by Osamu Tezuka.

astrophysicist - a physicist that studies the universe, such as planets and stars.

Atlas - a Greek mythological character who carries the world on his shoulders.

Back to the Future - a 1985 time travel comedy movie starring Michael J. Fox.

benders - an attachment that enables interface glasses to connect with other users.

Bennett, Tony - an American jazz singer from New York City.

beta - an early version of something, usually meant for testing to find potential problems or issues before a wider release.

billiards - a tabletop game (also known as pool) where players use wooden sticks to hit heavy balls into pockets on a specially designed game table.

birria tacos - A Mexican dish consisting of marinated and stewed meat, usually goat, beef or lamb, eaten with soft corn tortillas.

Birth of Venus, The - A depiction of the Roman goddess Venus emerging from the sea after her birth.

bite your thumb - a rude gesture similar to giving someone the middle finger, made popular in the play *Romeo and Juliet* by William Shakespeare.

Bollywood - the name for the film industry in the country of India.

Booth, John Wilkes - an American actor who shot and killed Abraham Lincoln in 1865.

brainwash - to make someone think in a completely different way than they previously thought, usually by unethical, coercive means.

Buddha - the spiritual teacher and founder of Buddhism, a religion from Asia.

Burj Khalifa - the tallest building in the world, found in Dubai in the United Arab Emirates.

bust - a sculpture of a person's head.

bustling - full of life, energy and movement.

cacophony - harsh, unharmonious sounds.

calibration - the act of fine tuning something to make sure it functions as it should when used.

callus - a thickened, hardened part of skin usually caused by rubbing against something.

celestial - relating to the sky or outer space.

Cervantes, Miguel de - a Spanish writer, author of *Don Quixote*.

Chaplin, Charlie - a silent film star from the early days of Hollywood, known for his character The Tramp.

chariot - a wheeled vehicle drawn by horses in ancient warfare.

chasing after windmills - to go after one's dreams no matter how they may appear to others, to tackle life head on.

Cheshire Cat - a character from Lewis Carroll's *Alice's Adventures in Wonderland*, known for his mischievous grin.

colonnades - a row of columns that support a roof.

Coltrane, John - an American jazz musician in the 1900's famously regarded for his saxophone playing.

Community Communication Office - a place where people in a community can get help and find resources.

Conan the Barbarian - a 1932 fictional fantasy hero created by Robert E. Howard.

condiments - something available to add to food to enhance its taste or compliment a dish.

conjunction - two or more things happening at the same point of time or space.

Connecticut Yankee In King's Arthur Court, A - an 1889 time travel novel written by Mark Twain.

contender - someone with a high enough score on the crown qualifier decathlon tests to compete for the crown and might serve as the philosopher king.

Continental Chamber - a meeting place for the Global Council, located in Earth City.

Copernican System - a model of the solar system that places the sun at the center, with the Earth and other planets revolving around it.

critical thinking - the ability of analyzing and evaluating information to make a judgement or decision.

Crucible, The - a 1953 play written by Arthur Miller about The Salem Witch Trials, also an allegory for McCarthyism, a time when the U.S. government persecuted people they believed to be communists.

cryptography - a method of protecting information and communications by using codes and algorithms.

crystal healing - the practice of harnessing the energy of stones and crystals to heal people.

curated - selected, organized and presented, such as putting together a collection of something for viewing.

Dali, Salvador - a well known Spanish artist of the 20th century known for his surrealist paintings, such as *The Persistence of Memory*.

decathlon - a series of ten tests or events where the winner is the one with the highest total points across all tests or events.

decor - decorations or furnishings.

demeanor - a person's outward behavior.

deterrent - something that discourages someone from doing something.

Dialogue Concerning The Two Chief World Systems - a 1632 book written by Galileo Galilei about the solar system. It compares the idea that the sun is the center of the solar system with the idea that the Earth is at the center.

DNA - short for deoxyribonucleic acid, a molecule that contains the genetic code that is unique to every individual.

Don Quixote - considered the first modern novel, it was written in the early 1600's by Miguel de Cervantes. It is about the adventures of a man with romantic illusions of being a knight but who gradually fades from his illusions to the reality of the world around him.

Durant, Will and Ariel - the authors of the historical work *The Story of Civilization*, an eleven volume set of books published between 1935-1975.

Earth City - a city just outside of Kathmandu, Nepal where the government of Earth is located and where the philosopher king resides and rules from.

easel - a stand or frame that holds an artist's canvas at an angle while they paint or draw.

eclipse - when the moon passes between the Earth and the Sun, blocking the light of the Sun and casting a shadow on Earth.

ecosystem - a community of living organisms in a particular area.

elaborate - a careful arrangement of parts to form a more detailed or complicated whole.

Elizabethan - occurring at the time of Queen Elizabeth I of England.

emanated - to give out or emit.

enforcers - officials tasked with enforcing the rules of the game of field ball.

enmity - intense hostility.

enraptured - filled with delight, extremely pleased by something.

equilibrium - when opposing forces, actions or influences are balanced.

ethics - standards of what is right and what is wrong.

euphoric - a heightened feeling of intense happiness or excitement.

exuberantly - in a way that is full of energy, excitement and happiness.

Fernando II de Medici - a patron and supporter of Galileo Galilei who lived in the 1600's.

fever pitch - heightened excitement.

field ball - a sports game played by two teams trying to get a ball across various barriers of a field.

fleeting - lasting a brief, short time.

Ford's Theater - a theater in Washington D.C. where U.S. President Abraham Lincoln was shot and killed by actor John Wilkes Booth in 1865.

Frankenstein - a 1818 novel written by Mary Shelley about a scientist creating a man-like monster.

fringe - not part of the mainstream, outside of the normal.

futility - pointless, of no use.

Gabilan Mountains - a mountain range in central California located in Monterey and San Benito counties.

Galilei, Galileo - an Italian astronomer who championed the idea that the Sun did not revolve around the Earth, but that the Earth revolved around the Sun.

Gatsby, Jay - the main character in the 1925 novel *The Great Gatsby* by F. Scott Fitzgerald, known for his lavish lifestyle.

giddy - a heightened feeling of being happy or excited.

Global Council - a council made up of one member from each of Earth's continents who are led by the philosopher king to govern the planet.

Godspeed - an encouragement to have a safe and successful journey.

Goldman, William - an American writer, author of the book *The Princess Bride*.

gothic - relating to a style of architecture in western Europe from the 12th to the 16th centuries.

Grand Duke of Tuscany - a male title of nobility from a region in central Italy.

grimace - a facial expression showing strong dislike, pain or disgust.

guerilla warfare - a type of unconventional fighting done by a person or a group who is outnumbered, involving tactics such as quick ambushes, sabotage, espionage and propaganda.

guild - an association of people with common interests who pursue shared goals.

Hamlet - a dramatic play written by William Shakespeare.

Hansberry, Lorraine - an American playwright, author of the play *A Raisin in the Sun*.

Hearst Castle - an estate built by media tycoon William Randolph Hearst and architect Julia Morgan in San Simeon, California in the early 1900's.

Hilltop, The - the elevated center of a field ball field covering three tunnels running underneath it; the place where new balls are dropped in a game of field ball.

hither - to this place.

Holy Grail - from the legend of a mythical object bestowing power upon its possessor, often used symbolically to mean anything special or rare that is worth pursuing.

Huckleberry Finn - an 1884 novel written by Mark Twain, fully titled *Adventures of Huckleberry Finn*, about a boy from Missouri who runs away from home with a runaway slave named Jim.

humanoid - having the appearance of, or being similar to a human being in shape.

hyperbolic - a geometry term used to describe a space where more than one line parallel to a given line passes through a point.

hypnosis - altering the state of consciousness of someone so they are suggestible and given commands they must follow.

illustrious - well known, respected, famously admired.

immaculate - perfectly clean, without any flaw.

immutable - unchanging or unchangeable.

imperative - of vital importance.

implications - the conclusions drawn from something, the likely consequences.

impressionistic - from the French art movement or style representing an impression of a moment, most often done with shifting light and color effects.

inaudible - unable to be heard.

indoctrinated - to have thoroughly educated someone into a set of beliefs or way of thinking.

infatuated - strong, passionate, often obsessive interest or attention given to someone or something.

intangible - unable to be touched, held or possessed.

interface - a technological computing device enabling a person to access information and programs.

IQ - short for intelligence quotient, a measurement of a person's intelligence.

Italian Cypress - a tree native to the Mediterranean region, also known as a pencil pine because of its tall, pointed shape.

jeopardized - putting something or someone into danger of losing or being harmed.

Julius Caesar - a general and dictator of the Roman Empire who was assassinated in 44 B.C., who was also the subject of a dramatic play with his name, written by William Shakespeare.

Kathmandu - the most populated city in the country of Nepal, also the seat of the federal government for the country.

Keaton, Buster - an American silent film star known for comedic action films.

keenly - intensely.

kerosene - a flammable oil often used in lamps in the middle to late 1800's.

King Jr., Dr. Martin Luther - a minister and civil rights leader in the 20th century who helped organize peaceful protests which led to the passing of the Civil Rights Act of 1964.

kinsmen - blood relatives, or from marriage, also a member of the same race or tribe.

Kitty Hawk - a beach town in North Carolina where the Wright Brothers successfully achieved powered flight.

Kurashiki - a city on Japan's Seto Inland Sea where the philosopher king Ethan Tanaka is from.

La Casa Grande - Spanish for "The Big House." It is the largest building in Hearst Castle at 68,500 square feet, containing 38 bedrooms, 30 fireplaces, and 42 bathrooms.

La Cuesta Encantada - Spanish for "The Enchanted Hill." It is the name of the hilltop that Hearst Castle is built on.

Latin - an ancient language spoken by the Romans and throughout Western Europe for many centuries.

lectern - a stand or desk that supports a book or script for a speaker or reader to use while standing in front of an audience.

limestone - a type of rock used in construction, especially in cement.

Lincoln, Abraham - the 16th President of the United States.

Lincoln, Mary Todd - wife of President Abraham Lincoln.

literature - written works, such as books, considered to have a significant artistic and lasting quality.

Lone Ranger, The - a 1930's fictional masked western hero who fought outlaws on horseback with his Native American sidekick Tonto.

M.I.T. - short for the Massachusetts Institute of Technology, a university in Cambridge, Massachusetts known as a leader in science and technology.

MacBeth - a dramatic work written by William Shakespeare.

magnetism - the motion of an electric charge resulting in attractive and repulsive forces between two things.

makeshift - a temporary substitute for something, standing in for the real thing.

mandala - a symbolic diagram meant to represent the universe, often used for religious purposes, meditation, or art.

McCullough, David - an American historian and author.

Merchant of Venice, The - a dramatic work written by William Shakespeare.

mesmerized - the experience of someone's undivided attention being fixated on something.

methodically - systematically doing something, in an orderly way.

metronome - a device that makes a steady click or sound that can be adjusted, most commonly used in making music.

Michelangelo - an Italian sculptor and painter known for his statue of David and his painting on the ceiling of the Sistine Chapel.

mijo - a Spanish term of endearment for a young person, especially a boy.

millennia - plural of millennium.

millennium - a period of 1,000 years.

Miller, Arthur - an American playwright, writer of *The Crucible*.

mischievous - causing trouble, playfully irresponsible.

Modern Times - a 1936 comedy film starring Charlie Chaplin.

monotony - a repetition of the same thing over and over again.

morality - a system used to determine what is right and wrong.

Mount Everest - the highest mountain on Earth, located along the Nepal and Tibet border. It stands 29,031 feet tall.

mumbo jumbo - meaningless or confusing language, often used to sound important or smart.

Naturalis Historia - a Latin work on the subject of nature written by Pliny the Elder during the time of the Roman Empire.

Neptune - the Roman god of the sea, fresh water, horses and naval victories.

neurology - a branch of medicine focusing on the nervous system, including the brain, the spinal cord and nerves.

New Delhi - the capital city of the country of India with a population of over 33 million people.

o'erperch - to fly over or mount over.

obscured - hidden from view.

observatory - a place to study objects in space.

obsolete - no longer around or usable.

omnibus - a collection of previously released work into one giant volume.

onslaught - a destructive attack or fierce show of force.

organic - grown without the use of synthetic chemicals or pesticides, without any genetically altered components.

ornate - detailed, created with complex patterns or design.

palpable - able to be touched or felt, tangible.

paradox - a seemingly absurd statement that may appear self-contradictory but when looked at closer proves to be true or accurate.

peace zone - one of the two end zones in the game of field ball, the area of the field players head to with the ball to score.

peasant - a person that rents land, usually to grow crops or raise animals, or someone poor, of a lower social class, often uneducated.

pendulously - to swing or sway back and forth, commonly referring to plants like vines.

pharmacology - the study and science of the use of drugs and chemicals on living organisms.

PhD - short for Doctor of Philosophy, considered the highest level of postgraduate academic achievement.

philosopher - a person who uses philosophy, the study of fundamental truths about life.

philosopher king - the most powerful leadership position in the government on Earth. The throne is open to the person who scores highest on a series of tests designed to locate individuals with the exact qualities needed to serve humanity.

philosophy - the study of fundamental truths about life.

pillars - tall, vertical, support structures, usually columns, that hold up or support a part of a building.

Pinocchio - a fictional character from a children's novel, *The Adventures of Pinocchio,* written in 1883 by Italian writer Carlo Collodi. Pinocchio is a wooden puppet who dreams of being a real boy.

playwright - a writer of plays.

Pliny the Elder - Roman author of the Latin work *Naturalis Historia*.

practical - concerned with the actual doing or demonstration or use of something as opposed to the theory or ideas of it.

Princess Bride, The - a 1973 fantasy book written by William Goldman.

promenade - a paved, public area for leisurely walking.

propensity - a tendency or urge towards doing something.

protocols - official rules or plans to be followed.

psychology - the study of the human mind and its affects on human behavior.

Ptolemaic System - the theory that the Earth is the stable, stationary center of the universe, with the planets and the Sun revolving around it.

Raisin In The Sun, A - a 1959 play written by Lorraine Hansberry about a working class African American family living in south Chicago.

rambunctious - energetic in a wild, noisy way.

rampant - something that has grown or is widespread.

rampart - a defensive wall, usually found around a castle or walled city.

Ray, Satyajit - an Indian film director, known for many films, including *The Apu Trilogy*.

recompose - to restore or return to a previous, more acceptable condition or state of being.

recuperate - to recover or regain strength or health.

refectory - a room used for communal (group) meals, usually in a religious or educational institution.

reinforced concrete - when steel rods or bars are placed inside of concrete (a composite material made of cement, sand, gravel and water) to make it stronger.

rekindle - light the spark again, to reignite something after it dies out.

reluctantly - hesitant, unwilling, without really wanting to.

Renaissance - an artistic and cultural movement of the 15th and 16th centuries in Europe.

resilient - able to last or withstand difficult or challenging conditions.

resonate - to strike a chord, to make a connection with someone.

ricocheting - to bounce off a surface onto another and back again.

rites – religious or social acts done in a ceremony or as a custom.

Robinson Crusoe - a novel written in 1719 by Daniel Dafoe about a man stranded on a deserted island.

Rocky Mountains, The - the jagged, elevated areas on a field ball field nearest the peace zones on either end of the field.

Romeo and Juliet - a dramatic work by William Shakespeare about two young lovers.

rosaries - sets of beads used in prayers and devotional practice among Roman Catholics.

rudimentary - undeveloped, basic.

RUN-DMC - a hip hop music group who helped push their musical genre mainstream in the 1980's.

Sagredo - a character in the work *Dialogue Concerning The Two Chief World Systems* written by Galileo Galilei, based on his friend Giovanni Francesco Sagredo. In the work, Sagredo listens to philosophers argue theories about the solar system and tries to decide who is right.

Salem Witch Trials, The - the accusations, hearings, and prosecutions of people believed to be witches in the late 1600's in colonial Massachusetts.

Salinas - a city located in Central California, in Monterey County.

Salviati - one of two philosophers in the work *Dialogue Concerning The Two Chief World Systems* written by Galileo Galilei. He argues in favor of the Copernican theory, and he takes Galileo's side in his book.

San Simeon - a city along the central California coast, home of Hearst Castle.

Sawyer, Tom - a fictional character from the 1876 book *The Adventures of Tom Sawyer* written by Mark Twain.

Scopes Monkey Trial, The - an American legal case in 1925 involving a high school teacher accused of violating a law making it illegal for teachers to teach human evolution in public schools.

self-conscious - feeling unnecessary attention about one's self, appearance or actions.

Shakespeare, William - an English playwright, poet and actor, known for his plays *Romeo and Juliet, Hamlet, MacBeth, Julius Caesar*, and more.

Shangri-la - an imaginary place considered to be an ideal, perfect utopia. The name originated from James Hilton's 1933 novel *The Lost Horizon*.

Shelley, Mary - an English writer of the 1800's, author of *Frankenstein*.

silhouette - a dark shape or outline over a lighter background.

simpleton - a simple-minded, foolish, gullible person.

Simplicio - one of two philosophers in the work *Dialogue Concerning The Two Chief World Systems* written by Galileo Galilei. He argues the Ptolemaic side of things (that the Earth is the center of the universe). His name is meant to imply he is simple-minded.

simulation - a computer generated model meant to approximate the real world, used in problem solving exercises.

Singin' In The Rain - a song written in 1929, made famous by the 1952 movie of the same name.

Sonnets - a collection of 154 sonnets (rhyming poems) written by William Shakespeare.

speculation - a theory or guess about something without having evidence to support it.

splotches - blobs, smears, or marks of something, usually liquid.

St. John the Baptist - a religious figure in Christianity who anticipated the coming of Jesus Christ, and later baptized him in the Jordan river.

Steinbeck, John - an American writer, author of many books set in the Salinas Valley, including *Of Mice And Men* and *East of Eden*.

Story of Civilization, The - an 11 volume set of books on Western and Eastern civilization written by Will and Ariel Durant, published in the 20th century.

studious - giving great attention to study, paying attention to the details needed to learn and understand something.

subconscious - a part of the mind operating below the level of mental awareness.

subjective - based on personal bias, feelings or taste. One's own opinion on something rather than taking into account the larger picture.

sublime - extremely good and beautiful, often of a spiritual nature.

Sudoku - a popular game involving the figuring out of missing numbers on a grid.

susceptible - open to influence or harm.

sustainable - able to be maintained over a long period of time.

symbolism - a literary term referring to a story's use of a person, object, or situation to represent something else, usually connected to a larger idea or theme.

tangible - able to be touched or felt, something real, solid.

tapestries - woven decorative fabrics used to cover furniture, walls or floors.

terminology - the specific words common to a particular technical subject, field, or profession.

terraformed - to transform a planet's surface so as to make it more inhabitable.

Tezuka, Osamu - a Japanese manga artist, the creator of *Astro Boy*.

thee - an old way of saying "you," often used in plays written by William Shakespeare.

therefore - and for that reason, consequently.

Thermodynamics, Laws of - a set of scientific laws dealing with the properties of energy.

thou - an old way of saying "you," often used in plays written by William Shakespeare.

thy - an old way of saying "your," often used in plays written by William Shakespeare.

Tibet - a region in the western part of Asia, annexed to China in 1951. It is also home to Mount Everest, the highest mountain on Earth.

Tibetan - belonging to an ethnic group of people native to Tibet, a region in the western part of Asia.

Time Machine, The - a 1895 science fiction novel written by H. G. Wells.

topical - an ointment used to aid in the physical healing or health of someone.

tortilla - a thin, flatbread typically made from corn or flour.

Tramp, The - a fictional film character portrayed by actor Charlie Chaplin.

transfixed - to be still or motionless because of something that amazes or frightens, to hold someone in awe.

Tree Top, The - the top floor of the John Appleseed Memorial Library located on the Alisal University campus.

Trojan Horse - a wooden horse used in the Trojan War to enter the city of Troy undetected in order to unleash a secret attack; also the iconic monument and building located on the Alisal University campus in Salinas, California.

tunic - a loose-fitting piece of clothing worn by men and women.

Twain, Mark - an American writer, author of *The Adventures of Tom Sawyer*, *Adventures of Huckleberry Finn*, and *A Connecticut Yankee In King Arthur's Court*.

tycoon - a very powerful and rich businessman.

Ursa Minor - a star constellation in the northern sky, also known as "Little Bear."

Valhalla - in Norse mythology, the celestial realm where the souls of Viking warriors go when they die.

vanquish - completely defeat or end.

vantage point - the position from which something is viewed.

viewscreen - monitor or electronic screen for viewing videos or images.

vigilant - keeping careful watch over something for protection from possible harm.

VR - short for virtual reality, a computer generated environment that appears real to an immersed user.

war zone - the area of a field ball field in-between two peace zones, where control of the ball is battled over.

Wells, H. G. - an English science fiction writer, most notably the author of *The Time Machine*, *The Invisible Man*, and *War of the Worlds*.

Willie - the son of Abraham and Mary Todd Lincoln who died of typhoid fever at the age of 11.

Wright, Orville and Wilbur - two brothers who were first to successfully achieve powered flight in 1903 in Kitty Hawk, North Carolina.

Zorro - a fictional character created in 1919 by Johnston Mc-Culley, a masked vigilante who defended the local people of California against corrupt villains.

ACKNOWLEDGEMENTS

I would like to thank the following individuals for their support:

Lenette Carus, Sage Carus, Norma Cortez, Danny Munoz, Alberto Murillo, Mariela Villaverde, America Tirado, Rosa Recio, Carole Eddington, Anna Flores, L. Micki Moss, Jody Graffam, Rachell Santiago, Larry Jaffe, Anthony Wells, Norma Matos, Jose Cabrera, Moria Dolan, Chris Deleon, William Reasor, Jaime Hardt, Leah Chalmers, Rebecca Danese, and Beau Hiner.

ABOUT THE AUTHOR

DAVID CARUS is an author and entrepreneur. He graduated from Georgetown University where he studied English Literature and Government. He wrote *Sage Vector and the Book of Space* to inspire people to seek knowledge to improve the world. He lives in Central California with his wife Lenette and son Sage.

Made in the USA
Columbia, SC
01 December 2024